INVASIVE

SHEILA JENNÉ

for my children

1

Robin

I was the first to notice the engines' roar had changed in pitch. A tinny whine grew over the throbbing growl they were supposed to be making. I jammed my thumb on the intercom. "Cliff, what the hell is that?"

There was a moment of silence as he checked. "Engine seven is overheating. Can we stop the burn for a few minutes?"

"Negative, we're too close to the planet now and going too fast. We need to keep burning steadily for the next thirty minutes or we'll overshoot."

"Um…" I could sense his panic even over the intercom. He might have gone to engineering school, but like most of the Greenies, he had had no real experience before the colony ship had left Proxima. In the two years we'd been underway, he had learned the quirks of the engines, but during most of that time we could always just shut the engines down and service them if necessary. Which had happened often, given what a bag of bolts we were flying. The *Resurrection* was an ancient colony ship, left over from the voyage from Earth to Proxima a century ago. The best the Disciples of Terra could afford: not much.

I had told them all that when they hired me to fly her, but they had simply nodded gravely and accepted the risk. It would *probably* survive the trip, and that was all they needed to know. Maybe the Greenies didn't care if we ended up swan-diving into the sun, so long as they did it while following their goddess's orders. But I cared, so it was on me to make sure we didn't die.

"Spray the coolant as fast as you can," I said hastily. "Don't spare it, it's not like we'll need it next week. That should buy us some time, and I'll try to run a new trajectory." I swiped my screen to bring up the nav program. Our current course stood out as a glowing yellow line, all the way from Proxima and to this new planet, Z169-alpha, or as the Greenies called it, Eos. We had been running as close as we could to the speed of light, but for a year now we'd been steadily decelerating in the hopes of hitting the tiny planet at the end at the exact moment our velocity was slow enough to swing into orbit. Like throwing a needle from New Proxima Dome and skewering a sesame seed in First South. No room for error. Certainly no room for faulty engines at the very last minute.

The whine of the malfunctioning engine was louder now, and the com buzzed. I ignored it, but the prophetess could override everything on the ship. She'd insisted on that. "Robin? I can hear a strange noise, is everything all right?"

"No," I hissed through gritted teeth, rapidly typing in new calculations. "But if you want to not die you're going to have to let me do my job, *ma'am*."

"Sybil is fine," she corrected, a faint note of offense creeping into her usually placid alto voice. "I'll leave you to it then. Please call me when you get a chance." Translation: *don't get confused about who's really in charge of this mission, even though we let you drive the ship. You work for me.* I hated that she expected me to call her Sybil. You don't pretend to be friends with the pope. The egalitarian act only worked if everyone pretended they obeyed Sybil just because they happened to agree with her at all times. But I didn't like the charade. I wasn't a Greenie and I wasn't going to play along. If she wanted to be treated like the leader, which she did, she was getting a *ma'am*.

The first trajectory I put in sketched a red path straight into the gravity well. Fuck. I tapped in another, the whine of the engines getting louder. The only reason Cliff wasn't calling, I felt sure, was because he was too busy spraying coolant. And it wasn't really working.

There! This time the dotted line was blue, meaning not fatal. It described a loop just outboard of the planet to keep from overshooting it, and by the time the loop was finished we'd have had an hour for the engine to cool down. I hoped it was enough. I punched the shipwide intercom. "Everybody brace for unusual grav vectors. Grab your kids." Grabbing a handle on the side of my station and hooking my feet into the metal loops that scattered the deck, I shut down all the port side engines.

Immediately the gravity shifted. It wasn't really gravity, of course; it was the inertia of our deceleration. Normally it pushed us forward as we decelerated, so the blunt cone of the ship was pointed backward and the engines were under our feet. With only half the engines running, suddenly the deck beneath my feet turned into a steep slope, and without the loops holding my feet, I would have tumbled down into the left-hand corner. I tried not to think of my kids down below. They were only nine and seven. They'd had a good fifteen seconds to brace, and they had been able to match that in drills, but what if they had been distracted? What if their dad hadn't been paying attention?

Well, at least none of the rooms on the ship were spacious enough for them to have very far to tumble. I called Cliff again. "Was I too slow? Is it burned out?" I chewed my lip as I waited for him to check. There were only nine engines; I wasn't sure we could land without all of them. Not with any sort of control. We needed to be able to slow our descent, or the ship would burn up on entry or impact too hard to survive. Maybe if we aimed for water … but then how would we get everyone to shore?

Cliff's voice crackled back. "It's bad but I think I can get it running. How long do I have?"

"An hour. When we finish this loop we *need* them all if we want to slow down."

He took a deep breath. "Yeah. Yeah, I think I can. I'll get Moss to help me."

"Get anybody you need." I flicked him off and called Sybil. "Everything's under control now. Are you all right down there?"

"Only shaken up a little," she answered calmly. "How long are we going to be tilted like this?"

"An hour. Is everyone going to be all right?" I imagined little Lily hanging diagonally off a handhold. How long could she keep that up? Was Aspen nearby to help her?

"There is some panic on the habitat level. People are concerned. Could you address them? After that I can lead everyone in a prayer of thanksgiving for our deliverance."

I rolled my eyes. *I* had saved the ship, not her goddess. She should be thanking me. Then again, it would surely calm the colonists. "Yes ma'am," I said, flicking off the channel. For a moment I just stood there, hanging onto the control panel with one hand while I knuckled my achy pregnant back with the other. Of all the comforts we'd left behind on Proxima, I missed artificial gestators the most. My first two kids had been born with little inconvenience on my part. This one was sapping the life out of me already, and it wasn't even born yet. At least when we hit orbit and turned the engines off, the thrust gravity would vanish and maybe my back would stop hurting.

Thumbing the intercom again, I started talking. "This is the captain speaking. Thanks for putting up with that. We had some engine trouble and had to shut off all the ones on the left-hand side for a bit. But no worries, we'll be able to bring them all back on in another hour, and then half an hour after that we hit orbit." I looked around the tiny control room, just under the blunt point of the ship's cone. One of the ship's few windows was here, thick reinforced plasteel, only two feet across. The arc of the planet slowly edged into view as we described our loop, tail end first, the nose turning toward the planet.

"I can see Eos from here, you guys, and it's beautiful. When we reach orbit you'll all get to look." I wasn't lying: it was truly lovely, more beautiful than Proxima had been by far. Proxima was a barren gray rock, dotted with green patches where the domes were. This was a white marble, with a band of blue and reddish-purple around the middle. It wasn't exactly a temperate planet. Glaciers covered most of the land mass, but the tropical zone was bare of ice. At the equator it would be perfectly livable. White masses of cloud streaked the light side; the dark side was completely black, visible only by the gap it made in the stars.

"Can't say for sure when we'll actually land, we'll have to check on the engines and see how long it will take for them to be ready. Plus of course picking out a landing site. But it'll be soon. Meanwhile, hang tight, expect the gravity vector to stay where it is for the next hour, and I'll let you know when to be ready for normal gravity to return."

I shut off the intercom and listened idly to Sybil's prayer. It was the usual stuff, thanking Terra, their goddess, for shepherding us to our destination and protecting us from harm. Funny word, shepherding, given that sheep were extinct so there hadn't been any shepherds since humanity had arrived at Proxima. What humans were left on Earth were shepherding mycoprotein by now. Earth's atmosphere wasn't friendly to much else, last I'd heard.

Behind me the door shushed open and Sybil climbed in. I hadn't noticed when her prayer had stopped. I half-turned, wondering if I should try to help her, but she navigated the handholds easily. She wasn't old, after all, even though she had the placidity of a quiet elderly woman. She was in her late forties and her hair, tumbling diagonally down her back and hanging sideways past her waist, was still almost all black. "I wanted to see the planet," she said by way of explanation. Her rich low voice, so compelling when she prayed, was beautiful even saying a simple sentence like that. No wonder people listened to everything she said.

She reached me and hooked her feet into the loops beside mine. Her face tipped back to gaze at the planet above. I looked down at her, asking, "Is it everything you hoped?"

"Everything and more," she whispered. "The goddess is rejoicing; she sees it and she knows this is her new body, the place where she will dwell at last with her people."

I looked away uncomfortably and scanned my readouts. My up-bringing was completely secular; I'd been rubbing shoulders with the Greenies for four years, but I was never going to get used to the goddess talk. They would drop it into the middle of every conversation. I had always believed in religious freedom, but bringing it up all the time was simply bad manners.

Sybil turned her green eyes to me. I couldn't help but meet them. Her gaze is intense and hard to ignore. "So," she asked. "Are *you* excited to land?"

"Space is where I feel most comfortable," I hedged. "I always have." Since the first time I'd gotten into the cockpit for a training run, it had felt right. So different from an atmospheric plane, where you had to consider the lift beneath the wings and the resistance of the air. In space, there was only the trajectory you started off on and the burns you made. If you didn't or couldn't burn, you could keep drifting forever, till your air ran out, and then your corpse would freeze … but even then, it would keep traveling off into the stars for eternity. Millennia from now it would drift right out of the galaxy, farther and farther into infinity.

That scared some people. To me it was like a drug. Half the tingling spice of danger, half the lure of the stars, which seemed to promise eter-nal happiness if you just kept your finger off the braking jets and followed them forever. I had always said no, and so I was still alive, but there was something seductive about listening to the temptation.

"I hope you won't have any regrets, once we touch down," she was saying.

I shook my head. "It's the tradeoff I made. One big voyage, further than I'd gone before, and then an end to it. It's better for the family, any-way. I didn't like being gone all the time on the asteroid-hoppers."

My hand drifted to my belly. That was another reason. Three chil-dren would never have worked out on Proxima. Even two had been a strain on our budget. On a space colony there weren't any limits. And since Aspen, my husband, was a Greenie, they had offered me the job.

Now I swallowed hard, looking past Eos's arc to the spangled black beyond. It would be goodbye forever to the stars and my career. The ship didn't have nearly enough extra fuel to lift again, and it wasn't built for it in the first place. The Greenies hadn't shelled out for landers or shuttles. I was going to have to land this massive beast, and then there was nothing for it but to leave it there. No space for me, ever again.

I tore my eyes away and forced a smile at Sybil. "Is there anything else, ma'am? Because I really have to …" I gestured at the panels. There wasn't really anything I needed to be doing, other than keeping an eye on our trajectory in case I needed to burn the maneuvering jets. But I would feel more relaxed doing that without her there.

"I really wish you would call me by my name," she said softly, turning to clamber back off the bridge. "We're all equal in the sight of the goddess."

"That's nice of you to say, ma'am." The door slid shut behind her and I focused back on my displays.

After a fraught hour, we were almost back where we had started. "Is the number seven cooled off yet, Cliff?"

"Yeah, it's—it'll do for half an hour, anyway. After we hit orbit you can come look at it and see what you think."

That didn't sound promising. We needed all nine engines functional to land. But at least once we were in a stable orbit, we could take as much time as necessary to make repairs.

I watched the displays, seeing the numbers for relative velocity and position count down, flipping the switches to engage the full engine bank at the right moment. Abruptly the pseudogravity corrected itself, the bridge floor flattening back out and my weight once again centered over my feet.

The final burn went smoothly and there had been no further strange noises when I finally shut the engines down. Gravity vanished. Finally my giant belly stopped squashing my bladder, that was a nice feeling. Then suddenly the pressure reversed and I had to grab for the emergency barf bag under the control panel. Humiliating. I had never been spacesick before, but pregnancy was doing all kinds of unexpected things to my body. At least there was no one there to see.

I stayed on the bridge till I had confirmed our orbit was stable, and then floated downstairs. It was time to check on Aspen and the kids.

I had met my husband a decade ago on Proxima Station. I lived there between ice runs, just long enough to unload, refuel, and jog a bit in the rotating gym so I didn't lose all my bone mass. There had been no point, then, in going home. I saved rent and an elevator ticket by sleeping in my cockpit.

I had spotted Aspen across the small cafeteria, struggling to poke the straw into his coffee pouch. The cafeteria was set up like a planetside one—all the seats on one side of the room, so that patrons could pretend that side was "down." The booth seats had seatbelts for the tourists, so they could sit up at the table the way they were accustomed without accidentally lifting themselves up when they reached for the salt.

I never used the belts. Those were for tourists. I hooked my stocking feet in the rails beneath the table, to be polite, but it wouldn't have really mattered if I'd had my lunch floating parallel to the table. Sometimes the old hands did that, but it tended to upset the management.

And there was that daft planetsider, successfully skewering the straw into the little foil hole, but managing in the process to squirt coffee in his eye. He clearly needed a hand. His good looks—broad, muscular shoulders; braided hair; brown skin spotted with unexpected freckles— weren't the reason. Well, not the only reason.

Unsticking my food pouches from the table, I got my heels under me and pushed off with just the right amount of force to catch myself lightly on the edge of the bench opposite him. I snatched a few napkins from the dispenser and swept them through the air, catching the errant coffee globs. "Don't worry about the waste," I said. "That shit's not worth drinking."

He smiled gratefully and accepted another napkin to wipe across his face. "I had hoped not to embarrass myself my first lunch here."

"Everyone embarrasses theirself the first time here." I slid into the seat and hooked my feet underneath the table. Velcroing my food pouches to the table, I took a drink of my own bitter coffee to cover an assessing glance. Business casual, that told me nothing but his class: updome professional. "Tourist?"

Grinning with embarrassment, he said, "I wish. Then there would be some excuse for my faux pas. No, I'm here for work." He managed a drink of the coffee and failed to repress a grimace. "Oh dear, that is strong."

"It sucks balls," I agreed. "I gotta drink it to stay awake with the hours I keep. But we all hate it."

"What do you do?"

"Pilot." I gestured to my gray flight suit. "Doing ice runs right now. You?"

"I'm a botanist."

I blinked. "Plant man? Bullshit. We don't have any plants here."

"That's the thing," he said, leaning forward enthusiastically. Good thing he was strapped in; zero-g was unforgiving about that kind of unconscious flailing around. "Right now you get your oxygen from a mechanical scrubber, and then the carbon is taken out of the sink and shipped planetside. Same with water reclamation, the nitrates are taken out of your urine and shipped down. Then all the food gets shipped up here. What's food made of?"

"I don't know," I said, face heating. "Plants and animals?"

"Carbohydrates and fats are made of carbon and hydrogen. Protein is made of that and nitrogen. All stuff you just sent down!"

"I mean, it's all by elevator," I said. "It's not a huge deal bringing stuff up and down."

"It takes up elevator space that could be used for goods," he argued. "Plus, if you wanted to build a station somewhere else, somewhere not at the top of the elevator, then how would you keep breathing and eating? Right now a deep space voyage is limited by how long you can bring your food with you. But a dome doesn't have that limitation. They grow their food at the same time as they scrub their air."

"Well sure," I said slowly. "But they have the space for it. On a ship or a station, there's not a ton of room for hydroponics. Not more than a little, anyway. And certainly no room for animals."

"What my team is developing is a genetically modified symbiotic organism—bacteria, algae, and fungi—that could scrub the air *and* waste-water and produce food without ever needing any planetside inputs." His eyes focused on the middle distance, as if he could see it already. "With enough sunlight, it could theoretically go on indefinitely, as long as the inhabitants of the station kept eating the organic matter. And it could be done in a small space."

I eyed him doubtfully. He couldn't be more than twenty-five. "You invent this yourself?"

He shook his head vigorously, sending his braided hair waving like an anemone. "No, I'm the grad student. You think the professors would come up here? No, they sent a minion to set up an experiment here, and come back for it next month and see how it's growing."

The conversation had left me humbled, but curious. I hadn't had the chance to finish high school; his big words and academic career left me feeling ignorant. But at the same time, he hadn't made me feel like he was trumpeting his superior knowledge. Instead he laughed at himself and let me show him the ropes of zero-g.

We were from different worlds, almost literally—my feet so rarely touched the planet as to make it hardly a home anymore. But his world intrigued me. If science could allow further settlement in space, open up further stars, it had to be worth something.

And I liked his enthusiasm. He was clearly in love with his work, the way I was with mine.

10

He had fallen in love a second time, without losing the first—with me. And a third time, which I didn't understand at all, with his odd religion. I wasn't entirely sure if that enriched him the way botany did, or stole something that should have belonged to me. If push came to shove, which would he choose? I was careful never to find out.

The personnel level was subdivided into a number of separate spaces, the better for everyone to keep themselves busy over the long voyage. I found Aspen and the kids in the playground. Colt, our nine-year-old, was doing the monkey bars upside-down, delighted to find they worked in every dimension. Lily, seven, quietly rotated around and around the fire pole, unwilling to let go.

Aspen floated nearby, watching. His many braids floated, mermaid-like, around his head. I couldn't help but smile. He'd always looked amazing in zero-g.

Aspen spotted me grinning to myself and carefully picked his way over, using the handholds on the wall. "You look pleased. Did you save us from a terrible fate with that crazy maneuver?"

I grabbed his arm and hauled him near for a kiss. "I did, actually. Were you all okay?"

"Oh, yeah. They listened very well. Lily was a bit scared, but when Colt showed her how to use the floor like a slide, she climbed down and tried it."

"You let them let go of the handholds? What if the vector had shifted?"

"You *said* it would stay the same for an hour," he countered, frowning. "I wasn't going to leave them hanging there for an hour."

I sighed. "Fair enough." I was hardly in a position to criticize, was I? I hadn't been here.

Just then a soft chime sounded. Lunchtime. You could count on Sybil to keep the routine going. Her calm leadership had kept the settlers from ever panicking, regardless of what was going on in the ship. I didn't have to like her to admit that.

"Can you take them in?" asked Aspen. "I need to talk to some people."

I nodded, calling to the kids. They looked absorbed, and if they chose to pitch a fit about stopping their play, I wasn't sure what I'd do. But luckily they came over almost immediately, Lily singing softly to herself, "Round and round, round and round."

Once we had sat down, things got thornier. The meal was grayish lumps of mushroomy substrate from the bioscrubber, spiced up a bit with bits of greens. Colt was carefully picking out the green and leaving the rest.

"You have to eat everything," I reminded him.

"I don't want any lichen today," said Colt, politeness a thin veneer over stubbornness.

"Colt, you know there isn't any choice on a spaceship. I know it's boring always eating the same thing…"

"It's not *that*," he said disdainfully. "Pine told us in religion class this morning that scrubber lichen has no soul because it's not Earth food. It takes away your connection to the goddess."

I bit my tongue to keep from cursing. What business had Pine telling the children any such thing? It wasn't like there was anything else to eat. "Sybil gave permission to eat this. This whole trip is to serve the goddess, right? And we couldn't do it if we didn't eat scrubber lichen."

He scowled and pushed the mushroomy chunks around with his fork. A sticky sauce glued them to the plate so they didn't drift away. "You're not a disciple of the goddess, anyway. What do you know about what's allowed to eat?"

My mouth drew together in a hard line and I jerked to my feet. A hard push off my seat brought me to the table where Aspen was talking with some of the others. Pine included. I leaned forward, holding onto the edge of the table. "Colt says he can't eat his dinner because it has scrubber lichen in it. Who's been telling the kids this stuff? They have to *eat*." I

12

looked at Pine, though I didn't want to call her out by name.

"I never said they should stop eating it," she said. "Only that once we arrived on the planet, we wouldn't have to eat soulless artificial food anymore."

I appealed to Aspen. "How can you let her call it soulless? That stuff is what allows us to be out here at all! It's a genius invention!"

He looked uncomfortable. "Well, I mean, Sybil does say the best food is Earth food … that it helps you connect with the goddess the most. I guess Colt got a little stuck on that concept."

"It's really admirable that he has such a delicate conscience," Pine said. "And at such a young age!"

I jerked upward, almost losing my hold on the table. "I think perhaps the conscience that you need to be worrying about is—"

Aspen hastily pushed away from the table. "I'll talk to him."

I took a deep breath and let it out through my nose. I cast Pine one last glare and turned around. She wasn't worth it. I was going to have to get along with these people for the rest of my life. I couldn't afford to make enemies.

2

Aspen

I picked my way carefully into the conference room, trying not to swivel my head too much. Despite the antiemetics I'd taken, every quick movement made me want to puke. But hey. I was adjusting to zero-g better than my daughter was. One look at the zero-g toilet and she had reverted to diapers. I only hoped she would give them up again after we landed.

My opposite number, Autumn, was there already. She was the head zoologist of the colony, an older woman with short, salt-and-pepper hair and a permanent friendly smile. "How are the goat fetuses handling orbit?" I asked. That's what passes for a greeting between her and me. Not because we don't like each other, but because both of us like our work more than almost anything else.

"It makes no difference to them," she said, smiling. "They're floating in amniotic fluid already. I'm more worried about re-entry. I put so many layers of shock absorbing gel around the tanks I'm pretty sure they could survive more g's than the ship can."

I grinned, climbing into a chair and hooking my feet around the legs so I didn't float off of it again. "You don't need to worry," I said. "Robin's going to set us down gentle as a baby."

"I'm sure. I just want to be ready for anything."

The door slid open and Sybil came in, followed by a white guy in his fifties—her chief acolyte, Hawk. Behind almost every visionary is some practical person, the one who pays the bills and balances the budget and everything else a prophet doesn't have the bandwidth for. Hawk was that for Sybil. He had very little charisma, but he didn't need it. Sybil had more than enough to run the Disciples by herself.

Robin liked him better than Sybil, because he was practical and not what she considered "too churchy." Given he was the number two guy in an entire religion, I thought that might be wishful thinking on her part.

Hawk nodded at me brusquely, dropped an identical nod to Autumn, and took a seat. Sybil gracefully slipped into the chair at the head of the table. That only left the one at the foot for Robin.

When she came in, she didn't take it. Instead she pushed off straight from the door, hooked her foot on her chair back, and brought herself to a stop floating above the table. It broke the illusion all of us had that we were sitting right-side-up, under gravity. Instead my mind flickered between possibilities. Was she floating upright, and we were bolted to the wall? Or maybe she was lying on her back and we were hanging from the ceiling.

I was used to the head trip, since I'd been visiting space with Robin since long before we left Proxima. The others, however, were clearly thrown by it. I cast her an admiring look. She knew well enough not to screw with people's heads when she didn't want to. Her position was a power move, to remind everyone she was better at this than they were, and it made me want to snatch her out of the air and kiss her—at the very least. I adjusted in my seat.

"I got the maps," she said, unrolling a long printout across the table and pinning it down (up?) with magnets. "These are the new photos taken by the *Resurrection*. Though there are few differences between these and the photos we already had, from the Hermes probe thirty years ago. Mostly just increased forestation in some areas. But that matters, because

16

I can't easily park this bucket on top of heavy forest."

Sybil nodded. "Can you mark the landing sites we discussed before?"

She gathered more magnets from the edge of the table and placed each one. "You can see this one is right out, it's all woodland now. But the rest are all adequate for a landing site. Whether they'd suit the colony is another question." She looked over at me and Autumn.

I followed her cue. "Yes, we've discussed a great deal whether we wanted to be along the equator or closer to the tropics. At the tropics, we would have a long, warm growing season but also a long, cold winter. At the equator, there would be basically two short growing seasons a year, corresponding to spring and fall at the tropics, but the two annual winters would be mild."

"Well, the year is long already, right?" asked Sybil. "Five hundred and …?"

"Forty-nine days, yes," I finished for her. "So the two growing seasons really would be adequate. And even in the winter, there would be little or no snow, so there are some cold-weather crops we could keep alive all year."

"That's definitely what we want to aim towards, then," Sybil said, reaching across the table to remove the magnets that were too far from the equator. That left six sites, scattered across the three visible continents.

"The Hermes rover landed here," Robin said, tapping the map. "So if we choose a site on the same continent, its data will be more valuable. We'll be dealing with the same plant and animal life it analyzed."

"For what that's worth," Hawk snorted. "In the ten days before it wandered into the tundra, it didn't see much."

"It saw plenty that was of interest to *us*," I said. "It was able to analyze hundreds of plant and bacterial samples in that time and verify that there don't seem to be any hazardous germs. And it's the whole reason we know level-three terraforming is necessary, to replace the native life with life from Earth. None of the plant life will be edible to us."

I felt a pang at this. I had seen the photos from the rover: tall, ferny violet trees; magenta shrubs; tiny star-shaped pink ivy. It was beautiful as it was, albeit indigestible. It would be a shame to uproot it all. But we had to, if we wanted to live there. Eos in its natural state couldn't be our home.

"What we don't know much about yet is animal life," said Autumn. "Hermes did get some glimpses of large herbivores, and where there are herbivores, there are going to be predators. We'll need to find a location where we can build some kind of stockade."

Hawk stabbed a finger at one of the magnets. "Why not that one? The valley looks defensible."

Autumn shook her head. "This one's better. The high plateau should be at least some defense against predators, *and* it's closer to where the Hermes probe landed."

Sybil lightly touched the magnet Autumn had indicated, smiling faintly. "The goddess is pleased with it."

Hawk scowled, clearly annoyed that his suggestion had been over-ruled. But he didn't say anything. Sybil might have spoken softly, but she wasn't prone to changing her mind.

"So should I plan a landing pattern for that one?" Robin looked around the table. Now that Sybil had spoken, nobody was going to contradict her. But there was nothing wrong with the site: close to the equator and with steep bluffs dropping away on two sides, to help protect us from predators. It was a perfect spot.

Sybil nodded and started picking up the magnets. "How long will it be before we can be on the ground?"

"At least a week," Robin said. "We have to do some work on the number seven engine to ensure it won't give us any more trouble during the landing."

After that meeting it was back to the residential level to pick up the children from school. I was still, until we landed, the full-time parent. The amount of botany needed by a ship in motion only took a few hours a day, not counting what my assistants did.

Pine, the head teacher, was frowning when I came in. "No more luck at the potty," she said.

Lily made an angry sound and threw a block. Without gravity, it careened off the side of the wall and almost hit one of the other kids before a teacher nabbed it out of the air. I took Pine's sleeve and drew her a little away. "She doesn't like you talking about it in front of everybody," I reminded her. I had told her the same thing yesterday.

"If it's so embarrassing, she does have the option of just using it."

"It's not 'just' for her. The zero-g toilet is very different from what she's used to. Did Ivy try helping her?"

"Of course."

I caught the junior teacher's eye across the room. Ivy was the best with Lily by a long shot. If she hadn't been able to get Lily to use the bathroom, it couldn't be done.

I went back up to Lily, using the edge of a bookshelf to hold myself in a low crouch at her level. "Come on," I said, extending a hand. "Let's get out of here."

"Let's blow this popsicle stand," she agreed, putting her hand in mine. It was our thing at dismissal, our little call-and-response.

Colt bounced along the walls to us. He was enjoying this entirely too much, careening off everything. I felt a little bad for the teachers, having to handle a roomful of excitable children without even gravity to settle them down. I couldn't imagine much learning was happening at this point.

"Dad, can I go to the playground?" he asked.

"Sure." This time of day, there were always adults there. And Colt was of an age where he'd rather play with friends than be with me. That way I didn't feel guilty about giving Lily all my attention all afternoon.

I did feel guilty, though. Just like I would feel guilty if I didn't. I had been an only child, but my parents weren't around much. All I wanted was to be present for my kids, but I hadn't really banked on one of them needing so much extra help. Colt had ended up being low-maintenance, but I always wondered if it was only because I had so badly needed him to be.

Lily clung to my hand and let me tow her through the corridors. After school, I always took her to the hydroponics level upstairs.

That was a tradition older than she was. As soon as I was old enough not to have a babysitter after school, I used to go to the arboretum on the way home every day. My mother never cared particularly when I got home or what I did, so long as I didn't make noise once she was at home. So I would wander the paths, throw myself on the grass, and stare upward at the light of the dome lamps filtering through the trees.

In under a week, I'd be on solid ground again, and with trees and plants all around. Hopefully we'd have time to study them a little before we had to start replacing them with Earth plants. That might not be what we were here for, but I itched to get my hands on at least a few samples.

Robin

It hadn't occurred to me I might not fit in the spacesuit. I had to exhale to do it, but I eventually got it fastened. Pregnancy was getting more ridiculous all the time. No wonder humanity had moved past it the instant it could.

Cliff followed me into the airlock, and we waited for it to cycle. "What do you think is the matter with number seven?"

I shook my head. "Could be anything. This thing is a hundred years old, and we've put some serious mileage on it."

The door cranked open and I led the way outside, clipping my tether to a hook beside the airlock. Eos shone above us—below us?—and we both paused for a moment to stare. Clouds swirled over the temperate belt around the middle, concealing the shapes of the continents.

"I can't wait to see sunshine again," he said, starting along the side of the ship toward the engines. "Down on a planet, where it just comes down all around you."

"Funny, I never knew you were a daysider."

"Yeah, my family is in agriculture," he said. "They came to Proxima in the first wave."

I fought a rush of resentment. Hadn't I known Cliff for four years now? He hadn't acted like a privileged ass in all that time, and he wasn't suddenly going to start now. Especially now that his updome family was far behind. "My people were fourth wave," I said quietly. "I always said, if there had ever been a fifth wave, maybe we could have gotten ahead. But nobody was left on Earth who had the slightest chance of affording the passage. It took my grandparents all they had."

"I would have thought you wouldn't want another wave. I mean the third-wavers always act like they wish they were the last."

I ran my hands over the engine. I couldn't see a problem yet. Groping along my belt, I took out my magnifier for a closer look. "It's stupid," I said. "The third-wavers made a huge fuss over the fourth wave, because they thought we'd take all their jobs. And we did—so they could move up to better jobs. Every planet needs a bottom."

"Pilot isn't what I would think of as a bottom-tier job."

I turned my helmet away so he couldn't see the look on my face. "My father was in debt his whole life, paying for that ship. He was in love with the stars, he didn't care that he couldn't afford it. Everything he earned went straight to the slip on it. So all three of us, plus my grandma, had to live on what my mom made in yeast extraction." I slammed the magnifier back into my belt loop and slid around the engine to look at the other side. I didn't want to talk about what it was like, down in the lower levels on the nightside where you never saw the stars. The cramped single room, the public kitchens and bathrooms, the noise of the man on the other side of the wall screaming at his wife, every single night.

Cliff didn't pick up on my annoyance. "So did he ever pay the slip?"

"Yeah. He actually did." I took my magnifier back out. "The very next month he stroked out. Weakened blood vessel in his brain, from pulling so many g's. He had to, to deliver enough cargos to get out from under that fucking *note*!"

Finally Cliff got the hint and stopped asking questions. I probably shouldn't blame him for not being able to read me in a spacesuit. But I still did. Privileged updomers like him never thought of the kind of things my family had learned from birth. Shaking my head, I focused on the engine.

The trouble with space travel was a simple physics problem. With nothing to push against, the only way to move at all was to throw something away. As we pushed out a stream of hydrogen or oxygen or whatever, we pushed ourselves forward with the same amount of force we used on the jet material. The problem was that any amount of mass we wanted to push out, we would have to carry, which increased the amount of thrust it took to move us forward.

The solution was to throw away the jet material one atom at a time, at near-light speeds. After all, it generated just as much force to throw small amounts away quickly as to throw large amounts slowly. We still had needed to carry a shit-ton of hydrogen—1 g for four years is a massive amount of acceleration to have to generate—but at least it wasn't so much we couldn't afford to move it at all.

A magnetic field, powered by the massive fusion reactor in the center of the eight engines, accelerated the atoms away from us to generate the necessary thrust. There weren't many moving parts, so not much could go wrong. But clearly something had.

Ah. There it was. A tiny gap in the delicate tracery of the cooling matrix. It was just a network of fine conductive metal that carried heat from inside the engine to the outside, where the large surface area would help it dissipate in the cold of space. But that tiny crack, barely visible to the naked eye, would stop heat from traveling along the metal. A large portion of the matrix wasn't being used at all, because the heat couldn't get over the crack.

"Hand me the microwelder," I said. "I found the bastard."

3

Robin

I took a deep breath. This was it. My last piloting job, and my hardest. I had never had to land anything before. I'd done about a thousand training sims by this time, and I knew the *Resurrection*'s responses like my own body's.

I could take her down. I knew I could. But my heart was still pounding. I'd never been this nervous before a burn before. Normally, I was entirely calm behind the controls. But this time I had five hundred people relying on me to get it right. Three of whom were my own family.

Thumbing the intercom, I began. "This is it, guys, we are ready to make our descent. I've had confirmation that all of you are safely secured. Please do not unfasten your restraints for any reason until we are safely on the ground. Sit tight and we'll soon be home."

Home. Could it be that? I remembered the day Aspen and I had gotten our first apartment, unlocking the door and stepping into the blank, empty room. It hadn't felt like home then, but before long it felt like we'd always been there. This planet, bare of human habitation, was just an empty suite of rooms as far as I was concerned, but I knew in time I would look back sentimentally on this moment and wonder how I had ever *not* been attached to the place.

My heartrate steadied, I finally sat down and fastened my own restraints. Normally I preferred to stand, but this trip would be bumpy at best. The engines would keep it from being a free fall, but we would have atmosphere to deal with. Yet another thing I had no personal experience with.

Touching the thrusters, I began to degrade our orbit.

It's a surprisingly long way from orbit before you even start to hit atmosphere. That part was easy. Later, as gravity started to tug at us, I fired up the engines to slightly push back. Still, we were falling fast enough that I felt barely any gravity. The time to decelerate would be later.

As the air around us got thicker, I could hear it shrieking against the metal hull. The friction of the air would degrade the metal; it was one of the many reasons the *Resurrection* couldn't be used again after we landed. The electromagnetic shielding worked well against errant space dust, not an entire atmosphere. Inside, the temperature started to warm up. I checked my gauges. Well within tolerances.

"How's number seven?" I called down to Cliff.

"Ehhhh …" he answered vaguely. "It's warmer than it should be."

"What the fuck?" I shouted. "We *checked* it!"

"I don't know," he said. "Maybe the atmosphere?"

I checked the readings. There was no camera out there; it would have gotten blasted off by the friction by now if there had been. But he was right; the temperature on the number seven was rising. Shit.

"Can you do what you did last time?" he asked.

"Can't. We're already out of orbit, and we have to lose a lot of velocity before we touch down." This was an understatement. We had started out moving at almost eight thousand meters per second, laterally. And we were accelerating downwards another nine point four meters per second every second. Not quite G, because Eos was smaller than Earth, but not enough difference to matter. "Better spray the coolant."

"I just sprayed everything we had left."

That's right. We had used it all up on the last crisis. I brought a breath through my nose and let it out. "Well we're just going to have to hope it holds itself together. I can't land this thing at eight thousand meters per second."

The scream of the atmosphere increased, and my seat jerked me side to side. We were hitting Eos's airstreams, carrying weather around in the upper atmosphere. It was clear at our landing site, but there are always high winds on a planet with an atmosphere. God, I wished I could have practiced this. Maybe a hundred times. But Proxima had no atmosphere, even if we had been in the habit of landing ships directly on the surface instead of bringing things down by space elevator. There was nowhere I could have practiced. Anyone who knew how to do it was long dead, and probably using a ship better suited to the job than ours. The *Resurrection* was supposedly able to land in an emergency, but of course it had never been tested.

I guided her on slow s-curves, as the sims had taught me, to lose some velocity. Down below, Colt and Lily would be strapped in on either side of Aspen. Lily, especially, would be scared. They had drilled the landing— every possible landing, including a water landing and a rapid evacuation. Every Saturday evening was emergency drills of every conceivable kind. But I couldn't help but worry. As I was realizing, simulations weren't the same as the real thing.

The temperature on the number seven kept inching up. Then suddenly it made a leap upward. "It's igniting!" Cliff shouted.

I clenched my teeth. "Shut it down!"

"I can't!" he cried. "I mean, I did but nothing's happening."

Of course—shutting it down was supposed to cut off the oxygen, but there was oxygen *outside* too. The fire was being fueled by the atmosphere.

"It's getting hot in here!"

"In the engine room?"

"Yeah, the wall is red." Suddenly he shouted wordlessly. The fire breaking through?

"Get out of there!" I shouted. "I'm shutting the fire door in three seconds. Mark." I counted off three seconds. No sound from him. Hopefully that meant he had obeyed? I shut my eyes and stabbed the button. Whether he had made it out or not, I couldn't risk the ship for him. If that fire got inside, it would devour all our oxygen. Even if the heat didn't kill us, we'd asphyxiate. I thought of Aspen and the kids, strapped in safely in the chapel. I had to protect them, and the rest of the settlers, first.

But now the ship was beginning to cant over, unbalanced by the massive flame spurt on one corner. In a moment it would start to spin. I switched off the four, five, and eight engines to try to compensate. Almost. I boosted the burn on the rest to maximum and the ship finally balanced out.

A chime on my panel alerted me to low oxygen in the main hold. *What?* I had *shut* the fire doors! Either they had malfunctioned and failed to shut completely, or I had been too slow and the fire had caught on something inside. But what? The ship wasn't made to be flammable!

Didn't matter. I punched the shipwide intercom. "Oxygen drill. Put on your masks." I released the button, chewing my lip. Everyone knew what to do. But I worried Aspen would try to put on Lily's first. It's what I would be tempted to do. And if he passed out before he had been able to do his own, or Colt's...

I shook my head. That wasn't my wheelhouse. This bridge was. I leaned forward as much as I could with my straps. Elevation was down to a thousand meters now, but velocity was still forty meters per second and only dropping slowly, with one engine spurting flames and three shut down. I couldn't boost the gain on the remaining engines any further. They weren't made for more than 20% over cruising speed. With Cliff down there, I might have overridden that. But not without him.

My teeth worrying my lip, I flicked the remaining engines on, simultaneously turning the maneuvering thrusters on full, all along the other side. Was it going to be enough? My instruments showed me the ground coming up below me, sketched in outline. Too fast. In retrospect I should have vetoed this landing site. It wasn't large enough. If we missed, and ended up hanging off the edge of the plateau…

With a terrible, grating roar, one edge of the ship met the ground. A second later, the seat below me rose up and slammed against me. It was like leaping off a roof and landing square on my ass. Then everything slid sickeningly sideways. My neck jerked against the straps. We were sliding, sliding toward the edge of the plateau.

A few seconds later, with a tooth-rattling jolt, we slid to a stop. The lights suddenly went out, replaced with the faint blue glow of the emergency lighting. I couldn't breathe. Things felt flat, but were we poised to topple over? At last I checked the display. We had stopped meters from the edge of the plateau. I drew in a long, shaky breath. We had made it. But only just.

For a second I was so overcome with shaking I couldn't move. I had done it. I had almost killed us all. Everything was fine. We could have all died. I covered my face, trying not to imagine the might have beens. Or, for that matter, what might still be going on down in the hold. If anything had gone wrong with the masks…

That thought stirred me to action. I reached out for the intercom. "Chapel, report," I barked.

Sybil's warm voice responded smoothly. "We are all right down here. Very shaken. Can we take off the masks yet?"

I glanced at the oxygen levels. "No. Your level, and everything below you, are depleted. I'm not yet sure why. I'm going to go see, and then try to restore oxygen." In that order. If there was a fire in the hold, it would be easier to fight the less oxygen there was.

"I will lead everyone in a prayer of thanksgiving."

Gingerly I unstrapped myself and grabbed the emergency oxygen mask from under my control panel. I felt sore all over, but there was no time to check myself carefully. Somewhere, down in the engine room, was a fire. And Cliff. He still hadn't checked in.

I climbed down the ladder and past the hydroponics deck and the personnel deck. The gravity felt strange, a little lighter than our standard acceleration gravity and a lot lighter than Proxima's. At last I reached the corridor that led down to the engine room. The lights along the edges of the walls were tinted orange: high CO_2, low oxygen. But I saw no sign of fire.

As I approached the fire doors, I spotted a shape on the floor and hurried over. It was Cliff. He wasn't moving.

Taking a deep breath, I took off my mask and clapped it over his nose and mouth. I held it there as long as I could stand, meanwhile checking over the rest of him. One arm and shoulder were blistered red, but the rest of him looked relatively undamaged.

I took my mask back for a few more breaths before giving it back to him. If he'd survived the fire only to asphyxiate when it had stolen all the air, I'd be pissed. But his eyes were starting to flutter. "Did the fire doors stay shut?"

I glanced behind me. "Look fine to me."

His next turn with the mask, he said, "They stuck. Wouldn't shut. The air was getting sucked out." With his undamaged hand, he gave me the mask back for a breath. When he got it back, he continued, "I managed to get them to shut, but it took ages and by the time I had done that, I was dizzy and couldn't make it to a restraint seat. So I just lay down right here."

I eyed him, stretched out like that. It was true, slamming straight down like we had would have just pressed him toward the floor. If he'd been standing he'd likely have broken both legs. "So you put yourself in danger to shut that piece of crap door?"

He waved his good hand dismissively. "If the ship is junk, we just have to make allowances. It would have sucked all the air out."

"It very nearly did," I said. "It didn't help that I had no idea the door didn't shut and so I didn't shut any of the other fire doors until the oxygen loss had reached the personnel deck. You should have *called*."

"Sorry," he said. "I had time for one thing. I picked one."

"I forgive you *only* because you're not dead," I said, getting up. "I'll get you a medic." I took a deep breath from the mask and left it with him. It was only about thirty more feet down the corridor to the next emergency station. My lungs were burning by the time I reached it—I was tempted to breathe, but the high CO_2 in the air would be worse than just going without. The new mask smelled of musty plastic, but the canister was full. Good. The emergency station also had an intercom, so I called up to Sybil to send the doctor down.

Going back over by Cliff, I passed him to put my hand on the fire door. It was only warm. Tentatively I turned the manual crank to edge it open.

"Ruining my hard work?" Cliff asked.

"I have to know if the fire's out. If it's gotten into the reactor we'll have to evacuate."

But no flames came pouring out, and I cranked the door the rest of the way open. The engine room was a mess of blackened metal and melted plastic. The curve in the wall where the number seven engine passed through the side of the room was distorted, and a gaping hole showed where the fire had exploded through. The whole inside of the engine was melted to slag. Useless. Not that that mattered.

Between the closed fire door and the outside of the engine being buried in dirt, the fire must have been smothered. But for good measure, I took down the fire extinguisher and sprayed the inside of the engine, as far as I could reach inside the hole.

When I got out, Hazel, our doctor, was kneeling beside Cliff, spraying a dressing on his arm. "Between the fire, the oxygen loss, and the unsecured landing, you're lucky to be alive."

"I know," he said, struggling to his feet. "I was about ready to meet the goddess, but I'm glad I don't have to yet."

"She must have something in mind for you," Hazel said, supporting him down the hall.

I hung back in the doorway. I had been meaning to join them, but suddenly I didn't feel like it.

Restoring oxygen was next on my list. The bioscrubbers were too slow to clear the carbon dioxide before everyone's masks ran out. The backup scrubber ran off the reactor, which had shut down when we land-ed. I had no idea how long that might take me to fix. Emergency power wouldn't be nearly enough.

But what was I thinking? We were on a planet now. A planet with breathable air. I hurried to the nearest computer terminal.

It took some doing to convince the computer that it was safe to open all the airlocks, yes, *both* doors. But it eventually realized there wasn't hard vacuum on the other side and opened the locks.

When I reached the personnel level, Lily and Colt came running to me, trailed by Aspen. For a second I couldn't speak, just squeezing the two of them against me. What could have happened…

"You're all right," said Aspen, engulfing me and the kids. "What about the baby? Have they checked?"

I froze, the blood draining from my face. I hadn't even thought. Whose crazy idea was it that we could do without artificial gestators? What sort of insane idea was it to keep our babies inside us, where they were stuck in any terrible situation we were?

Pulling myself free of his arms, I snapped, "Well it's not my fault if it's not, I did the best—I did the best I—" I started to cry.

"Hey," he said gently, but hanging back a little. Afraid I'd bite his head off? I wanted the hug back. "Hey, it's okay. We'll go find Hazel, I just saw her."

"You don't know how bad it was!" I shouted. "How close we came! It's not okay! I thought maybe everyone was—that you …" I trailed off. Four big brown eyes were staring up at me over their masks. I took big gulps of air, dashing the tears out of my eyes with both hands.

Just then I felt a big kick. A strong kick, a healthy one. My hands went to my belly. The anger seeped out of me. It was okay. It was okay. Everyone had lived. Tears streamed down my face, but I didn't yell any-more. I reached out to Aspen mutely.

He wrapped his arms back around me. "You did good, okay? You did fine. We're all safe. Everybody got their masks on. A little bumped up. Colt says his butt hurts, so Lily's probably does too."

"*My* butt hurts," I laughed shakily, dragging my wrist against my nose. "My whole back. Right up to my skull." I crouched down so I could see Lily's face. "That landing was a little hard, wasn't it, sweetie?"

"*My* butt hurts," she said, in exactly the tone I'd used, fiddling with the ear of her stuffed bunny.

"I know, baby. It'll feel better soon, I'm sure." I straightened up. "Look, the orange lights are going out." I pulled my mask off and took a lungful of air. It was cool, with a sharp tang of smoke. I had hoped to smell flowers or something, our first breath of real planet air, but the scent of the fire covered everything.

Colt took his off and crumpled it up in his hands. "Can we look out the window? I wanna see the planet."

"Of course we can." I took his hand and Lily's and led the way.

There was already a little crowd gathered around the window. Sybil turned as we approached. "Did you see this?"

We edged in beside her. It was evening, and the sky was an interesting purplish gray. But strangely, the ground was spattered with glowing gobs of red.

It took me a second to realize what I was seeing. It wasn't some strange new glowing plant. It was fire. The earth had stopped up the engine tube and smothered the fire inside, but the fire on the outside had caught in the ground cover and was slowly edging across the plateau. I wondered how far it would go.

"I'm sorry," I found myself stammering. "The engine was burning … I couldn't get the fire out." I felt like a monster, having set the planet on fire, the very first thing I did.

Sybil looked at me steadily for a long moment before turning back to the window. "It's for the best, I suppose. To terraform the planet, the first step is to remove the native life. This will give us a head start at that."

I turned to Aspen, incredulous. "Doesn't it release too much carbon, though? Won't it screw up the climate?"

"It's already on the outer edge of the habitable zone here," he said. "A carbon dioxide blanket might be a good thing. But don't worry, wildfires run out eventually. They hit a river, or it rains. It'll go a few hundred square kilometers at most."

That still seemed like a lot. I looked out at the darkening scene, as the lines of red spread outward, away from the ship. It didn't feel like a good omen.

Interlude

Mrrka, Eldest of all of the woodland nation, keeper of eighty-seven generations of memories, stirred from her sleep. Beside her, her mate, Tsaft, slumbered on.

Carefully slipping out of bed, Mrrka gazed down at her. It was pitch black in their bedroom, but her eyes could see the heat of Tsaft's body, the gentle curve of her tail and her ears. They had been together, by now, twenty years, and had begotten each other's children. Back in the day their love had been a terrible scandal—the heir to the Eldest with a second child, a nobody! But over the years it had become comfortable, easy. Though not, for that, any less intense.

On all six legs, Mrrka padded upstairs and outside. It was early yet, barely after sunset. A good time for hunting, though with her high rank and extensive lands, Mrrka hunted only for sport. Later that night, the peasant family that hunted and cooked for her would bring her something to eat.

She loped into the clearing and stood upright, throwing her head back to gaze at the sky. The stars hung low and bright, a perfect night to read them for a hint at her daughter's future.

The natural philosophers were saying these days that astrology was only superstition, but Mrrka still enjoyed it. Something about lining up the events in life to the patterns in the stars made everything seem much more orderly and safe, as if it were meant to be. When Mrrka's daughter Kisht had come out of the pouch for the first time, Mrrka had cast her stars. They said she would grow to be prideful, loyal, ambitious, and she certainly was.

Today had been the first great earthshaker hunt of the dry season, and Kisht had been honored at the feast afterward as the one who had struck the first blow. It had been a proud moment, and more than one young person had paid special attention to Kisht. And why wouldn't they? As the daughter of the Eldest, she would be an advantageous match for anyone. Kisht had seemed to show interest in one in particular, the daughter of another old family, and the two had danced together a dozen times.

Mrrka felt she ought to be happy. If Kisht had found love, and simultaneously a socially-appropriate match, who could complain? But Mrrka couldn't help but wonder how much of Kisht's choice had to do with love, and how much had to do with class-consciousness. Kisht had always been adamant about family pride, about who was appropriate or not for the family to speak to. *Perhaps she is compensating for my disgrace*, Mrrka thought.

The scandal around her marriage had not fully died down by the time Kisht was old enough to hear it. People talked, saying that Mrrka would be Eldest someday, she ought to know better than to select a second child with no lands or memories at all, no matter how beautiful or kind.

Kisht loved Tsaft, but she had become aware early in life that others thought there was something wrong about her parents' match. Perhaps that was why she had gone so strongly the other way, toward propriety. Kisht never did anything improper.

It isn't that I could ever reject her choice of mate, Mrrka rationalized to herself. *It's that I worry there could be a better mate for her, and she would miss out if the person weren't from an old family. That's all.*

She focused back on the stars. Perhaps there would be an answer there. If the blue planet, the one symbolizing love, was in Kisht's constellation, that might mean a match made at this time would be fortuitous. Then Mrrka could relax, trusting that this noble girl might truly be a good mate for Kisht. But if the large white one were nearby, the planet of mistakes, it would suggest Kisht might be making an error. And if so, would it really be so terrible for Mrrka to intervene somehow?

She found the blue star that pointed north, and from there went searching for the planets. But before she could find any of them, she saw something quite different. An object like a star, but visibly moving. And not blue or white, but red, red and flaming. It came slowly at first, gradually growing larger as it arced down in the sky. Mrrka realized suddenly that it wasn't slow, it was only very far away. But as it came closer, it also came faster, not like a star at all.

Mrrka's mother had once seen such a thing, she suddenly remembered. Ancestral memories were like that. You wouldn't be aware of them at all, and then a sight or smell or thought brought them back, and you would remember suddenly, exactly as if it had happened to you. It took time and practice to recognize the difference, to know what had happened to you, your mother, or your great-grandmother.

But she could not linger on the memory, because the object was growing closer by the second. Just as it was almost close enough to make out its shape, it dropped below the tops of the trees that ringed Mrrka's clearing. Dropping to all six, she dashed after it. If it really was falling to the ground, she wanted to see it happen. Then perhaps she could finally answer the question of what sort of thing it was.

She broke free of the forest at a small ridge. Below was a large, flat plateau, barren of trees, part of the common. It was a good place to hunt grazers, but not for much else—no one wanted to live where there were no trees.

Looking around, she spotted the falling star again. This time it was clear it was no star, nor an animal. It was shaped like a cone, falling bottom-first out of the sky, but the bottom was spurting flames. It reminded Mrrka of nothing so much as a cauldron with a fire going underneath. And it still grew larger, and larger. It was like a mansion, dug up out of the ground.

At last the thing reached the ground and plowed into it, leaving a deep furrow in the earth. Mrrka's ears twitched and centered on the sound it made, a horrible grinding screech. It ground to a stop, and for a moment it seemed that the fire beneath the cauldron had gone out.

But then she saw the heat spreading away through the ivy and realized it had only moved on. The red flames followed quickly, pushed by the wind. That, at least, was something Mrrka did understand. A brushfire, here in the dry season, could be a disaster. And she didn't have her hunting horn with her to sound the alarm.

Dropping down again to run, she raced through the woods. Everyone must be gathered. She would direct some to begin digging a trench, others to divert the river. Trees might need to be felled. It wasn't the first forest fire she could remember: she knew how it could be stopped. But every minute lost would increase the danger.

4

Aspen

I paused a moment before stepping out the airlock. A new world. And I had the privilege of being one of the first to set foot on it.

My boot crunched on the ash underfoot. Bending to inspect it, I said to Autumn, "Looks like this area was covered in low vines or grass. Only a few large trees here and there."

"No surprise," she replied. "That's how it looked in the satellite image."

"I wish I could have seen it intact."

"Saves us a lot of time that it isn't."

"I suppose." I tried to sound casual.

All my life, I'd sought out nature when I was upset, or lonely, or bored. From my parents' potted plants to the Disciples' temple garden, being near plants always made me happy. They didn't ask difficult questions, make demands, or yell at you. Yet, unlike my mother, they were always *there.* They were rooted down, and that made them dependable.

Of course my main role here on Eos was to grow Earth plants. But it would be years before a really flourishing ecosystem would get off the ground. I hadn't realized till this moment just how much I'd been looking forward to walking in a real, living forest. Not an arboretum, and still less the cramped hydroponics lab that had been my only refuge for years.

But I couldn't let any of it on. Autumn would never understand; none of them would. Because wanting to see this alien forest would seem like a lack of devotion to Terra, whose Earth-origin seeds and embryos we'd spent so much effort bringing here. The goddess didn't like alien life, that was a truism by now.

So I cleared my throat, gave a sharp sniff, and kept walking, talking and gesturing to Autumn and the agricultural interns as I went. Here would be the main vegetable garden, here the wheat and corn, here the alfalfa for the animals, there the paddock and barn. Might want to build the stockade here; obviously we'd expand out past the fence in time, but first we'd need to know what kind of hazards were out there.

That job done, and a plan quickly drawn up by my most capable assistant, Willow, I let the others get on with other tasks while I tested the soil.

The shovel went right in when I stomped on it, turning up a rich, dark loam. I almost laughed out loud. It really could not be better soil for farming, and by pure luck too. Not like we could have done a soil analysis of the landing sites from space.

The soil was veined with mycelia, or something very like it. I took a few samples, along with vials of the soil itself. If it carried the same kind of nutrients with it that Earth fungi did, I might just leave it there. Plants were happier with mycelia nearby, ferrying nutrients here and there and trading molecules with their roots, but they didn't, strictly speaking, need to be from the same planet.

No worms in this soil, but there were little burrowing buglike creatures and something like a tiny underground lobster. I looked for Autumn, but she already had a collector's net and was going after flying bugs. Ah well. Maybe there would be time to study the native plants at least a little bit, later on.

Robin

I crawled out of the reactor housing and started stripping off my radiation suit. Balling up the gloves, I threw them on the floor. It could have been worse, was all I could think of to cheer myself up.

When we had slammed into the ground, the superheated plasma inside had escaped the field that trapped it and splashed all over the inside of the reactor. All of the delicate components inside had melted. I was no nuclear engineer, but with Cliff's help I'd managed some minor repairs on the reactor as needed. This? This was well beyond either of us. Even a Proxima mechanic would have told us to scrap it and get a new one.

The bright side was that the housing containing the reactor had done its designed job and kept the plasma inside. There were melt marks all over the inside, but the housing was a foot thick and made of a heat-resistant alloy. It had kept us all from a fiery death.

For that, I gave it a respectful slap as I left the engine room. She did good.

I found Aspen by the airlock, giddy from his walkabout on the planet's surface. "It's amazing out there," he said. "I can't wait to show it to you." I smiled, but it must not have reached my eyes, because he immediately asked, "So how's the reactor doing?"

I shook my head. "It's not doing. It's dead. There's nothing I can do for it. That was a hard landing and it was never expected to receive anything more than one g."

He pulled his stunner out of his belt and stowed it in a cabinet. "No reactor? I had just assumed the low power in the ship was temporary."

"It's temporary in the sense that it's running on battery. It won't last more than a week at the rate we're using it."

"But there are solar panels, right? Why aren't we getting any power from them?"

"Burned off in the descent," I said. "Like a lot of things. We didn't worry about that because we didn't expect to need them."

"This isn't going to fly," he said, eyes wide and worried. "The emergency power is totally inadequate for the hydroponics. The bioscrubber is suffering too. The CO_2 killed off a lot of the fungus and the lack of light is starving the algae. We don't need the scrubbing function but we absolutely have to have food."

He was right; power was not optional. Till we were living off the land, months from now, we needed the ship's power almost as badly as we had in space. I took a second to think. "We have solar panels in the hold for use in the colony. We can make a kind of solar farm. Fuel the ship that way."

He nodded slowly. "Okay. Okay. Yeah, we can do that. I'll ask Sybil."

"I was going to ask her," I protested. "If you think that will work for you, I'll just take care of it myself."

Glancing to the side, he said, "It's okay. I can do it."

That was his tell for avoiding something. "You think I can't?"

"I think you and Sybil don't get along very well."

I shrugged. "We get along fine. You don't have to take it on yourself to manage her and me arguing."

"But I don't *want* you to argue," he protested.

"Don't worry. I can be cool. Haven't I made nice with her for four years?"

"I'm not sure I'd call that making nice," Aspen muttered, at a volume I could plausibly pretend I hadn't heard.

I chose that option. Fighting with Aspen over the other woman in his life never ended well. "I'm going to go find her. Show me around outside after?"

I could see him consciously put aside the disagreement, and a smile broke out among the freckles. "Meet you at the airlock."

I found Sybil in the chapel, which was really just a big room with rows of seats and walls painted to look like a forest. She was kneeling on the ground, sitting back on her heels and half bent over, waves of dark hair falling forward over her face.

I grimaced. A religious person could hardly signal *leave me alone* any louder. But this definitely qualified as an emergency, and she wasn't holding anything like office hours since we'd landed. Reluctantly, I came up the aisle and sat next to her on the floor. Surely at some point she'd look up.

There was a small, choked sound from her and I looked up. "You okay?" I murmured, low, though we were the only ones in the chapel.

Her head came up, hair shaken back and away. Her face was wet and teary. "Robin," she said, and sniffed. "I assume you need something."

"I do, kinda, yeah, but I can come back later."

She shook her head, though I didn't know whether she meant *no, now is fine* or *no, don't come back ever.*

It was all the opening I was likely to get. "The fusion reactor was damaged in the landing. It's permanently offline."

She made a little choking sob. "Of course."

I didn't know how to respond to that. "I need your permission to get out the solar panels that we have in storage and set them up to provide power to the ship. We need power, you see, for the—"

"Was this a terrible mistake?" she interrupted.

Way to touch my exact insecurities. "I don't really think the hard landing was exactly avoidable, given the problems with the number seven engine."

"No, I mean." She waved her hand vaguely. "Leaving Proxima. Coming here. Everything."

I stared at her. This colony had taken years to plan and further years to get here. The work of hundreds of people. Every penny the church had ever had. Everybody had had doubts at some point—except her. Sybil had been the one pushing from the very beginning, demanding we had to do this, had to get a new home for her goddess, had to build a new world full of living Earth ecosystems. It was her whole thing.

"Well, *I'm* glad to be here," I said uncomfortably. "Plenty of room, finally. And the kids will be able to play outside."

"Terra asked it," whispered Sybil roughly. "She asked it, but will She help us do it? Did we do it wrong somehow? Did I displease Her?"

"I don't know," I said, nonplussed. "What did you do?"

"My best," she said, breaking down into tears again. "I have only ever done my best, and what she asked of me."

The conversation was getting away from me. Clearly she needed a spiritual counselor of some kind, but I had no idea who counseled the prophet herself. I cleared my throat. "How about we solve the problem of the solar panels first, and then I go get, uhh … somebody for you to talk to."

"I don't want anybody," she said forlornly. "You think anybody can handle seeing my weakness?"

It was a valid point, perhaps the first sensible thing I'd heard her say. In a place like this, the one thing everybody needed was confidence in her leadership. "Well, in that case you might want to leave the chapel," I pointed out. "People are always coming in. Why don't you go to your room. Before you go, could you just tell me if the solar panels—"

"I don't *care* about the solar panels!" she snapped, sounding like Colt on a bad day. She got to her feet and turned toward the exit. Over her shoulder she said, "Ask Hawk."

I let out a heavy sigh and went looking for Hawk. That, at least, was easy. He was in the cafeteria, the other largest room on the ship, pinning up schedules and work lists. I went straight up and explained the problem.

He frowned. "That's unfortunate. We certainly will have to take out the solar panels. Here." He pulled one of the work lists down, made some quick scribbles, and put it back up. "There. Coral knows where they are, and now she'll have a team of six to help her. You think that will be enough?"

I smiled. After the uncomfortable conversation with Sybil and the goddess talk, this was just what I needed. "Absolutely. Thank you, sir."

Unlike Sybil, he didn't correct me. I hurried off to go catch up with

42

Aspen.

I stood at the airlock, blinking in the bright sun. Aspen's team had set up a ramp leading down to the ground, but I still hesitated.

Aspen, seeing me, hurried over. "Got the solar panels worked out?"

"Yeah. And I didn't fight with anybody, either."

"Come on, then." He held out a hand.

I couldn't seem to untangle my hands from each other. "Are you sure it's safe?"

My eyes were fixed on the vast blue dome overhead—the *sky*, I reminded myself. It might look like a solid blue ceiling, but there was nothing actually there but miles of atmosphere. Nothing between me and space.

I struggled to catch my breath. I was standing in an open airlock, and there was nothing sealing in the atmosphere. A lifetime under domes, a career of carefully checking the suits and cockpits between me and space. I knew to be responsible for my atmosphere. Every molecule carefully sealed tight.

Here there was nothing. No dome. No glass. My lungs burned, convinced that the air would be ripped away, sucked into the vacuum. It was madness to live here on the bare face of the planet, without protection.

Aspen's hand on my elbow brought me back to myself. "It gave me a shock at first, too," he said. "You get used to it. It's just like a big blue dome."

"Maybe *you* got used to it," I groused. "I grew up in the bottom levels. There wasn't any dome to look at." But I tore my eyes from the sky and forced my lungs back to work. There was enough gravity here to hold the atmosphere all on its own. A magnetic field, too, to keep the solar wind out. Humans had evolved under just such a sky. It was perfectly natural.

The sight of the ground just depressed me. It was burned and blackened, no sign of the beautiful scenery we had all seen from the rover. "The soil is incredibly rich," Aspen said, leading me down the ramp. "Better than bare soil, because the burned carbon is so helpful. In a week we can start planting seedlings. I've already got them sprouted in the hydro lab, so we won't lose any time. Though I'm going to bring in soil to test whether the engineering I've done is right."

His enthusiasm made me smile. We had just spent two years where I got to do the thing I loved most, and he had been stuck tending lichen. Now it was his turn. I watched him talk as he poked around in the soil, not really listening. This was his life's dream, even as it was the end of my career. I only hoped I could be half as supportive as he had been. I didn't have much confidence in that.

After ten minutes, it was time to beg off. "I know you've got a million things to do. I'll let you get to it."

He sighed, looking like a boy who'd been told to come in from playing. "Yeah, you're right." He kissed my hair. "You'll be okay?"

"I'm sure there's tons of stuff for me to help with."

My first thought was to help build the fence. It was priority number one on Hawk's work lists, and they had gotten thick posts sunk every couple of meters, halfway around the clearing.

I headed over and volunteered. But the man supervising them was skeptical. "Should you really be lifting things?" He gestured at my belly.

I looked down at it. Hadn't pregnant women kept planting and harvesting and whatever the whole nine months, back in the old days? "I'll be fine."

But the very first beam I tried to drag into place, a muscle screamed in my lower back and I was forced to put it down. "I told you," said the man. "My wife carried both of ours naturally, it's no joke."

Next I went back into the ship, thinking I could help watch the kids. But Pine gave me a skeptical look. "It's not that I wouldn't appreciate the help," she said slowly. "But it's just, well, we're very careful about the influences the children receive. I mean, we're trying to give them a proper goddess discipleship. That means education in our faith," she added quickly.

"I know what it means," I said shortly. "You're saying you don't want a heathen like me around my own kids."

"Well, it's not just your children here. You can take Colt and Lily for the day if you want. But the other parents, they entrust their children to our school, and they're expecting a certain thing." Her large blue eyes gazed fixedly at mine, as if to stare me into submission.

I turned away, because there was nothing else I could do. Of course the colony school had its own policies. I hadn't needed to know that before. I had never been at loose ends like this.

In the end, I wound up back on the bridge, kicking back in the crash seat with my feet on the blank controls. Was this going to be my life from now on, complete uselessness?

It was hard enough losing the stars, the only thing I had ever wanted to do with my life. My dad had always begged me not to follow in his footsteps, but I couldn't help it. The very first time I was old enough to meet him at the orbital station, I had been hypnotized. And of course, once he had died, it would have seemed like sacrilege to sell his ship. He had bought it with his life, and I could finally make a living on running cargos, the way he never could.

It hadn't been easy. Not one single step of the way had. The zero-g physics and the orbital mechanics, when I had never finished high school. Being a young woman surrounded by grizzled old men. Figuring how not to get ripped off buying fuel and repairs, and finding cargos that actually paid. How could I have given up, after how far I'd come? My seventeen-year-old self would have been ashamed of me.

But life changes you, and of course there had been reasons. So many reasons. Aspen. The kids. When Colt was born, I had switched to short trips, just two weeks at a time, with lots of time at home, but Colt was a baby. He had no sense of time. At first he had cried when I left, and then he had just gotten used to it and made up his mind that Aspen was the only parent he really wanted.

And then Lily. Lily was . . . I took a deep breath against the rush of feelings that sprang up when I thought about her. About how things had been. Suffice it to say she had coped with my absence worse than Colt had. The doctor was telling us what she really needed was space, and access to nature. Couldn't we move to a larger apartment on a quieter street? Maybe buy a membership to an arboretum? And of course, she needed a predictable schedule with both parents around.

Well, we couldn't have had both. If I had quit my job, we would have had to downsize, not upgrade. As it was we only had 700 square feet, barely enough for our own kitchenette. Proxima real estate was at a premium, since it had to fit into the domes available. And I worried we'd get evicted if Lily couldn't stop screaming.

When Aspen had gotten into the Church of Terra, it had seemed—well, say it. Like an answer to a prayer. They had a little nursery school that was affordable and small, that didn't mind adapting to Lily's needs. They had a little infant prayer room full of potted plants, where it was always quiet. Lily stayed in there for hours, gently stroking the leaves or softly humming. At home, she spent less time screaming.

Aspen told me about the plan to colonize a new planet almost as a side note. Like he didn't care much one way or the other. But I could see the hope in his eyes. Finally a chance to work with plants in a whole new environment, to stop engineering ever-better kinds of algae and actually do something new.

And I…well, I could look around myself. Proxima was crowded and getting worse. It was too easy to fall through the cracks, and who would be the first to fall? Lily. Right back down to the tunnels, where I had come from. Aspen, born comfortably middle-class, never understood that. How easy it was to end up there, or how bad it was once you got there.

Every other colony had a million requirements. No genetic anomalies was always top of the list. Only the Disciples of Terra didn't care. They weren't trying to build a perfect world. They wanted to recreate Earth, in all its messiness. A home for their goddess, who had apparently been the spirit of Earth before it had gotten too toxic for her. The theology seemed a little weird, but I hardly cared.

And more kids. We were both only children; Proxima was such an expensive place to try to raise kids. Two had stretched us, but both Aspen and I had always wanted more if we could. I liked the idea that after we were gone, they'd have each other. Little pieces of us running around, giving each other a hard time. The Disciples were all about that. Repopulating this new Earth with new people.

But now it was time to pay up. I had loved what I did. I had loved it so damn much. And I had no fucking clue what I was going to do with myself now. Having a baby wasn't a *job*. My body was doing that part for me. What was I going to do with my brain in the meantime?

Behind me, the door slid open, and I jerked upright, scrubbing at my face with my sleeve. Stupid hormones. With a hard sniff and an attempt to smile, I got up and turned around.

It was only Cliff, his arm in a sling. "I have been looking everywhere for you," he said. "I thought maybe you'd be at loose ends too."

I grinned, this time sincerely. "Nice to know I'm not the only useless person around."

"Gosh, if you put it that way, I'll leave you to it!"

"You got a better idea?"

"Yeah, I had the idea that you and I could go exploring. They've looked at everything on the plateau, but I was thinking we could go past that and see how far the burn zone goes, maybe catalog some native plants."

"You ask permission already?"

"I asked Hawk. He said it would be great because we could map out where good trees are, for building with. I have a couple of stunners in case we run into any wildlife."

"You've thought of everything," I said, heading for the door. "Let me just say goodbye to Lily."

It turned out that was a stupid idea. She had expected not to see me all day, while she was at school, and so she refused to look at me when I stopped by her group. They were watching a show about pandas, one of her favorites, and when I tried to touch her arm, she squirmed away.

"Okay then, enjoy your pandas," I said softly, creeping away.

Cliff was waiting awkwardly in the doorway. As we reached the airlock, he asked, "So, is there…you know…something up with her? I've always wondered."

"You don't have to be embarrassed that you noticed," I said. "It's hard to miss."

"Couldn't afford a gene check before she went in the tank?"

I swallowed. I had had this same damn conversation so many times. "Actually, we did check. When they told us she'd be autistic … well, obviously they told us to flush her tank and try again. But it just felt … well, who's perfect, you know? And which of us would even be here if anybody had been that careful? After all, I was never gene checked, none of my family was. So if she wasn't good enough, maybe I wasn't good enough. And I'm just not willing to say that anybody's not good enough to be alive."

"You should tell that to Sybil," he said. "She'd like that. She's always saying nature is wild, it's messy but that's how it was meant to be."

We passed the fence workers, who smiled and waved. "Not sure I buy the idea of 'meant to be,'" I said slowly. "Things are what they are. Sometimes how they are sucks. If it had been something painful, something that could have killed her, we'd have started over. But this? It's not a big deal, really. She's only different. Different doesn't mean worse."

He chuckled. "You really do sound like Sybil."

We crossed a wide expanse of ashy plain. After a while it started to get rocky and slope uphill, and there were more charred trees. For a while it took all of our attention just climbing over all the obstacles.

I turned and looked back. Big mistake. The ground fell away below us, toward the sweeping emptiness of the plateau. Our ship, our colossal ship that had been our whole world for four years, looked small. Beyond, where the cliff fell away, I could see masses of purple vegetation stretching out, it seemed like forever. Too far to see clearly where it met the sky.

I felt like a bug, clinging to the naked skin of the world. My head spun. "I gotta sit down."

Cliff sat down beside me and handed me a water bottle. "Sorry, we should have taken a break before now. This is a long walk and obviously neither of us is in shape."

Sure, I'd go with that excuse. "I guess you're more used to the open spaces than I am," I said, waving at the expanse beyond. "Farm kid."

"Well, sort of," he said. "But the fields under the domes are . . . not like this."

"Nothing is like this."

"I guess Earth was. Back before."

I shrugged. We'd all seen a million pictures and videos. Sure, there were wide spaces and greenery. But somehow I'd never grasped the *vastness*.

Getting to my feet, I started climbing again. Cliff shouldered his pack and followed. Eventually the hill leveled out and we reached a wide, shallow creek, where water trickled over the jumbled stones. Here the burned area ended, and across the water was the living forest.

Between the stones and a number of fallen tree trunks, we got across with little trouble. For a moment we just stood and stared. The living forest was somehow less frightening than the burned-out land had been, perhaps because it blocked off the sky. But at the same time, it was even further from anything I had yet experienced. Not orderly like a garden or arboretum. In a way it reminded me of an alley back home, down in the tunnels, with shop fronts and buskers and ladders and booths everywhere. Utterly random and messy, but in a way that suggested a deeper pattern.

The largest trees were tall and straight, with white bark and shiny, red-violet leaves sprouting directly out of the trunk. Scattered among these were shorter, purple trees with ferny leaves. Where sunlight fell through the trees, there was a sort of creeping pink ivy, with star-shaped leaves.

Cliff recovered first, digging out his camera and taking pictures of all the plants. "Your husband is going to want to see all this stuff."

"Do you have any bags to take samples in?" I reached for the ivy to break off a leaf.

"Don't touch it!" he snapped. "Sorry. It's just, we don't know if it's poisonous yet. Use the bag to protect your hand." He tossed me a roll of them.

"I wasn't going to eat it," I said. "Could something be poisonous if you just touch it?"

"Oh yeah," he said. "There were Earth plants that were."

"I don't know anything about Earth plants. Not unless they were brought to Proxima."

"That's the kind of thing they teach us at Greenie school."

"I thought you guys were all about idealizing Earth. You know, the perfection of nature and all that. Not plants that hurt you if you touch them."

Cliff took the sample bags from me and stuffed them back in his bag. "Not a bit. Nature is a mess. Don't you ever watch the animal videos they show every night? It's all polar bears killing seals. Or if the seal gets away, the polar bear babies starve. It all works out in the end, kind of a naturally-correcting system, but it's not very nice for the seals."

"Or the humans."

He shrugged. "Not always. But that's the problem, you see. We tried to escape it and tame it so we'd never get hurt, and in the end we killed it. But it turned out, we needed it."

"Only we didn't really, did we? We've gotten on fine without Earth. And engineered better plants and things, that work the way *we* want them to."

Shaking his head, he led the way further through the trees. I cast a glance backward, trying to impress on my mind the way we'd come. This place would be easier to get lost in than the tunnels, and no friendly streetwalkers to ask for directions.

"That may be how it looks at first, but *ultimately* it's eventually going to—" He broke off. "Oh my god."

I hurried to catch up, trying to guess from his tone whether he saw something dangerous or something beautiful. It didn't sound like either.

When I came up beside him, I stopped dead. In the clearing beyond was a huge…thing. It took me a second to figure out what it was. "Is that an animal skeleton?"

He nodded. "Fresh."

The animal had been about the size of my first apartment, with six stubby legs and a long neck. But most of the flesh was gone from its body, so all that was left was red, stringy stuff clinging to its bones. Dozens of batlike creatures clung to the bones, eating what was left of it. Cliff took out his camera and started taking pictures, but without coming any closer.

"Natural causes, you think?" I managed to say weakly. My only experience of meat was the solid, even-textured blocks of vat beef I used to get from the store. This was…not like that, except for the metallic smell. The tattered flesh that still coated the bones was streaked with white tendons. Altogether too close a reminder of my own flesh, and what it might look like if you peeled half of it off.

I swallowed hard, so as not to gag and embarrass myself in front of Cliff. All those nature videos, this would be old news to him.

"No," he said, pointing. On the ground a little distance from where it was lying was a huge smear of red blood. "Some predator took it down."

"What kind of a predator could tackle *this*?" Automatically I had lowered my voice to a whisper. "It's fucking enormous! Look at that tail!"

Cliff stuffed his camera back in his bag. "We should get back."

I nodded. I didn't want to hang around where a predator like this could be roaming.

5

Aspen

I tried to find Sybil and talk to her, even though Robin had told me she was leaving everything in Hawk's hands for the moment. Most likely, she was hiding herself away completely. She did that sometimes, perhaps a few times a year. Whether she was sick or taking personal prayer time, no one had ever found out. It didn't seem proper to ask.

But I felt like I needed to at least try, and not just to talk about the practical issue of the dead reactor. I wanted to talk about how this planet made me feel. How sad I was about the fire. Was I going to be able to handle managing the terraforming project, if one bald patch made me so morose?

I knew Earth life was what mattered to Terra. And Earth life was what I most deeply wanted, too. But I always felt wistful when I saw the pictures of Eos landscapes. It felt like the real version of all the Proxima fakes—gardens and arboretums skillfully mimicking real forest. Not one human alive had ever seen a wild forest, till we'd come here. And now Robin got to go exploring it while I was stuck looking at the burned patch.

I paused outside Sybil's bedroom door, steeling myself to knock. I wasn't afraid of her, but I didn't want to bother her either.

I had a sudden memory of my childhood. My mother had been ... busy with her own life, let's say. She didn't like to be bothered much. But I'd had a terrible nightmare and was scared enough to try waking her.

I had stood out in the hall, raised my hand to knock—and chickened out. What if she was mad? What if she rubbed her temples in annoyance and told me a child my age shouldn't still be waking her up in the night?

After several minutes of agonizing in the hallway, I had gone back to bed, to stare at the shadows in fear until morning.

But Sybil wasn't my mother. She had always been so much more open, more available. I could knock. Only just as I raised my hand, I heard voices and paused. I recognized Hawk's clipped tones. "You can't just stay in here forever. The people need you."

"They don't need me," Sybil's voice responded bitterly. "They need someone better."

"You can't be this way," he insisted. "Stop feeling sorry for yourself. You have a duty."

She gave a short, sharp laugh. "Sorry for myself? Is that what you think this is?"

"I don't know what else to call it, when suddenly you seem to care more about your feelings than your flock. We're trying to build something here. Something that was your idea in the first place!"

"It was never my idea," she said coldly. "It was Terra's. I'm surprised at you."

"You'll have to forgive me." His voice was formal, angry. "I don't understand what that's like, since she doesn't deign to talk to me."

I realized suddenly that I was eavesdropping, and beat a hasty retreat. My own problems would have to wait. I didn't want to be like Hawk, nagging her to come out when she wasn't ready. We were all adults here. We didn't need her to be constantly available. She was allowed a break like anybody else.

I went back to the lab and studied my new samples. Nothing like getting lost in science to clear my head. Life from another planet! I might not be able to roam the woods, but there would be copious microorganisms even in my soil samples.

The mycelia, or mycelia-analog I should say, were slightly different from the Earth version structurally, but they seemed to fill the same ecological niche. For the most part, the nutrients they ferried around were the same as the ones our plants would need.

The soil teemed with nitrogen-fixing microbes, microscopic nematodes, everything good soil should have. I divided the rest of my sample into pots and planted a few fast-growing seeds in it. No better way to tell if it was viable for our plants than to try it.

That was the fun part of my day. At any rate, it had cheered me up enough to be ready to look at the bioscrubber. I opened up one of the grow tubes to have a look. Each had a core of permeable substrate, through which nutrient solution bubbled, and a shell lined with bright grow lights. Between those layers was the scrubber lichen itself, greenish-brown scales like fungi jutting out from a log.

It looked, if anything, worse than yesterday. Whole patches of the stuff were fully gray, and in places the inner tube was visible. The lights still weren't shining as bright as they should; I hoped once the extra solar panels were set up, they'd brighten.

Robin came in while I was checking on each tube, coming up behind me and wrapping her arms around my waist. "How's the scrubber?"

"Bad," I said. "I know Coral is setting up the extra panels, but she told me even all together they won't put out anything close to what the reactor did."

"You don't need all that," she said. "We use energy like it's going out of style because the reactor puts out so much, but it's easy to reduce usage. Have people turn out the lights when they leave the room, that kind of thing. You leave it to me. I'll go over everything and see what we can cut."

"I just hope it recovers at all," I said, not entirely comforted. "A natural ecosystem bounces back from almost anything; it's not adapted to our needs, but it's great at surviving. But this, this is a hothouse flower.

It was created for a controlled environment. It's not so controlled in here anymore."

She stared at it, chewing on her lip. It couldn't be lost on her that this was the majority of our food still, and would be for months yet. "Are we going to be all right?"

I shook my head slowly. "I *think* so. Hopefully it will adapt to a lower algae population in time. But I can't be sure, so I *really* have to get the plants going." My eyes went back over to my pots of dirt.

"I'll help," she said, striding over and hitching her butt onto the counter. "Put me to work."

I grinned. "Do you never get *tired*?"

"I'm exhausted, but if you don't make me climb up another mountain, I'll be fine."

I handed her a stack of small pots. "So how was that?"

"Terrifying. Pretty. Weird. We saw one of those megafauna—it was huge. Bigger than in the pictures. It was dead. Cliff thought it was killed by a predator, but if so, it was a big one."

"Not necessarily. Could have been a pack of small ones."

"I don't know if that's less frightening, or more. Would you rather be attacked by a hundred regular sized chickens, or one giant chicken?"

"Chickens are dumb, I'm pretty sure I could handle either." Just having her here in the lab with me made me feel so much better. Plants are comforting, but there's something to be said for a person to talk to.

She packed the little pots with soil, and I tucked in the tiny seeds. Peas. Spinach. Radishes. Nothing pops up so fast as a radish. If these did well, we could eat them in a month. If they didn't, though, I might need to tinker with the genes to get them to flourish. The soil had slightly different levels of each nutrient, and you never really know how plants will take to that till you try it.

"I brought you samples," she mentioned after a while. "I feel a little bad that I got to go and you didn't. So I brought a little of everything."

I leaned in and kissed the tip of her nose. "You didn't have to do that."

"Gotta let the botanist do botany."

I wrote the last radish label, stuck it on, and moved on to labels for the spinach. "I shouldn't waste too much time on that. This is what I'm here for." I gestured at the pots.

She looked surprised. "But this is all new plant life. If we're going to be getting rid of most of it, don't we have to study it before it's gone? Of all the planets people have surveyed, only a few of them have any life at all, let alone this much."

I shook my head. I knew what she'd say if I said what I was really thinking. *I feel guilty about wanting to study these plants? I feel like I'm cheating on Terra for taking any interest in Eos life?* She hardly needed ammunition to start complaining about my religion.

Eventually I said, "It's Earth life that's the endangered species. Its whole habitat has been destroyed, the ecosystems aren't systems any-more. If we can get past peas in pots, and actually create a thriving Earth ecosystem…won't that be the more exciting thing to study?"

"Is that what you think, or what Sybil thinks?" asked Robin. Just as I said. I tried not to argue religion with her because I didn't actually want to convert her, but she didn't always give my beliefs the same respect.

I shrugged. "We're not a top-down kind of religion. Anybody can hear the voice of the goddess."

"Even you? You're hearing voices and never told me?" She gave an amused smile.

Pulling out another stack of pots, I unstacked them, one by one, onto the table. "I wouldn't say I hear any words, no," I said at last. "Not like Sybil does. But when I meditate, I do feel something sometimes. A presence. A sense of peace."

"Sounds nice." There was a wistfulness in her tone. Robin had never had much peace in her life. She could use some more than anyone I knew.

"More than nice," I said, feeling better as I thought of it. "I was des-perate for it, back when I first got involved. When Lily was little. I felt like I was slowly losing my mind. Meditation made me feel like myself again."

"It wasn't the free babysitting during the services?"

"Well, that *too*." I opened another seed packet and shook the little specks out into my hand. "And talking things over with Sybil. She's really very wise. She helped me find my peace with life as it's happened." I finished the row of pots and paused for a moment, looking up at her. "You should talk to her sometime. Might find it helpful."

"No thanks." She made a face. "I just—she rubs me the wrong way, or something. And you know she'd only try to convert me."

"She isn't like that."

"She always is, when she talks to me. She just can't turn the goddess talk off, ever."

I shrugged. "Well, don't if you don't want to." For a minute we worked in silence. Then I said, "You know, meditating isn't the most spiritual experience there is. To me it's this."

"Getting dirty?"

"Working with living things. Their complexity and interdependence. To me the implausible hypothesis is that the whole system *doesn't* have a soul. Because you can see they're more than the sum of their parts."

"You're a poet at heart," she said fondly. She finished the last pot and dusted off her hands. I'd never seen her with dirt on her before. Engine grease, yes.

Some people clean up nice, but Robin grimes up good. The messier she is, the more I love her. She wasn't one to dress up, but I liked that about her. Her lanky shape always looked amazing in a flight suit, hair cropped close to the skull to fit in a helmet.

I wondered briefly what she'd say if I shut the lab door and offered to take her right on the lab counter. She wouldn't even have to move, I could just get in between her knees and—

With a sigh, she slid down off the counter. I wondered if she'd been thinking along the same lines, before she remembered we were boring married people now and had jobs to do. "I'm gonna go see what I can do to cut power use around the ship." She gave me a kiss, a deep and slow one, resting her wrists on my shoulders to keep her dirty hands off my clothes. "Good talk."

6

Robin

I spent a week crawling around the ship, prying open vent panels and arguing with computer safeties, to reduce the energy usage. Successfully, too—about seventy percent of what they usually drew was optional now. I put the fans on a reduced schedule, blowing through the ship to refresh the air morning and night. More than that wouldn't be necessary.

Lights, too, could be reduced, though many of the rooms had plants in them. Half ornament, half to free up space on the hydroponics level. The lights in those rooms had to stay on full. But they were in use frequently anyway.

Between the solar panels and the reduced usage, we had an energy surplus at last. A small one, but if we let it stack up in the battery for a while, we'd have a nice cushion in case of emergency or cloudy weather.

The next week was spent on putting together a transmission package home. Almost everyone in the colony had someone—parents, siblings, old friends—back on Proxima. People we'd never see again. I had each person come record a video and give me the names of the people it was for. The transmission would have to bounce around a number of satellites before it could make the trip to Proxima—our own equipment wasn't strong enough to travel a distance of lightyears—so it would be almost a decade before the messages would arrive.

Some of the recipients might be dead before the videos got there. It was a reality we carefully didn't discuss when I recorded the videos. A message for your ninety-year-old grandmother? Of course, of course, she'll be delighted.

I recorded an official log to head the whole thing up—the historical record that Proxima would keep of our successful landing. To be followed, as long as our antenna still worked, by successive logs of our progress as a colony. We might be out of physical touch with Proxima forever, but communication was still possible.

I finished compiling the whole thing and got up from my bridge chair. Nothing stopping me from sending it now, but I'd better check with Aspen. The energy usage would be massive, and if there was a better time for me to do it, I could easily wait.

When I got down there, Autumn was in the lab along with Aspen, squinting into a microscope. "Well, it looks like this isn't my field after all," she declared, waving Aspen over. "Look! Oh, hello, Robin."

She flashed me a sunny smile. She had been a redhead once, but now her hair was mostly gray. Most of the colony was younger families or young, single people, but Autumn and her husband weren't the type to want to settle down to a boring retirement. Her energy for zoology made her seem like a kid, sometimes.

"What have you got?" I asked.

"Well, I *thought* I had a bug," she said. "Since we can't go roaming around, and the goat incubators don't need much care, I thought I could at least study the insect life. But it's not a bug at all. It has some independent motility, but it's really some kind of seed or pollen. At least that's what it seems like to me."

Aspen straightened up. "Maybe a bit of each," he said. "What I would guess is that the reproductive phase of this plant is, effectively, an insect. I mean, insects are a lot better at finding a breeding partner and a place to lay eggs than pollen is. Maybe what we're calling 'trees' are really just a sessile adult phase of the bugs. Like a coral."

"But it's structurally like a plant!" she said with excitement. "You've got to study it!"

"Can't," he said, walking away from the microscope and back to his workbench. "We have only so much of the growing season left and a month till your goats come out of the tanks. I need to get these plants in the ground asap. You study it if you want to, and I'll pitch in when I can. Maybe you can tell me how to keep them out. I've got purple plants springing up all over the place."

"Why not use the locusts?" said Autumn. "I'll defrost some for you. Wouldn't take you long to gen-mod the bacteria to go with them."

I looked from one of them to the other. "What's a locust?"

"Oh, they're a bug used in terraforming. These ones are already engineered to eat only purple things. What you do is engineer bacteria to put in their stomachs, which will break down the native starches into a carbohydrate that the locust can digest. Then, during phase two, we'll release them to defoliate as much as we can of the planet."

"Is it okay to take them out now?" Aspen asked. "I don't want to screw with phase two."

"Oh, I've got a million of them. I'll thaw out a thousand as soon as you can get the bacteria ready."

"All right. I'll try and get that done tonight. I've got two hundred pea embryos to clone this afternoon." He made a note on his notepad—the man couldn't brush his teeth without writing it down and checking it off again—and looked up at me. "Did you need something?"

"Wanted to check your energy needs." I explained what I wanted. "I need pretty much the whole output of the solar panels for a few hours. Is that going to hurt the bioscrubber?"

He frowned. "Yeah. Low power hurts it, no power is going to be a serious problem. It doesn't have a night cycle. To say nothing of all these seedlings." He gestured to the rows of pots sitting under grow lights. "These get eight hours of darkness every night without a problem, but your panels won't be giving you any power at night either."

"To say nothing of my tanks," said Autumn. "The oxygen pumps need to work without a break or the goat fetuses will suffocate."

"Okay," I said. "Scratch that plan."

"But you need to send that message," Aspen argued. "Proxima knows we should have landed by now. When it comes time for them to get our message, they'll worry we've all been killed."

Not something any of us wanted our loved ones to think. "No, I can work around your needs. Now that I've cut power usage elsewhere, you're only using about seventy percent of what we make, even now you've got it going at optimal power. The rest is stacking up in the battery. If I wait awhile, I'll soon have what I need. Shouldn't make for more than a week of extra worry for everybody back home."

I turned to go, but Aspen caught up with me as I reached the ladder. "Are you doing okay?" he asked softly.

I focused on his chin. "Sure, why wouldn't I be?"

"Just worried that, with that job done, you'll be bored."

"Nah, I'll find a work crew. There's a shit ton of work to do."

"Not the kind of work you like."

I shrugged. I really didn't want to get into it, not here, not now, and preferably not at all. "It is what it is. Anyway this way I'm always free when the kids need me. Nothing I'm doing from here on out that's urgent, or can't be done by somebody else."

That's what I was doing, two weeks later. Work that could have been done by anybody else. Grunt work. Digging rows upon rows of little holes. I couldn't remember what Aspen had said they were for. Tomatoes?

It was hot, truly hot this time, and sweat trickled down my forehead. You never had a hot day on Proxima. A balmy seventy-four degrees, forty-five percent humidity—at least where the environmental controls were working right. Down in the tunnels it was more like sixty-five, and condensation sometimes collected on the walls. I was used to that. This had to be close to ninety, and the sunlight scorched the back of my neck.

A shadow fell across the baked earth. I sat back on my heels and squinted upward. It was Pine, the head teacher. "Can I borrow you for a minute?"

"Sure, what's up?" I dropped my spade and followed her. I had a good guess which kid she needed help with.

"We're ready now to take the kids outside, now that the stockade is complete. It's going to be difficult for everyone, because they don't remember being outside the ship before. So we broke everyone into very small groups."

"You need me to take Lily out by herself?"

"Or watch her in the ship. She got as far as the airlock, looked out, and panicked. She's back in the schoolroom now and won't come out."

I blew out my breath and rubbed my forehead. Full-on meltdown, probably. I wished Aspen were available, but he almost certainly was working. At best I could calm her down. But sooner or later, she was going to have to come out of the ship. We needed to move everyone out, so we could stop wasting energy on lighting and ventilating the whole thing.

As promised, she was in the schoolroom, hiding behind a potted cherry tree. Her daddy's girl, wasn't she? Always wanted to be around something growing. Her bunny's ear was in her teeth, and she chewed on it while rocking back and forth. Bright side, she wasn't crying.

"Hey baby," I said softly, kneeling down on the other side of the cherry tree pot. "How's it going?"

"Oxadrul," she muttered. "Oxadrul, oxadrul." Gibberish to me.

I slowly reached my arm around the pot and touched her shoulder. She jumped only a little. "Was the open door scary, baby?"

"Oxygen drill," she said. "OXYGEN DRILL!"

I glanced toward the door, where Pine was still waiting. "She said that before," said Pine.

Chewing my lip, I considered. I certainly understood why the open door had upset her. She knew, just like I did, that the doors on a ship are supposed to stay shut. I just wasn't sure how to bring her past that panic. I knew how air stays on a planet even without an airlock. She didn't. Maybe in the computer's databanks there would be a video that explained…?

Then it clicked. It didn't have to be that complicated. "Are you asking for your oxygen mask, baby?"

Lily stood up and reached out her empty hand. "Oxygen drill?"

"Come on, we'll get one for you."

Pine gave me a skeptical look as I passed her on the way to the storage lockers, Lily's hand in mine. I shrugged. I had no problem with putting a bandaid on the issue for now. Eventually, once she was used to the outside, hopefully she wouldn't need it, but if she felt like she needed it now, who was I to say no?

With her mask firmly in place, and one on me too (she was adamant about that) we re-entered the room with the open airlock. She stopped dead at the rim of the door and stood still for a long time. Her big brown eyes roved over everything: the ramp, the fields where I had been digging, the workers putting up a house some distance away, her classmates milling around. I just waited. There was a lot to take in.

"Plants?" she asked after a while.

"There will be plants here soon," I said. "But right now all of the plants are outside the fence."

She fingered her bunny's ear and looked around a bit more. Finally she stepped over with one tentative foot. I leaned on the side of the hatch, chewing my lip, trying to stop myself from saying anything or hurrying her up.

She stepped her other foot over and promptly sat down on the ramp, just rocking gently back and forth. After about ten minutes, she got up, touched my arm, said, "Goodbye baby, be good at school," and hurried over to catch up with her class.

I took off my oxygen mask, stashed it in my back pocket, and blew out my cheeks. Crisis averted. Even Aspen couldn't have done better. Once I'd caught Pine's eye to make sure she knew Lily was back with the class, I went back to the fields to dig more holes.

At the end of the first row, I glanced up at Lily. She was crouching on the ground, scraping at the dirt with a stick. At the end of the second row, I glanced again.

Lily was gone.

At first I stayed where I was, scanning the group of children more carefully. Maybe she was actually one of the kids running around and playing? But no, there was no sign of her brown cheeks or the two fat braids on the top of her head. White kids, redheaded kids, curly-haired kids. No Lily.

Not wanting to overreact, I got up and dusted off the knees of my jeans. My lower back twinged painfully, but I tried not to hobble as I went over to the school group.

"Pine," I said softly, "did somebody take Lily inside?"

Her eyes widened and she cast a furtive glance around the group. "Let me just check real quick."

She went around through the group, whispering to each other teacher. All I could see was head after head shaking. No one knew where she was.

I frowned. Surely they knew to watch her closely! They knew she wasn't great at following directions or staying with a group! But then again, she'd never had anywhere to wander before. All of the habitat level was safe for her to be, and the hatches to the other levels were normally code-locked.

Pine came back to me, looking worried. I drew in a breath, prepared to bite her head off if she started in with any kind of defensiveness. But instead she said, "No one has seen her. I've sent two teachers to look for her." Briefly she squeezed my hand. "We'll find her as fast as we can."

"I'm going to look inside," I said.

It was the most likely possibility, I thought as I rushed from room to room on the habitat level. If she was scared, she'd go back where it was familiar, right? But as I left room after room, I couldn't take my mind off the other possibilities. What if she got in the way of the building crew and was crushed by a beam? What if she fell into the foundation hole of another building site?

I found Aspen in our tiny bunkroom, changing his shirt. "Spilled nutrient solution on myself," he said, grinning. "But I think the bioscrubber is starting to adapt to a higher fungal ratio."

"That's good," I said absently. "Have you seen Lily?"

He stopped with one arm through his shirt. "Why? Is she missing?"

"She wandered off from her school group ..."

"Out of the classroom?"

"No, outside."

"She went *outside*?" He pulled his shirt the rest of the way on. "Today? I had a whole plan for introducing the concept one day at a time ..."

"Well you might have clued *me* in! Pine came and told me they were all going outside today and could I help get her to come out, and I did. It's like you've forgotten that I'm supposed to be dealing with kid stuff now! You just expect me to know!"

"You know you can't just shove her into new things. That's not a big mystery that you've never been introduced to before."

"I know, but she seemed okay with it ..." I hung my head. He was right, though I'd never admit it. I had been so focused on the goal of getting her outside, not even considering the possibility that I could just say no, not today.

"Let's fight about it later. Where have you checked so far?"

But a few minutes later we met back up at the airlock, empty-handed. She was nowhere on the habitat level, and the hatches to the other levels were locked, as they should be. Together we hurried out to see Pine, who shook her head. "They searched the entire colony. There's not a lot of places she could be hiding! And we passed the word all over to keep an eye out."

My eyes went to the stockade, with its giant gate. It was the only possibility left, one I'd tried not to think about. "She couldn't open that, could she?"

"It's not meant to be childproof," said somebody. "It's just a metal latch about yea high."

I strode over, Aspen hurrying on my heels. "She wouldn't have done that," he was saying. "If she was scared she'd find a place that felt safe. Not take on a new challenge."

I shook my head, furious with myself. "No, you see, she asked about plants. The teachers had said there would be plants outside, and like an *idiot* I told her they were all outside the fence."

He said nothing till we reached the gate. Sure enough, the latch was open. The gate itself was shut, but that was no surprise. Lily was compulsive about shutting doors and cupboards. I felt a sob, or a scream, starting to bubble up and bit down hard. "I'm going out there. I have to find her."

"Not alone!" he burst out. "Hawk said it's dangerous…"

"Dangerous enough I'm not waiting around twenty minutes for Hawk to organize a team." I gave him a quick, dry kiss. "You get some more people together and send them after me with stunners and radios and a first aid kit and anything else you can think of."

He stood there, looking stricken as I swung the gate open. "Be careful!"

"Always," I said. "I'll get her. She can't have gone far."

Once I got out there, I realized that didn't help very much. A seven-year-old girl couldn't cover much ground in twenty minutes, but she could have gone in any direction, while I had to somehow check all of them. "Lily!" I called, uselessly. She didn't even come when I called her on a good day.

I crouched down and looked around, trying to put myself in Lily's shoes. What would she think and feel? The bright sky, that would bother her. She'd never seen anything as bright as the sun, or seen a shadow as sharp as the one it cast. Then there was the hot air, uncomfortable even to me. A few insects droned around. And the smell of ash was stifling. Any one of those things would be a lot for her to handle. For a moment I forgot the intent of this exercise and just wallowed in guilt for having subjected her to the outdoors so suddenly in the first place.

Pulling myself together, I scanned the hillside, imagining all I wanted was a glimpse of plants. Which way would I go? There were big violet trees uphill, but would Lily recognize those as plants? Off to the side, there was a way down, alongside the plateau. Green flowers shone in the distance. That's where she would go. I started off, calling from time to time as I went.

Here, the charred trees were enormous, some fallen, others leaning against each other. I tried to avoid walking under them, but there wasn't always a choice. Peering up and down, I checked under and behind all the trunks I could. A cool wind started to blow, making the hair on my arms stand up. I would never get used to this place and its constantly changing temperature.

On and on, and I couldn't see any sign of her. Had I come the wrong way? I didn't want to turn around just fifty yards short of finding her, but at the same time if it was the wrong way, the longer I kept at it, the further Lily was going in the other direction. There seemed no right answer.

I had promised myself to turn around in another minute when I spotted the first sign of her. It was the oxygen mask, dropped carelessly on the ground. I wondered if that was a good thing or not. Had she calmed down enough to realize she didn't need the mask, or was she so panicky she couldn't tolerate it on her face anymore?

The way passed out of the burned area and into the forest, across a small gully which was easy to scamper down. It would probably be easy for Lily too, and she'd definitely be aiming this way.

The forest here was dense and bushy, with rose-colored briar bushes everywhere. I followed whatever gaps I could, figuring Lily wouldn't have tried to push through the thorny plants. In the trees above, birds, or whatever this planet had instead, were screeching shrilly at each other. Not helpful, when it came to listening for Lily.

Or, for that matter, for any approaching animals. The big herbivores would stomp loudly enough for me to hear, probably, but whatever predator stalked them might be quiet. I tried not to think too hard about it. I didn't have a stunner so there wasn't going to be anything I could do. It was just, I'd be damned if I let Lily spend one more second without me than she had to.

Finally I started to hear a familiar noise, barely audible over the screeching of the birds. A long, sobbing wail, the kind that makes your throat hurt in sympathy. I broke into a run, shoving through brambles that cut my arms, to zero in on that sound before she stopped.

I needn't have worried. Lily kept crying the whole time it took me to find her. At last I burst through another patch of briars and saw her huddled at the foot of a tree. Her bunny's ear was in her teeth and nearly chewed clear through.

I knelt down beside her, wrapping my arms around her shoulders and squeezing tight. "Shh, baby," I said. "Mama's gotcha." The top of one of her braids jabbed me in the throat, but I didn't shift.

After a while her sobs subsided enough for her to try to talk. "No plants," she said. "No *plants*!"

"These weren't the plants you were expecting, huh baby?"

"No plants."

"Yeah, I know. These ones are different. I get it. It's because they have purple stuff in them, instead of chlorophyll. You know how chlorophyll helps plants eat the sunshine? Well these ones like to eat purple light instead of green light, so they're a different color." I was probably getting it wrong. But I did know talking botany to her was how Aspen calmed her down. And it seemed to be working.

"You know what we should do?" I went on. "We should get some little green plants and plant them all over the colony. Inside the fence. Then we can look at them whenever we want without having to go on long walks. And they'll be just like the plants we're used to."

She let me help her to her feet. Slowly we started back uphill. Luckily I had that one cue for direction to go off of, since at the end, when I was running, I hadn't exactly been keeping track.

We had nearly reached the little gully when she stopped dead, staring into the trees. "Kitty," she said.

I looked around. Couldn't see anything strange. "What do you mean, baby?"

She tugged at my hand, trying to pull me off the trail. "Kitty!"

I followed her gaze and this time I spotted it. It was hard to make out any kind of outline, but I saw the eyes, large and yellow, with vertical pupils, like a cat's.

Tugging her hand, I tried to hurry Lily away from it. By the size of the eyes, whatever creature they belonged to was bigger than the two of us together. But she stood fast, staring at it.

Taking a deep breath, I knelt down beside her, staring at the animal. It was close enough that I could have thrown a rock and hit it between the eyes. If I blinked and looked at it a bit sideways, I could begin to see the shape of it, though its color blended exactly with the violet and gray undergrowth. Kind of like a ... centaur? Or a llama. It had a long body, with four legs, and then an upright section of its body with two more legs. And it was just standing there, looking at us.

For a moment I contemplated trying to drag Lily away physically. But between the hill and my giant belly, I wasn't sure I could. "We can't play with the kitty," I whispered. "Daddy is waiting for us at home. He was going to plant some seedlings today."

Reluctantly she turned away from the animal and let me lead her back the way we had come. I cast a look over my shoulder at the thing, hoping it hadn't only been waiting for my back to be turned. But instead it gave a slow blink and then ducked its head at me. For all the world, it looked like a deliberate gesture.

I turned and climbed up the slope. The gully was steep for Lily, and both of us slid a little on the sandy earth on the way down. Then she needed help getting back up again. Picking our way through the fallen, charred tree trunks on the other side, I began to worry. She had crossed the original distance quickly, but going back would be slow. If she got tired, she could and would plop right down on the ground and refuse to continue. And what if that creature chose to follow ...?

As we rounded another massive trunk, I spotted Aspen and Hawk, on their way down. I waved, but didn't shout; I didn't want to draw the creature's attention. They spotted me and hurried down.

Aspen scooped Lily up easily, squeezing her to his chest. He gave me a look of relief and gratitude, too overwhelmed to speak.

"Where was she?" demanded Hawk.

"Down where those trees are," I said. "We saw the predator, I think. A big creature, the size of a horse, maybe? It's on the other side of that gully and through some trees. I didn't see it following us, but I want to get back as fast as we can."

Hawk nodded and led the way back. With Aspen carrying Lily, we made good time. "You'll have to draw a picture of this predator for us when we get back," he said, as we were coming up on the stockade. "We'll be looking for ways to reduce their population in this area."

"Are you sure that's a good idea?"

He threw me a quizzical look. "Why wouldn't it be? They're certainly a threat, and we will have to come out here to get wood. Not to mention terraforming this area once the colony itself is fully developed."

"I just . . ." I hesitated to put it into words. "I mean, are we sure it's not intelligent?"

"Why in the world would it be? Most scientists believe intelligent life is extremely rare. And we've seen no sign of any civilization on this planet. No cities, no farms, no industrial pollutants."

"It looked . . . kind of aware to me."

"You mean it was wearing clothes? Using tools?"

"I mean it was watching us. It sort of . . . nodded at me."

"Animals have all kinds of gestures like that," he said. "Some birds nod almost incessantly. And as for watching you, why wouldn't it? It would want to keep an eye on anything moving through its territory."

I sighed. He was almost certainly right, and yet I felt an instinctive revulsion at the thought of killing the creature. The feeling sat uncomfortably in my mind next to my fear of it, the thought that it could have devoured Lily by the time I had even gotten there. But it was how I felt, all the same.

When we got back to the colony, Lily turned down the offer of transplanting seedlings and opted to go back to the schoolroom. Once she'd made herself a little nest out of blankets and turned a nature video on the vidscreen, she curled up comfortably, snuggling her bunny.

I stood in the doorway, watching her. Aspen wrapped his muscular arm around my shoulders and gave a tight squeeze. "God, what a day."

I nodded. "I'm sorry. This is my fault. I'm not good at being in charge of them."

"I'd say you clearly proved that you are."

"Are you kidding?" I forced my voice to stay quiet. It was never safe to assume Lily wasn't listening. "I *lost* her."

"You *found* her," he said. "Okay, you didn't know how to introduce her to something new, but that's something you can learn. But you did great in a crisis, and that can't be taught."

I ducked my head. "Not really that different from landing a flaming spaceship, I guess."

"Apparently not." He was quiet for a while, gently rubbing his thumb back and forth along my shoulder. "I just wanted to say—I'm glad you're here with them. I'm glad the kids get to watch you be the badass you are, and maybe pick up some of that."

I leaned against him, a warm glow starting under my ribs. *I'm glad I'm here with them too,* I should have said, but I couldn't quite make myself do it.

I still wished I were back in space.

Interlude

The Elders were meeting, and Mrrka found herself outnumbered.

The meeting was held at Mrrka's mansion, because it was the largest den in the region. Her meeting room, large enough to host a feast or a ball, was decorated in fine claywork and softly lit with phosphorescent fungi. Plenty of light for their eyes, though daywalking creatures would have found it murky and dim.

A dozen Elders crouched on four legs around her heavy wooden table. "It seems the object that fell from the stars is some kind of vehicle," Mrrka said. "The creatures inside have come out and are building nests out of wood."

"So they're some kind of bat?" asked one of the others.

Mrrka gestured dismissively. "They're not really like any other creature we could compare them to. If anything, perhaps like some kind of tree-climber. But quite a bit larger, and it's obvious they are intelligent to build with such complexity."

"If they are intelligent, then the fire they started is an act of war!" That was the Second Eldest. She and Mrrka had been rivals—or, at least, their families had been rivals—for generations. Mrrka could remember dozens of quarrels with the Second Eldest, many around this very table. Also they had mated a time or two. But those had been other lifetimes, long ago. This scion of the house, Fesskh, was much less friendly.

"I understand some of your estate was affected," Mrrka allowed. "But their vehicle was on fire when it landed. It may have been an accident."

"Even if so, we can't just let them build nests all over the common!" the Second Eldest protested. "That plateau was prime hunting ground. The poor in my district rely on it."

"You'll have to allow more share-hunting on your estate," Mrrka said. "We all will."

"That's a temporary solution. The long-term solution is to declare war on the newcomers. From what you say, they are small and soft. Bare-handed, we could defeat them."

"We don't know what weapons they have," someone put in nervously.

"We could catch them unawares. It wouldn't be difficult."

Mrrka could hardly listen. All she could think of was the youngling she had seen. Four-limbed and bald, with no ears to speak of, but recognizably a child. It had struck her with a sense of familiarity and sadness, which it had taken her a moment to pin down. At last she remembered: one of her ancestors had lost a child, just about that size, newly out of the pouch. She had gone on to have another child, but the memory of that pain remained fresh.

At first, Mrrka had wondered why the ancestor had chosen to preserve that memory. She could have let all that pain pass into forgetfulness. But finally she had understood: it had been the mother's way of preserving her child's life. If she couldn't have lived, if she would never grow to hand her memories down to her own child, let her at least be remembered by her sister, and her sisters' daughters, forever.

In any event, that memory might be why she felt so protective of the invaders. Everyone else thought of them as the ones who had brought the fire. And they were. But they were also the mother and child who had walked by her campsite, when she had been startled awake by their crashing through. It made them seem much less terrifying.

She raised a hand for silence. "We are not declaring war on them."

Everyone around the table stared at her. The Second Eldest began to protest, "But they are a *threat*—"

"Of course they are, and we have to be rid of them. That's obvious. But I am not convinced they mean any harm. They may simply be stupid and ignorant. In the sphere they came from, perhaps things are not harmed by fire. Or perhaps there is no fire, and they did not know it would spread." She flicked her tail in a shrug. "Our goal should be to discourage and frighten them, so they return where they came from."

"And if they don't go?"

She spread her hands. "In that case, I suppose we shall have no choice."

7

Aspen

I wrenched yet another pink vine out of the ground and dropped it in the bucket. Despite myself, I couldn't help but feel a grudging respect for the native life. It was absolutely dogged in its determination to re-establish itself in this burned-out patch.

The tiny seed-flies had multiplied into veritable swarms, planting vines everywhere. Autumn had identified a second, slightly larger species that was the seed of a plant we'd dubbed razor briar, for obvious reasons. Those ones had to be pulled out with heavy, gauntlet-like gloves.

In ecology, environments could be defined as brittle or non-brittle. Brittle environments easily became desertified or waste land, failing to re-establish their native life after an environmental insult like clear-cutting. Non-brittle environments sprang back fast.

This was the far opposite end of the spectrum from brittle. It leaped back into life overnight, and the pink and purple growth had to be uprooted or hacked back daily. With seeds spread by motile "flies," it was impossible to prevent them from appearing unless we somehow roofed over the entire colony with mosquito netting. Autumn's locusts were trying their best, and even the schoolchildren spent some time each day pulling weeds, but they could hardly keep up.

And, sap that I am, I was impressed. I hoped the goddess would understand I wasn't being disloyal to Her. I just felt the native plants' determination was a virtue even She couldn't help but respect.

Autumn stomped over with a handful of weeds to shove in my bucket. "The bugs are definitely worse today," she said, straightening up and waving them away from her face. They never bit, but getting one in the eye was almost as bad.

"I think they're responding somehow to the fire," I said. "I can think of several possible mechanisms. Maybe they're triggered by heat or increased carbon dioxide. Or even signaled somehow through the mycelial network. We know trees on Earth can react to things happening miles away, through changes in the mycelia."

She considered that. "If so, maybe when this area is all filled in with our plants, the bugs will settle down."

"I hope so. My alfalfa isn't doing well, with how much I've had to stomp around in it, pulling up weeds. Today I planted some kudzu out by the chapel. At least it's edible in a pinch. And the goats can snack on it when they're ready."

At that moment, Hawk walked up with two thick plastic-bound booklets. "I'm distributing scriptures today."

I straightened up, giving him a puzzled look. "The Disciples of Terra don't have scriptures."

"It's some of Sybil's sermons I had printed up. Look." He opened one, showing me chapter and verse numbers, coupled with dates. "We had recordings of most of it, and I thought, while she's indisposed, it would be nice to be able to keep her words present with us."

Autumn looked skeptical. "Indisposed?"

Hawk shot her an annoyed look. "Not that it's your business, but she's ill," he said shortly.

I thought back to the conversation of theirs I'd overheard. He hadn't sounded like he believed she was ill. He sounded like he thought she was malingering on purpose. Or had he thought he could chastise her into health?

"Is she going to be all right?" Autumn asked. "You're not printing these because you're worried she'll …"

"She's in no danger," Hawk said, flipping the booklet shut and handing us each one. "I'm just trying to nurture our spiritual health in this time." He stalked away.

I tucked my booklet under my weed bucket and went back to work. "I can't imagine actually reading that."

"I don't know," said Autumn, flipping through hers. "It might be helpful. It's not like I can remember everything Sybil's ever said."

"I feel like part of the point is getting it from the source. You know? We're not one of those religions where the prophets are all long dead, and we all have to argue what they really meant. We can just ask her."

"We won't always be able to," said Autumn. "I mean, sure, she's fine now, but by the time your kids are grown, we might be telling our grandkids stories about her. Every religion has to grow up at some point. Getting things in writing is probably part of it. And this way she can correct anything that's wrong while she's still here."

After Autumn had gone inside, I kept thinking about what she said. Of course Sybil wouldn't be around forever. She wasn't *old*, but she was older than Robin and me. Someday we'd have nothing but a book.

For me, Sybil was a huge part of the point. She made everything make sense. She was always—well, almost always—there to talk to. But that couldn't be the whole point. That would make it a cult of personality. Sybil hated those.

I wondered if Hawk had ever checked his scripture idea with her before going ahead with it. He was a practical man, not a spiritual one really. If there was a spiritual problem with getting Sybil's words out of a book, he wouldn't be one to notice it.

Hawk was one of Sybil's "practical recruits." Robin hated that Sybil did that—targeted specific people in specific fields for evangelization. She felt if people wanted to join, they would do it on their own. But in reality, most people don't think about changing religions unless someone personally asks them. It wasn't like we could force anybody to convert if they didn't want to.

I'd been in the church for a year before I'd realized their strategy. I'd joined because a botanist friend of mine had invited me. Obviously the church has a lot of botanists and zoologists; people who study life for a living are already halfway there. It's easy to explain to a botanist that life is more than a collection of cells. We already see that every day.

Sybil kept asking me to invite Robin, but somehow the timing was never right. She was always out on an ice run on Sundays, and if there was a weekday event, she was too tired. Finally she came to the temple picnic...exactly once. "I love that you love it," she'd said, politely, when it was over. "But I just don't get religion. It doesn't interest me."

Sybil wanted me to keep trying, but I dropped the issue completely. I can't count the number of arguments I've won that way, by letting them be and giving Robin time to think over my side instead of coming up with reasons I'm wrong. But this time I suspected she'd never come around. She doesn't have that need for anything beyond her. And besides, what use is a goddess of growing things to someone born to soar through vacuum?

When Sybil finally announced the great plan, the dream of finding a new home for Terra, I wanted nothing more than to say yes. But I tried to mention it to Robin carelessly, like I could have gone either way. It was a decision that would affect our whole lives. I didn't want her to do it because of me.

"What's the catch?" she asked. "I know colony charters get snapped up fast."

"Well, um—it's already covered in vegetation, according to the astronomers. It'll almost certainly be toxic to humans, so they'll have to clear it away before they can plant anything. Where there are plants, there are animals, which may be unfriendly. Everybody who wants an open sky is looking for a ticket to Carson's Planet. It's nice there and the only life is harmless microbes. This place—well, it's kind of a shot in the dark. And one of the guys in the planetary survey team is part of the church, so we got our application in first."

"Makes sense." Robin finished the last of her whiskey on the rocks—her after-bedtime drink, in those days. "It's too bad. It seemed like a really nice bunch of people, from what you said."

"Um." I took a nervous gulp of my own drink. "Sybil wanted me to talk to you about that."

She stared at me for a moment, processing. "She wants you along."

"Well. Us. I mean because you…"

Robin brought her feet back to the floor and sat forward, putting down her glass. "Because I'm a pilot. This whole thing. She targeted you because she wanted me to fly her there, and you to work with the biosphere."

"Don't get mad."

"I'm not mad." She took a slow breath through her nose, a sure tell that she was but was trying hard not to be. "But—doesn't it sound mercenary to you? They converted you just to get to me?"

"You don't know that's why."

"This guy who just happened to be on the planetary survey team. You think he joined the church on his own initiative? Does your church *just happen* to have every single specialty you need in a colony?"

I was silent. Since she put it that way, it felt kind of obvious. "I'm sorry I brought it up," I said at last. "Don't worry, we don't have to even consider it."

She held up a hand. "I didn't say I wouldn't consider it. But I don't want to talk to *you* about it. This isn't your idea and I'm not arguing with your priestess by proxy. Tell Sybil I'll talk to her."

I don't know what they talked about, but Robin eventually did agree. She saw, like I did, what it could mean for our family. And, skeptical as she was about the church, she'd decided Sybil didn't mean any harm.

I asked Sybil, next time I saw her, whether Robin was right. Had our family been targeted on purpose? And Hawk, and everyone else?

"Terra isn't just the goddess of the Cambrian explosion," she had said. "She's also the goddess of the Permian extinction, and of everything that survived it. You don't survive by ignoring the practicalities of the world as it is. So of course we try to convert people who we think could help us. If they're not interested, we train those we do have. But everything for our goal. Everything for a new home for Terra."

She had a point, and I had let it go. But I wondered sometimes what had convinced a man like Hawk to convert. He never seemed that spiritual. But he'd made himself useful enough to rise to the number-two position in the church. Perhaps just because of what Sybil had said—we needed to survive, and to do that we needed a practical man.

That didn't mean I was going to read his photocopied scripture.

8

Robin

At breakfast a few days after Lily's adventure, Cliff sat down next to me. "I fixed the latch on the big gate," he said, around a bite of lichen scramble. The stuff wasn't much like eggs, but the people in the kitchen insisted on dressing it up as if it was. Oh well, it wasn't like it could pass easily for meat either, and yet we had lichen burgers at least twice a week.

"How high is it?"

"About as high as my head. You'd have to reach up a bit."

"Good. Lily has been showing some interest in going out again. Maybe she will try it today." I said it lightly, because I meant it lightly. Maybe. She would if she wanted to. This time I wasn't going to push so hard.

"And there's the other kids to think of," he said. "You can tell kids not to go out till you're blue in the face, but some are still going to want to try it. I would have. The more forbidden something was when I was a kid, the more I wanted to do it. Kids have a death wish." He took a swig of synthetic caffeine beverage. "Though it'll be less dangerous out there soon. I spent most of yesterday trying to figure out something to keep the predators away. Hawk insisted I do that ASAP."

"Humane traps?" I asked hopefully.

"I only had spaceship parts to work with. I'm making a kind of electric fence. It's a really fine wire that goes the whole way around the colony, running off the ship's power grid. The voltage should be enough to kill them quickly, at least I hope it will. I'm going to switch it on this morning and make sure it works."

I stabbed at a gray lump. "At least it'll be safer out there."

After I'd finished, I went back to our bunkroom to wake the kids and get them fed and to class. Always better to get myself ready early, I had found. With some toast and cafbev in me, I could handle the inevitable foot-dragging and last-minute crises. Once they were settled in their classroom, I went outside to check on the fields and see if there was anything I could help with.

Every day lately, Aspen had had another set of seedlings to plant: beans, peas, radishes, squash. He was like a kid on Christmas morning about it. And as long as he was planting, there was something for me to do, and a day when I didn't have to feel like dead weight on the colony.

When I got there, though, no one was working. Instead there was a crowd of people standing around, chattering nervously. I pushed past to get to Aspen. "What's going on?"

He gestured to the field in front of him, where we had spent all the day before planting pumpkin seedlings. Only there were no seedlings today. Every plant had been broken off. The stems stood up bravely for an inch or two, and the leafy tops lay on the ground, withered.

"They're all like that," he said hollowly. "Must have happened hours ago, the tops are completely dead."

"So you can't ... stick them back on?"

He shook his head. Kneeling down, he sifted the soil through his fingers. "My only thought is that it's some kind of cutworm. Just went down the row and nipped them all off. But I can't find any sign of one now."

I crouched beside him, not sure what to look for. Then I saw a mark in the soil and leaned closer. "Is that … some kind of footprint?"

"Paw print, more like," he said, leaning over to see. "You think some kind of herbivore? Though how would one get over the stockade? Must be some amazing climbers out there."

The print was about the size of my hand, with four splayed toes. "Wouldn't an herbivore have *eaten* all of these?"

"Maybe they tried them but didn't like them."

"And then went on to take a bite of every single other plant around?"

A shadow fell across the print. I glanced up. Hawk. "What are you suggesting, Robin?" he asked in a low voice.

I rose awkwardly to my feet. "That print looks like it could belong to our predator. If they were intelligent, and if they wanted to be rid of us, wouldn't they go for our plants?"

Leaning in so as not to be overheard, he hissed, "I don't want you talking about that crazy theory."

"Why, because you've already put out a trap for them?" I glanced over his shoulder at Aspen, hoping he'd come to my defense. Of course he didn't. In Sybil's absence, Hawk was his religious leader. He wouldn't question him any more than he did Sybil.

"Because it's a ridiculous idea and one that will spread panic," he snapped. "You think all these people can handle the thought of being on an alien planet that's populated with people who hate us? We may as well give up now, if that's the case."

I fell silent, a little stung by his tone. He wasn't wrong, it didn't look promising for us if we had enemies out there. At the same time, if we did have enemies out there, putting out that electric fence was one of the stupidest things we could possibly do. They'd know we meant them harm.

Raising my eyes to meet Hawk's, I gave him a rebellious glare. So much for having an ally, a practical man who could see sense. He wasn't seeing sense now, which made him no better than Sybil, only less diplomatic.

His cold blue eyes met mine without flinching, and eventually I turned and strode away. Aspen hurried to walk beside me. "He's not entirely wrong," he ventured.

"I know that, but he's enough wrong that I'm seriously worried." I paused and turned to him. "Do you really think my theory is that crazy?"

He looked at the ground. "I don't. You could be right. But on the other hand, what can we do if you're right?"

"Find more information! Try to communicate with them! Something!"

"Hawk won't allow that."

"I know." I continued stomping off, toward the ship.

"Where are you going?"

"Over his head. To Sybil."

"She's not seeing anyone."

"She's going to have to." Surely she wasn't still moping like she'd been that day in the chapel. And yet, nobody had really seen her since then. Maybe what she needed was a little tough love from me.

Aspen touched my arm, getting me to stop and look him in the eye. "Promise me you'll listen to whatever she says."

"Why? Because she's the prophet of the goddess?"

"Because she's a wise person and knows what she's doing. She got us here."

I frowned. "*I* got us here."

"You know what I mean. She worked out this whole plan, got the settlement council to give us the license, got us the *Resurrection* at a steal. She didn't do all that by being stupid." He dropped his hand to mine, squeezed, and released. "Just don't do anything impulsive or crazy. I think interrupting Sybil is probably the right call, but just *leave* it at that, okay?"

I hadn't even thought of what I might do after talking to Sybil, or if she refused to listen to me. But he wasn't wrong to suspect I might try something on my own. It wouldn't be the first time.

Because this could be a disaster, and I didn't have Aspen's faith in divine guidance. I wasn't just worrying about the harm we might do to an intelligent life form. Those creatures were dangerous, and it seemed they already meant us harm. But sneaking in while we were safely shut up in the ship for the night, that was nothing. Harassment, or a warning, or perhaps just suspicion of our strange green plants. They hadn't hurt anyone. Thus our electric fence was an opening shot. It could start a war. We had to know what we were dealing with before we made a move like that.

"I won't do anything *crazy*," I said. "You know me. When I'm impulsive, it's always a good impulse."

He rolled his eyes and kissed me. "I wish that reassured me." But he let me go, turning back to inspect the rest of the fields. He had a lot of work ahead of him, with about a month of work on those seedlings lost. Our growing season was ticking away. And the scrubber lichen was still a little anemic. Aspen still wasn't sure it would survive long-term. We *had* to have another source of food at some point.

It was his version of the crashing spaceship: the time when the whole colony lived or died based on how good he was at his job. Luckily he was very good, and was keeping a cool head besides. But I had to leave him to it and distract him as little as possible.

Inside the ship, I rapped smartly on Sybil's door. There was no answer, and I raised my fist to knock again. I could keep pestering her for quite some time; I wouldn't be cowed by her like the Greenies.

But before I could get in a second knock, the door slid open. Sybil looked different than I had ever seen her: long black hair swept into a messy bun; knit pajamas instead of her usual elegant clothing. There were dark shadows under her green eyes.

She looked up at me in surprise. "Robin. I didn't expect you to come."

"I need to talk to you," I said. "Can I come in?"

She stood aside from the door, waving me inside with a perplexed expression. "Are *you* looking for guidance from the goddess?"

I blinked. "No, of course not." There was a chair across from her single bunk, which I took.

She sat on the bed, tucking her feet up under her. "Silly of me. You know how my thoughts always go straight to Her. You surely have something else on your mind."

I told her briefly about the predator, the electric fence, the footprint. "Hawk insists I'm wrong, but what if I'm right? If we hurt one of them, they'll want to get even."

She covered her face with her hands. "I'm sorry. Everything has gone wrong since we came here."

"None of that is *your* fault," I said automatically. But of course everything was her fault, since the entire trip had been her idea. Still, she hadn't forced me to sign up for it. "We've handled all the disasters so far. I think we'll be all right. I just think we need to check my theory somehow. We need to try to communicate with the predators, and if they are intelligent, we need to work out some kind of treaty."

"Treaty?" she repeated, aghast. "What kind of treaty could there possibly be? We need to terraform the entire planet."

"Well, if there are people here, we're obviously going to have to share…"

"That wasn't the plan. We're creating a new Earth here, not carving this planet into bits. It's Terra's will."

I bit my lip and looked at the ceiling. If she kept talking about her stupid religion I might scream. It was one thing to get spiritual guidance from it. A completely different thing to make decisions about terraforming a planet that way.

"Look," I began. Then I did look at her, and cut myself off. Tears were pooling in her eyes. "Are you okay?"

She scrubbed at her eyes. "It's just—well, you know."

"I don't, actually. You've been in here for over a month."

"It's just so hard. Everyone leaning on me emotionally. Everyone wanting something. I have to hide or it never stops."

And here I was, wanting something from her. Guiltily, I sat on the edge of the bed next to her. "Is there anything I can do? Who supports you, when you're supporting everyone else?"

She took a long breath in, let it out through pursed lips. "Terra. In theory. Though I'm having a bit of a dark night of the soul at the moment. It happens."

88

"I wouldn't know."

"I know she's there. I do. I believe it, anyway. Like the light from the bottom of a well. But my soul is clouded; it can't get through." After a moment she patted my hand. "I shouldn't be complaining to you. I promise I'll be all right. I just need to ride it out."

I could tell when I was being dismissed. "Okay, well. Sorry to bother you, I guess. Can I at least go outside and try to find out if—"

"Hawk's in charge," she said wearily. "Do whatever he says." Getting up, she opened the door for me to leave.

Outside her room, I stood for a moment in despair. Between Sybil and Hawk, nobody was going to listen to me. I imagined an army of predators pouring over the stockade, bristling with weapons. Obeying Sybil wasn't going to prevent that future.

But that didn't mean there was nothing I could do.

Most everyone was outside at the moment. I slipped into the supply room, grabbing a backpack, a stunner, a radio, and a thermos. The kitchen was empty also, so I snuck about a dozen lichen burgers out of the fridge.

I stashed the pack in my bunk and went outside, blending into the crowd of people working. It seemed they had abandoned the fields, since there was nothing to plant right now, and were mostly working to help build a house for Sybil. I wondered if she would bother moving into it.

Without the strength to lift the beams or the skill to build anything, I spent the morning running around fetching nails and tools. Everyone was used to me by now, and my habit of inserting myself into work teams I wasn't on to keep myself busy.

It was also a good way to keep from bumping into Aspen. I told myself the reason was that he would be absorbed right now in starting new seedlings and shouldn't be bothered. But I also didn't want him to try to talk me out of my plan, as I knew he would.

At last everyone came inside for midday prayers. I tagged along with them, peeling off to grab the backpack. At the door of our room, I turned back. I had to at least leave a note.

Babe, I couldn't get any help from Sybil and this really had to be done.

I will be very careful, and hopefully be back in a day or two. I love you.

I chewed my lip. I ought to add a message for the kids, something that would make them not worry. But what could I say? They were all out of the habit of me being gone for weeks at a time. Aspen was still their favorite, but they would want me to be there too.

Finally I added, *Sorry about leaving you with the kids. I just need them to be safe.* I signed the note with a star and left it on the bed.

Once outside the colony, I walked slowly, looking carefully for Cliff's fine wire. Finally I spotted it, about waist height. Only the glint of sunlight made the fine thread visible. On my knees, dragging my backpack beside me, I crawled under, leaving plenty of room.

I was tempted to disconnect the wire, but Cliff would surely be checking on it often. So I scrambled back to my feet and kept moving.

A few hours later, I was beginning to question my decision. I had given no thought at all to my ability to handle the wilderness since, after all, I'd been out in it twice already. The first time I had been terrified, the second time too anxious about Lily to notice much how uncomfortable it made me. This time I was pretty well inured to the open sky, the uneven ground, and the many odd noises from the wildlife.

What I wasn't used to was staying out in it for any length of time. My heavy outdoor boots chafed around my ankles, and the backpack felt heavy despite the reduced gravity. As I trekked deeper into the forest, tiny bugs started swarming around my ears, never landing or biting, just ... *hovering.* They seemed to prefer emitting their ultrasonic whine directly outside my ear canal. Once one got in my eye and I had to fish it out. Its tiny body, wings bedraggled after the dunk in my tears, was no bigger than a sesame seed, but it had left my eyeball feeling scraped and raw.

The undergrowth was dense, including some nasty bushes with magenta needles and stems like razor wire. This couldn't be the right way. If there were any sort of intelligent life form around, they'd have cleared this menace out first thing. I abandoned the course I was on, down past the spot I had found Lily, and tried going uphill instead.

This did get me clear of the swarming bugs and the razor-wire bushes, but by this time it was getting uncomfortably hot, even in the shade of the trees. The air felt like a damp towel across my face. I drank most of my thermos on the first gulp.

I was finally getting into a fairly clear area of the forest when I was startled by a deafening crack. I hit the ground before even thinking about it. Was a tree coming down? An avalanche? An explosion?

Cold wetness splattered my arms, and finally I got my head together. A thunderstorm. That happened on planets. We had had rain many times since the landing, but I had always stayed in the ship. Lily liked to trace the droplets on the window with her fingers.

Actually feeling the water hitting my skin was another matter entirely. I hated it. Keeping my head bent so the drops stayed out of my face, I hurried through the trees, looking for some shelter. This part of the forest was no good for it; the dominant kind of tree in the area had thin, fringey leaves that served only to gather the drops and splash them down in big gobs.

The light had dimmed, except when lightning flashed. I learned to watch for it, as a warning for the thunderclaps. Even with advance notice, they still made me jump, but at least I didn't duck and cover like an idiot.

Unless, of course, that was what one was supposed to do. Lightning did strike people sometimes, right? How did one avoid that? Or was it just random, "like being struck by lightning," oh yeah. Shit.

As I made my way uphill, I encountered more and more patches of bare rock, where the soil had apparently eroded away, leaving vertical walls of striated gray stone. Usually I could walk alongside them until I reached a more passable way, but when I saw one that curved inward slightly, I made a beeline for it instead. It appeared to be the closest thing to shelter anywhere around.

Huddling close to the rock wall, I was able to stay mostly out of the rain. Unless the wind gusted, and then I got a spatter of it full in the face. It didn't matter, I was soaked to the skin anyway. I peeled off my shirt and spread it on top of my backpack. I was cold in just my bra, but it beat feeling the clammy fabric glued onto my arms.

I rested my forearms on my knees and watched the falling rain. This plan was turning into a disaster. I had trusted in my ability to make quick decisions and carry them through, but maybe that only worked where piloting was involved. I knew nothing about surviving in the wilderness. It had been pure hubris to assume I'd simply figure it out.

To make things worse, I had seen no sign of any kind of civilization. Was I crazy to even theorize such a thing? How could an intelligent species be entirely missed, first by the Hermes probe, then by the rover, then by our orbital analysis, and finally by me, trekking through the bush? Humanity had never encountered one before; scientists were starting to speculate that we had simply gotten incredibly lucky and evolution didn't usually go that route. But if there had been one, surely they would need roads and houses and things. Even if they were primitive, somewhere they ought to have some kind of village.

If I was wrong, then I was miles from the colony, in a forest full of deadly predators. Alone. In the rain.

Except, I remembered, I wasn't alone, exactly. I was pregnant. Which made this ten times as stupid. For a second I imagined Aspen's reaction if anything happened to me. His wife and future child, in one day. No. I couldn't take any chances.

Unzipping my backpack, I took out the radio. It was time to make a plan to get back. "Robin Morrison to Eos Colony, checking in."

Silence.

"Robin Morrison to anybody, please respond."

Nothing. I checked the channel. This was the one they always used to call each other around the colony. Hawk had a radio on his belt all the time. And they would have noticed by now I was missing. How could they not answer right away?

I smacked the radio, tried again. The light still came on, so the rain hadn't gotten to it. But there still wasn't any answer. I dropped it on the ground between my knees. Either the range wasn't adequate or there were too many mountains around. Not something I was used to dealing with either. Since I had fallen into this damn gravity well there was nothing I was good at anymore.

Exhausted with self-recrimination, I eventually dozed, still sitting up. When I awoke, it had finally stopped raining. It was almost pitch black, but here and there were glowing green patches on the tree trunks. Glowing moss or fungus, probably.

I scrambled to my feet and put my still-damp shirt back on with a shiver. Without the sun's warmth, the temperature had dropped at least twenty degrees. I checked the clock on the radio to see the time, but it was still set to ship's time—two in the afternoon. I wasn't sure what that would be in Eos time. The days weren't quite the same length and I had stopped keeping track.

Didn't matter, really. I was rested enough to go on, even though my feet, legs, and back all ached. And anything had to be better than sitting here in the dark. I threw the radio into the backpack and took out the stunner. Not only did I want it ready to hand, it also had a flashlight mounted on the barrel, for exactly this kind of situation. Better luck stunning a predator if you could see it.

The first step was to try, somehow, to get my bearings. I had a vague understanding that I had gone north some, then northwest some, but once I had started up the hill, I had stopped following any clear direction because of all the outcroppings of rock. So the first thing to do was to get somewhere I could see the sky, and try to figure out which way I was pointed. After that I should try to strike downhill and south-southeast. Probably.

Eos was loud at night, it turned out. Screeching cries, hoots, rattles, whines. It wasn't constant or anything. It would be eerily quiet for a while and then *SCREEEEAW!* The first one I heard made all the hair rise on the back of my neck. But after a few, I started to catch the pattern. One of the screeching creatures was in a tree a bit behind me, and another some distance down the hill was answering it.

After some vague wandering roughly downhill, barely avoiding twisting an ankle on the rocky ground, I broke out into a clearing and shut off the light. It took a moment for my vision to adjust, but at last the stars glowed to life. I let out a shaky breath. They, at least, hadn't changed a bit. I could spot the Milky Way, Sirius, Deneb. Old friends, even if they weren't in their usual constellations.

More importantly, I could see three of Eos's five small moons. None of them was much bigger than a star, certainly not bright enough to see by, but they were spread in a straight line across the ecliptic, west to east. It took a minute, remembering how Eos was oriented in relation to the other stars, but I finally worked out which way was west and which was east. South, it turned out, was directly behind me, straight up the hill, but that wasn't going to work. I headed east.

By the time I had wrapped far enough around the hill to start heading downward again, the nervous tension between my shoulderblades was starting to unknot. I was even getting bored. The circle of light my flashlight cast was enough to keep me from tripping or smashing into a tree, and the rest of the world might as well not exist. Nothing to see, no color to anything, just one foot in front of the other.

Which is how I got scared out of my skin when an animal jumped out at me. There was a sudden crashing away to my right and there it was, plunging down the hill in a panic. It was a leggy beast, like a deer with six legs. I stood there gasping at it, too startled to run or raise my stunner.

Luckily, it seemed to have no interest in me. Its ears were pinned back and the whites of its eyes shone in my flashlight. Running from something? I slowly stepped sideways and put my back against the nearest tree, stunner in my shaking hand.

But no predator appeared. I heard some odd cries from up the hill, and that was all. Perhaps whatever had been chasing the hexadeer had been afraid of my light.

Soon enough, I found myself back among the razorwire bushes, and at last crossing the gully that led back into burned ground. I picked up a bit of a charred branch and held it in front of me. The sky was beginning to lighten, but the ground was still mostly dark. I couldn't take the risk of blundering into the electric fence.

I scrambled up the slope till I reached the plateau. From here, I could see pink streaks beginning to fan out across the eastern horizon. I caught my breath. I had never seen a sunrise before. Proxima didn't have them. I switched off the flashlight on my stunner so I could see it better. After a moment, I tore my eyes away. Better get home sooner rather than later.

Suddenly, I heard a crackle and a brilliant line of light etched itself on my eyeballs. For a second all I could see was the afterimage, a purple horizontal line, with a squiggly bulge in the middle. It had been close, perhaps twenty feet away. I hurried toward where the light had been, realizing it must have been Cliff's fence going off. Hell of a lot of voltage on that thing, to make a light like that.

There, just on this side of the fine, silver wire, was one of the predators. It had been traveling on all six legs this time, more like a cat than a centaur, and had gotten under the wire easily. But its tail must have brushed the fence at the very last moment. All the translucent fur was burned off the end.

It moved slightly, and I jumped, grabbing for my stunner. But it didn't seem able to stand, and I drew closer again. It rolled slightly onto its side, fixing me with its enormous yellow eyes. As before, I could swear the expression was intelligent. "I'm sorry," I said, and I meant it. This had been exactly what I had come out here to prevent. But how could I make it, or its people, understand that this hadn't been what we meant to happen?

It gave a complicated rumbling hiss. Speech? Or was I reading into it what I had expected to hear? "I'm sorry," I said again. "I can get the others, and we can try to help you…"

With a single quick movement, it reached out with both forepaws and seized my face. Tendrils on its fingers dug into my eyes, nose, and ears. I tried to pull away and found I could not move; my body did not seem able to obey me. I opened my mouth to scream, but a tendril sneaked in and stole away the sound.

For a moment I felt my brain was being scrambled: I saw flashing lights, garbled sounds, nothing that made sense. I did not know when I lost consciousness.

Robin

I awoke in a warm room with gray, squared-off walls. Someone had draped a heavy cloth over me. My gaze flitted around the room rapidly, looking for something, anything familiar. Even the colors didn't look right.

A creature walked into the room, something with four limbs, bald everywhere but the head. It spoke, but its words were incomprehensible and muffled.

"I demand to know where I am!" I shouted, but the creature only raised its hands, making more meaningless sounds. This enraged me. Didn't it know who I was? I was…I was…

My mind stuttered and refused to give up the answer. It infuriated me still more. I leaped to my feet, meaning to grab the creature by the shoulders and shake it, but the cloth tangled me up, and when I tried to stand I couldn't seem to remember how to put my feet. I crashed painfully to the floor.

The creature shouted and another one came in. I hissed at it, trying to scramble to my feet, but something was wrong, where were the rest of my feet?

The second creature spoke and my head flicked up. That sound, something in that sound was familiar …

Everything snapped into place, and I looked around me. There was Aspen, a worried furrow between his eyebrows, stepping toward me. Beside him, Hazel, saying, "I'm not sure you should get any closer, she's not herself."

I glanced down, taking in the tangled sheets, my filthy clothes. "Why am I on the floor?"

Hazel frowned. "What do you remember?"

I tried. "I don't, I don't remember how I got here …" Everything was hazy bits. Flashes that disintegrated into nothing when I tried to focus on them. Like a dream that had been so complex and involved while it was going on, only to fade instantly.

"Before that," said Hazel. "You were in the woods?"

I inhaled. "Yes. I remember the woods. I was coming up the hill, I was almost home. There was a sunrise." I could see the afterimage of the bright flash, almost, if I closed my eyes. "The predator was there. It was hurt. It seemed like it was trying to talk to me."

"We found you beside its body. Cliff's fence went off." Aspen looked haunted. "I hadn't known it was even there, I would have told him to shut it down. I thought it had gotten you."

I stood up, darted over, buried my face in his chest. "I'm sorry. I'm sorry, I'm sorry. You must have been worried sick."

"I was!" He wrapped his arms around me for a moment. But then he pulled back to look at my face. "I thought this was the whole reason we came here! So we would *be* together. For the kids, every night. Colt just kept asking and asking where you were and I just had to say, I don't know. And then he finally went down but Lily kept saying 'I don't know? I don't know?'"

I hung my head, tears prickling my eyes. "This was for them! If there were people actively sabotaging us, intelligent people, then I *had* to get to them before we hurt any of them." Raising my head, I looked him in the eye. "And I was too late."

Hazel stirred uncomfortably. "I'm going to tell Hawk you're awake. He wanted to talk to you." She left the room.

Aspen shook his head. "I don't know what to think. You think the creatures are intelligent, but you're the only one who thinks that."

"I'm the only one who's seen them!"

"We've all seen the creature now. It just looked like an animal to me. If it were intelligent, wouldn't it be wearing clothes?"

"If you had fur that camouflaged you that well, why would you cover it up? Especially not when you were sneaking around spying on us."

He conceded that point with a tilt of his head. "I'm just saying, you should be open to the possibility you're wrong."

"And you should be open to the possibility I'm right."

"I am!" he protested. Typical. He wanted credit for supporting me but without actually getting on board, not when Hawk had told him the opposite.

Speak of the devil. The man himself appeared in the doorway. "So you're finally awake," Hawk said, eyes narrowed. "I'm sure I don't have to tell you, I'm not happy with your excursion. I specifically said no one was to go outside the stockade, except in groups and with my permission."

"You and Aspen both," I said breezily, heading toward the door. "I've already had an earful from him, you don't need to chime in."

Aspen's dark eyes widened with hurt as I passed him.

Hawk stood firmly where he was, so I couldn't get by. "I have just been around the colony looking for damage. Turns out the well has been destroyed. The lid was smashed and the pump and purifier thrown to the bottom."

"So that's what she was doing here."

Hawk's eyebrows knitted together. "She?"

I paused for a moment. Why did I feel so certain it was a she? "Well, the creature's definitely not an it. Not if she was smart enough to know the well was her next reasonable target."

I glanced at Aspen. He was nodding slightly. Hawk, on the other hand, frowned. "Or it just likes to smash things."

98

"You'll believe anything rather than that it's intelligent!"

"I meant what I said earlier," Hawk countered. "If you go spreading this idea around the colony, there *will* be consequences."

"Like what?" I asked. "Not let me go to chapel?"

"You may not be part of the church, but you are part of this colony and signed the charter. The agreement was that *we* are in charge. That includes any consequences we decide are necessary."

Aspen sighed and rubbed his forehead. "Of course she's going to do as you ask," he said. "She didn't spread it around before."

I flashed him an annoyed look. If I wanted to face off with Hawk, that was my business. But I supposed it would get Aspen in trouble with the church if I was too much of a problem. "I'm not going to," I said. "Can I go now?"

Hawk finally stood aside and let me go. "But no more unauthorized excursions," he called after me. I didn't turn. On that question, I wasn't ready to give any promises.

10

Aspen

The ruined well turned out to be the least of our worries. Hawk brought me outside to show me the rest of the damage: our solar panel farm. Every single panel was smashed; a sunburst of cracks spreading out from the middle of each. Stomped? Hit with a rock? Robin was right, it looked suspiciously targeted.

"Is there any chance of salvaging them?" Hawk was asking Cliff, who had come along.

Cliff picked up one carefully, but shards still slipped off and shattered on the ground. Peering at the underside, he gave a low whistle. "Nope. The damage goes clear through."

My lungs constricted. I needed that power. I was feeding the entire colony on that power. And with so many seedlings destroyed yesterday, it would be a long time before we had any outdoor crop to live on. Especially if creatures kept coming into the stockade to destroy anything I planted. "You can make more, right?"

Cliff shrugged. "Not really sure. I've never had to before. I'll have to check the computer, and see what I can make with the fabricator."

"How much battery do we have?" asked Hawk.

This, at least, I could answer. Robin and I had been carefully rationing it out. "They're full now," I said. "Though at our current usage, we'll be out in three weeks."

"Find a way to cut that down," said Hawk.

I wanted to protest. Wasn't that what Robin had already done? But it wasn't like there was any other option. We needed that power to live.

Hurrying inside, I found Autumn in the lab, checking on the gestation tanks. "Don't look so frantic," she said cheerfully. "You'll recover those damaged plants soon."

I shook my head. "It's not that." I filled her in about the panels. "My first thought was, maybe we should cancel the goat project. For now."

She looked stricken. As well she might. "Cancel the goat project" was a sanitized term for flushing the tanks. And Autumn would be the one cleaning up bloody, dead goat fetuses. A horrible thing to ask of someone who loved animals like she did. "I know," I said softly. "I don't want that. But we might not have power for both the tanks and the scrubber. And with how things are going, there isn't going to be anything for the goats to eat. We have plenty more ova in the freezer, right?"

"When the batteries go out, the freezer won't work either," she pointed out. "This might be our only chance to have any animal at all."

My stomach sank. We had had so many plans, such a careful food web planned out. Chickens and pigs. Songbirds and salmon. Cats and dogs. It wasn't the whole Earth ecosystem, but it was as much as we could get our hands on. All in a freezer that was running on batteries. Sybil's dream, Terra's new home, defrosting.

Autumn reached over to squeeze my arm. "That's worst case, right? Best case is Cliff works out something else. And I would hate to flush four months of progress only to find we didn't need to."

"How much time have they got left?"

"Three weeks. But I think I can have them out in a week and a half, with steroids. I mean it's not ideal, but they'll live at that point."

I took a deep breath. "Okay. We'll see what else we can shave off. We can certainly move all the potted plants outside, at least. I'll talk to Robin about the rest."

She left to check on the gestators, and I started moving all the spindly seedlings I had left onto a cart. Talking to Robin, now there was the last thing in the world I felt like doing.

It's an unspoken rule of our relationship that I don't fight with Robin. She fights with me. Sometimes I think she must have come out of the gestator with her fists up. I'm the person to defuse, de-escalate, be the calm person who makes her shoulders come down from around her ears.

I didn't feel like being that person right now. Lily hadn't gone to sleep till two in the morning, and I hadn't been able to sleep for some time after that for worry. And then they'd woken me at six telling me the fence had gone off, and Robin was unconscious.

In a normal world I would have taken the day off to rest and process. But I didn't have that kind of luxury. I'd been overbooked already, before last night's destruction. I was *tired*.

I was also, no matter how much I pretended not to be, furious. She hadn't had to do any of that. If she'd listened to Hawk or Sybil or even me, she wouldn't have. She deliberately hadn't told me because she'd known I wasn't going to agree to it.

I loaded up the last seedling and sighed. I'd plant these out first before talking to her. Everything on my to-do list was about equally urgent, but the thought of telling her how upset I was with her made me feel sick to my stomach. The thought of talking to her without mentioning it was even worse.

11

Robin

That afternoon I rooted through cabinets and drawers until I found the satellite pictures of our landing site. They were printed on thin, glossy plastic which could be washed clean and put back in the printer. Everything on the *Resurrection* was reusable or recyclable. It had to be.

I laid them out on the table in the conference room and sat down, frowning. Something was bothering me. I had entirely made up my mind that there couldn't be an intelligent native civilization on Eos, because if there had been, I would have found it. At least, that's what I had thought when I made my way home last night. And I hadn't really had any hard evidence I was wrong. But somehow I had woken up more sure than ever that they were out there.

With a finger I traced the route I had taken. On the map, it really didn't look that far. Yet if there had been anyone around, that was a long way to go without stumbling on a single house or road.

"Except that the entire route was on the common," I muttered to myself. And then stopped. The common? I knew what I meant by it, I meant common land where landless people might hunt. But what made me think there was any such thing?

I yanked open a drawer and grabbed the little magnets I had used to mark landing sites, such a long time ago. The glob of them overflowed my hands. Pulling one out, I scanned the map. Where would a house be?

Without hesitation I snapped it down. It was a spot on the hillside above the plateau, perhaps five miles away. I knew it from the creek that went by, with another smaller creek flowing into it. There was a clearing near that spot, I knew that clearing. It was right by my home, where I'd grown up.

I pulled back my hand, puzzled. I hadn't grown up there. I had grown up in the tunnels, far downdome, on the nightside. Near Elevatortown. There were no creeks, or clearings, or anything remotely reminiscent of that spot.

Yanking another magnet off the bundle, I tried again. Where might an alien live? *Snap.* Again, entirely without thinking, I had found another spot. Some distance from the first one; both of our estates were large.

I shook my head slowly. Was I losing my mind? Hazel had told me about my delirium when I'd first woken up. Perhaps I'd been more traumatized by my experience than I had thought. Or one of the plants I'd brushed against had dosed me with hallucinogens. I examined the cuts all over my arms from the razorwire bushes. If it had some kind of toxin on it, that stuff was inside me now.

One by one, I placed all the rest of the magnets. Each of the spots felt deeply familiar, I would even have memories associated with them, but when I tried to remember what they were, they slipped away.

Taking out a felt tip pen from one of the drawers, I marked x's as I picked up the magnets. I couldn't leave this out. Somebody might think I was planning something.

I wasn't entirely sure I wasn't.

There was a gentle tap at the door. I jumped guiltily and gathered up the photos.

"There you are," said Aspen. "I was looking for you."

I glanced quickly at the clock. Not time for school to be out. "Something up?"

"Did you, uh. Did you check back in with Hazel at all? Make sure everything's fine now?"

I nodded. "Clean bill of health."

I'd asked if there was any way she could test my brain. Hoping she'd think I meant the delirium and memory loss, not this weird sense of deja vu I was having now.

"It's not that unusual to lose some time when you faint," she'd said, but she'd run me through a number of tests. All fine. I wasn't sure if that made me feel better or worse.

The doctors of my childhood, when I ever managed to get in to see one, always treated us down-domers like we were angling for drugs. Knowing something was wrong with me but having tests show up clean made me feel like I'd been caught in a lie. Which was why I hadn't told her about most of it.

"Good, good," said Aspen. "I don't know if you've heard, but, uh, we're needing to find a way to cut energy use again. The solar panels were smashed in this latest raid."

I felt the bottom fall out of my stomach. After all that work. This was the backup of the backup of the backup already. Nobody planning the colony had thought we'd lose the reactor and two sets of solar panels.

"We're getting close to having a little more food outside," Aspen continued. "They didn't destroy any more plants this time, and I was hoping to be off the scrubber lichen within a month or two. But we *need* power for the gestators and the freezers. Can you think of anything else we can cut...?"

"That damn wire," I said pointedly. It didn't take much actual energy to run, so long as it wasn't actually discharging, but I wanted to be rid of it.

"I'll certainly ask," said Aspen, with a tone that implied it was asking for the moon. Which, given how hostile Hawk had been to the whole idea of aliens, was probably accurate. "What else?"

"Our best bet is to step up construction as much as we can," I suggested. "Take the load off the fans and lights inside." I ran my tongue around the back of my teeth, considering each slice of our power-use pie. The lights and fan were good-sized slices; without those we'd have … another week on the battery?

"But is it safe to sleep outside?" he asked anxiously. "I don't know if you got a good look at the creature. It was big. Claws and teeth say definitely a predator. I know you don't like it, but it's probably for the best we got that one before it got any of us."

My gaze snapped to his. "How can you say that?"

"I don't know, maybe because I'm imagining that thing getting into our bunkroom at night?"

"You don't know her!" I cried out, surprising even myself. Then I stopped. For a second, for the briefest second, I remembered seeing the alien. She hadn't been dead when I'd seen her. She'd been alive. But now I couldn't remember the image, what she had looked like alive, what I had said or done.

Aspen only looked puzzled. "Neither do you, or anybody else."

I shook my head. "Never mind. I just—never mind."

12

Robin

"Tsaft." My eyes flicked open. I could still feel the shape of the word I'd woken up whispering, but it had no meaning to me.

The kids were still asleep in their bunks on the opposite wall. Aspen was up already. He was burning the candle at both ends as he tried to make up for lost time on the seedlings. I had just had the most beautiful dream, and I couldn't remember any of it. At least, I knew it was about … well there was a feeling of … anyway it must be related to that word I had said … whatever it was …

I gave up and got out of bed. I was beginning to get tired of this feeling, like there was a word on the tip of my tongue, always darting away and hiding behind other words which I *knew* weren't it.

Through breakfast, and getting the kids ready, I kept worrying at the problem, poking it and prodding it in my mind. Well, two problems. First, why I was having such odd mental experiences. But more importantly, how I could test my map. I thought I knew where the aliens might be living, but maybe I was just crazy. I would have to go there to be sure, and going there might be suicide if I was right.

Plus, of course, Hawk had been very specific not to, and he would surely find a way to punish me if I did. This wasn't Sybil, who would frown and sigh and eventually put up with whatever I decided to do. Hawk was a normal human leader, capable of laying down the law around here.

And more importantly, there was Aspen. He hadn't yelled at me, but I could tell he hadn't forgiven me either. If I was going to go out again, I would have to do it with permission. A thing I clearly wasn't going to get.

Lily gave me a lot of trouble getting ready for school. No surprise, after getting off the day before yesterday and finding me not there. "Go ahead and walk over by yourself," I told Colt, who gave me a quick squeeze before heading out the door with one backward glance. Poor kid, I always expected him to adapt to his sister, and he always had, but someday he was probably going to get a complex over it.

I knelt on the ground by Lily, who had melted into a small, teary puddle on the floor. "Baby, look. If you don't want to go to school today, you don't have to."

If I had thought it was going to be that simple, I was sharply disabused of that notion. She redoubled the shrieking, kicking at the bulkhead with her feet. One fat braid, which I had barely gotten done in the first place, started to unravel. We were actually moving backwards.

"I think I understand," I said slowly. "You don't want to miss school, but you're also worried about missing me."

This time the answering sobs were less scream and more cry, which meant—at least, I thought it meant—I had hit on the right problem. The solution might be more difficult.

Or not. I grabbed my alarm clock from beside the bed and started reprogramming it. It was a simple gadget, but at least it had a timer mode. I punched buttons till it read 4:00:00.

By this point Lily had raised her head and was watching me. I pressed start and handed it over. "See, look at those numbers counting down. When it all reaches zeroes, the whole way across, that's when I'll be back. It'll be lunchtime and I will be there to eat lunch with you."

She took it hesitantly. I wasn't entirely sure she'd gotten all that, but hopefully after a few days of this she'd catch on. I put her bunny in her other hand and wiped the tears off her cheeks. "Want to go to school?"

She looked at me, at the clock, and at the door and finally nodded. Success.

Once she'd been dropped off, I took a casual stroll outside and past the gate. A large man was standing beside it: Flint. Normally he was with the construction teams, but today he was just standing there. A guard. No luck.

Plan B was to try talking to Sybil again. She let me into her room without argument, which seemed a good start. I had thought she might have been offended yesterday.

"Hawk told me about your excursion," she said, perching on the edge of her bed. "I don't know whether to be relieved you came back safe, or angry you tried it against my advice."

She didn't sound angry. Her green eyes looked across at me steadily. Calmer, I thought, than yesterday. "I just had to know what was out there."

"And you came back none the wiser. So." She shrugged. "Do you want some cafbev? Tea?"

I sat down. "Real tea?"

She gave a sharp chuckle. "You'd know if we had that."

"Never mind, then." The stuff we had was made from herbs, spiked with a little synthetic tea extract. It tasted even less like tea than the cafbev tasted like coffee. At least the cafbev was bitter enough to strip paint, just like the old station coffee I was used to.

Sybil got up, poured herself a cup of hot water from a thermos, and added a tea packet. "Something happened to you out there, didn't it?"

I blinked. "What do you mean?"

"You have a very different energy today. Different than you've had the whole time I've known you. You're usually so simple. Red aura, I guess I'd call it. But today you're swirling and complicated." Turning from the counter, she caught my eye. "Don't look surprised, I've always had a sense."

I watched her settle back on the bed, blowing on her tea. Her movements were graceful but unsophisticated. You didn't notice it when she was among her disciples, because she created the standards for everything, but she probably wasn't born to any kind of privilege. Her coloring and features were familiar to me from down in the tunnels: that light brown skin that was a mix of everything, no way to trace now where any of us were from.

Not for the first time, I wondered how she had ascended to the leader of such a popular cult. The real story, not the hagiography I'd been told. Charisma was definitely a part of it. Maybe the rest was her skill at reading people.

"You're not wrong," I said. "Hazel says that when I woke up, I was delirious."

"She says? You don't remember?"

I tried. I could catch—a feeling? Maybe? Not a good one, I didn't think. "No. Hazel says I was hissing and snarling and trying to leap at her. I just remember finding myself on the floor."

She took a sip before resting her cup on her knee, regarding me. "Those memories are almost certainly still there. You just can't access them."

"Why wouldn't I be able to access them? I remember everything else."

"The mind is a funny thing. Sometimes the ego deletes things it can't accept. Or it strings together events into significance even when they aren't connected. Makes us feel certain when we ought to be doubtful. Until the ego is quiet, we can't see things as they are."

Privately, I thought that sounded like bullshit. "Well, the ego is me, right? So I can't just turn it off."

"Meditation can be helpful."

"That's what Aspen says." I shrugged. "I'm really not spiritual. At all."

"Everyone is spiritual," she said. "We all *are* spirits. You need to get in touch with yours."

I hadn't come here for this. I had been trying to break the ice for some kind of conversation about the aliens, and somehow she had grabbed the wheel of the conversation away from me. But I found myself asking, "How do you meditate, anyway?"

She explained, briefly, her method, and I tucked it away to maybe try sometime. Sometime when no one was around. I emphatically did not want Aspen thinking I was getting into his faith. I just wanted a way to maybe recall these things that kept nagging at me.

"Maybe I'll give it a shot. Sometime." Then, as if I was thinking of it for the first time, I said, "I had a very interesting time in the woods. I suppose you would think of it as a spiritual experience. Just made me think, maybe your problem is that you're here, in a tiny metal room. You might have better luck connecting with your goddess if you could get yourself in a better frame of mind. Surrounded by nature."

She lowered her empty cup to her knee. "You know, you're completely right! I hadn't thought of that at all, and I should have. Perhaps in the hydroponics lab…"

"I was thinking outside the stockade."

Shaking her head, she got up to put her cup away. "Oh no. She's the goddess of Earth, not of here. She doesn't like gen-mod lifeforms, and she wouldn't like alien lifeforms either. It must be Earth life. After what happened to the fields outside, basically the only Earth life around is the hydroponics. Well, and us."

13

Robin

I picked the bridge for my meditation spot the next morning, after the kids were at school. No one went up here anymore; it had gone from control tower to disused attic. I hadn't been up here since I'd sent the message home.

Parking myself in the crash seat, I pulled up my legs under me and closed my eyes. What had Sybil said? "Get out of the driver's seat of your mind." Well, that was ironic. Anyway, I was a pilot. The driver's seat was really the only place I was comfortable. I liked to be in control. Control is good. Then you can handle whatever happens.

I took a long, slow breath from the belly, like she had told me. *Out of the driver's seat. Be an observer of what is happening within and around you.* I pictured myself stepping out of the seat, a pilot's seat like the one I was sitting in, only just behind my eyes. My avatar perched on one of the control panels along the edge of the room. "Here I am!" I announced. "Just watching! Not doing!"

"You're talking," I imagined Sybil saying. "Talking is doing."

I shut up and watched. I watched myself take deep belly breaths.

I watched an itch trickle down between my shoulder blades. I watched myself open my eyes. I watched the shadows creep along the ground from the oblong window above my head.

I watched thoughts arise and pass away: Lily's face. Aspen's voice. Worry about what was outside the colony. That one almost broke me out of it, but I breathed in and out and let that thought go. Later. When I was in the pilot's seat again.

I watched a face come into my mind. An alien face. Not the one I had met. She had tufts of hair at her ears and her eyes were brilliant blue. Beautiful. I felt the warm feeling I had had from that dream; it felt like a rush in my gut, quick heartbeats, flush. Love? The image wavered as I caught myself trying to label, to judge. *Tsaft.*

She ducked behind a magenta bush, and I followed. Or someone followed; I was only observing. I knew I would be in trouble if I spoke to her, but I couldn't resist. She was so beautiful.

The memory faded and another swam up: worry and fear. I had to go to where the star had fallen. I had to see. I was afraid at first, but then curious. Two strange creatures passed close to my campsite, and I froze, staring. A large one and a smaller. A child?

I gasped and the visions vanished. That had been me. Me and Lily. How could I be remembering me and Lily?

Putting my feet down, I leaned my elbows on the control panel. That was enough meditation for one day, more than enough. I was exhausted and my ass hurt. But Sybil had been right, I had been able to remember a lot more this way. This time the images were still in my mind, not fading away. I remembered seeing Lily and me walking through the woods, but not knowing who we were. It was like a recording from another perspective.

The alien had seen us that day. So that would have been her perspective. Why would I be remembering things she had seen? Had she done something to me before she had died? I felt a faint itch in my mind. I thought maybe she had. After all, I remembered nothing after a certain point. But like hell was I going to try to remember that today. It must be

114

nearly lunchtime.

❧

A few days passed. I tried to do enough work around the colony that nobody missed me or wondered what I was up to, before slipping away each day to meditate. Every time I remembered fresh things. More faces, though no new names. Nothing really useful.

I remembered the constellations and what they were called. Running swiftly after a prey animal, all six legs eating up the ground. A pounding rainstorm on the roof of my home, dry and dark while outside the trees lashed in the wind. Cozy; I liked that kind of weather.

Or, *she* had liked it. Whoever's memories these were. I hadn't remembered her name yet, or much about her life. I wasn't even sure she *was* a she, though some of the memories with babies in them made me think of her as a mother. Maybe that was why I had automatically used that pronoun.

I told Aspen none of this. I didn't like the thought of keeping a secret from him, but it seemed so hard to explain or justify. In the end it was easy, because he was too busy and distracted to get curious. Each night he came into bed after I did, kissed me, and was asleep before I'd even had the chance to ask about his day.

Four days after my encounter with the alien, Sybil pounced on me. "I've been looking everywhere for you," she said quietly, falling into step beside me. "We need to talk."

I let her pull me into a little room alongside the kitchen piled with dirty pans. With lunch about to be served, nobody was working on these at the moment. "What could you possibly want to talk to me about, ma'am?"

Hurt creased her brow. "Ma'am? I was thinking we were past that now."

"You were off the clock then," I said. "Looks to me like you're back on the job."

She gave a tiny smile, which threatened to overtake her face if she stopped holding it back. "Yes. Your idea of praying around nature was a good one. I could *feel* my soul opening up again."

"What is it that you want with me?"

The swinging door flung open and someone came in with an armload of dirty trays. "Oh! Sybil, I'm sorry, I didn't realize you were in here."

"Don't mind me," she said sunnily. The kitchen worker deposited her trays in the sink and left beaming. Sybil turned to me again. "I heard you've been hanging around by the gate. Flint told me."

My shoulders drew up involuntarily. I had walked by *one time*. How closely was she keeping track of me? "Didn't know walking around was a crime."

"It's not," she reassured me quickly, putting her hand on my arm. I looked at it. She didn't take it off. "But you do want to get back out there, don't you?"

Narrowing my eyes, I moved my arm away. "Why are you asking this?"

"Because I want to let you do it," she said. "I want you to take me with you."

Now *that* was unexpected. I stared at her for a moment. "Why?"

"Because you might be right. What if there are intelligent creatures out there? I want to know. Hawk has no curiosity about it."

"Hawk answers to you. You could just have him put together a team."

"No one's been out as far as you have," she argued. "No one else has seen them. You've got the best chance of anyone of actually finding them."

I looked down, chewing my lip. There was something fishy about this. A lot of somethings. Like what had changed to make her suddenly interested. Or why she was hiding in a scullery when she could have simply approached me at lunch. Was this secret? Secret from whom?

But on the other hand, if I turned her down, I might not get another chance. I didn't even want to ask too many questions, for fear she'd change her mind. "When?"

"Now, if you can. I've got everything ready."

I shook my head. "Won't work. I promised I'd eat lunch with the kids." Lily had gotten the hang of her timer; no way was I screwing that up with a no-show. "After that, though."

She gave me a beatific smile. "*Thank* you. I will meet you after, near the gate."

Aspen wasn't at lunch. No surprise to me; he was working without a break these days. But Colt and Lily arrived with their classes and made a beeline over to me. "Today we learned about why ruminants are important for ecosystems!" Colt declared without prologue. "That's why we are growing *goats* and they will be *born* soon and we'll get to play with *baby goats!*"

"That's right baby, they're growing in the tanks in the lab upstairs," I said. "That's why Daddy's working so hard right now, so that there's food for them to eat by the time they come out."

"Can't we just not decant them till they're ready?"

"Nope, when they're done growing, they have to come out. Like cookies. You can't keep a cookie waiting in the oven or it burns."

Lily clutched her timer. It was counting down the last seconds. When it beeped, she shoved it in my face. She had decided only I was allowed to turn it off.

I silenced the beeping and put it on the table. "Kids, I'm going to go on another trip. Can I count on you to be good for Daddy?"

"Can I come this time?" Colt demanded. "I want to see the purple trees!"

I shook my head. "It's not safe out there for kids."

"Not fair," he groused. "Lily got to."

Lily just shoved the timer back at me. I rubbed her slick hair, where it ran up to the fat pigtails. "Let me see, baby, I gotta figure out how long I'll be gone." Chewing my lip, I put in twenty-four hours. If we didn't find anything in that long, we'd better give the whole thing up. "I'll be back when this goes off. Be good for Daddy and the teachers."

Aspen, when I found him out in the fields directing the replanting of the damaged fields, was harder to convince. "Hawk said you can't."

"Sybil said she wants me to."

He leaned on his shovel, eyeing me. "You don't trust her."

"No. But you do."

I could see the wheels turning behind his eyes. He didn't want me to go. He didn't think it was safe. But on the other hand, he wasn't going to say no to the prophetess. I leaned on the religious argument, feeling like a heel for doing it. "She seemed to think it was what the goddess wanted her to do."

He blew out his breath. "Well, be *careful*, okay? You both need stunners. Don't touch the plants. The ones with magenta ferny stuff will give you a rash, and that's just from the half dozen we even tested. You have radios?"

"Sybil has everything. I'll make sure she's got what we need."

"Okay," he said, leaning in for a kiss. "Just—"

"Be careful," I finished. "No repeats of last time."

He nodded. "Radio me often."

I trailed my fingers along his cheek before turning to go. Something about his cheekbones made me want to do unseemly things to him. When had we last had sex? A month ago? More? Between the shit pregnancy was doing to my hormones and the amount of time he was spending on the plants, that had been put on the back burner. But *God* he was easy on the eyes. And other parts.

Sybil waited near the gate, half-hidden by the frame of the schoolhouse the workers were building. At her feet were two bags. "What did you pack?" I asked, unzipping one.

"Everything we need," she said. "Radio. Stunners. Food. Thermal blankets."

I nodded. Those would have been smart to bring on my last trip. I took out a stunner and shoved it into the elastic band of my pants. "Is the electric fence shut off?"

"Did it myself."

"All right then." I shouldered my pack and followed her to the gate. Flint was there again today and opened it with a smile and nod.

Once we'd passed out of earshot, ducking under the dead wire, I asked, "Why so secretive about this?"

"What do you mean? I didn't tell you to keep it secret."

"You're hiding in closets and behind construction sites."

"Oh, that." She stepped over a burned log. Already it was festooned with pink ivy. "I've been in my room for weeks. People have been politely waiting for me to come out all that time, wanting to tell me about their spiritual life or their fights with their spouses or their problem with their children. If I had let myself get spotted, we'd never get out of here. As it is I have been answering questions all morning."

She had an explanation for everything. "Does Hawk know?"

"I left him a note."

So no. Like me the other day, she'd chosen to ask forgiveness rather than permission. I wondered why. After all, he was supposed to be her acolyte. If she wanted to go, he couldn't stop her. But perhaps he was protective of her, like Aspen was of me. "I've wondered," I said. "And you obviously don't have to answer. But are you and Hawk ..."

"No," she interrupted, laughing. "It's been useful to let that rumor go around. Keeps the ladies from thinking I'm stealing their men when I talk to them. But I don't even swing that way."

"Oh." My face heated. I hadn't even considered that possibility.

"Before you ask, I'm not with anybody else either," she added. "Only Terra." Her voice grew softer as she said the goddess's name.

"That's hardly the same thing."

"It is to me. I was in a very dark place when she came to me. I was supposed to be the first child in my family to go to college, but instead I wound up having a nervous breakdown. Too much of other people's feelings. Too much insistence on a single right answer, when life is much more complicated than that.

"So I found myself alone, in a white room, with no blinds for fear I would strangle myself, and that's when she came to me. I could see a pattern underlying everything that lives. The veins in a leaf, just like the veins in my wrists. The curl of a shell like the curl of an ear. We are all part of one thing, and that thing is Terra. I really see her as a person. A person who would be able to understand what it was like to feel hollow, broken, torn apart. Because Earth was. Her own body was.

"I know you'll laugh at me, Robin, but I think what we have is as important as any relationship. She has my whole heart."

"I wouldn't laugh at you," I said. "I had no idea you'd gone through all that."

"I usually leave the mental illness out of my life story," she said. "People have an irrational prejudice. I say an illness."

That was the second time in as many minutes that she'd admitted to misleading people. She never lied, did she? But she certainly knew how to get people to believe the wrong thing without lying.

"Is that what kept you in your room for so long?"

She nodded. "I take a lot of meds to function as well as I do. But nothing's perfect. There are more modern options, but all of those assume that mental health means not hearing voices, even kind ones. The doctors called Terra's voice part of the illness and promised to make it go away, and I—" She hesitated, as if unsure how much of the story to trust me with. "I couldn't be sure they weren't right. A voice can be genuinely divine and also coming from a part of the brain that's broken. A kind of receiver the human mind wasn't meant to have. So ... I take a handful of meds every day, and sometimes it isn't enough and I break down for a week, or a month. Hazel knows. Hawk, too, but he doesn't cut me much slack for it."

Her voice turned a little bitter on that last sentence. "He doesn't cut anybody much slack," I agreed. All of my encounters with him lately had been unpleasant. I wasn't sure if that was his fault or mine.

Unconsciously I lengthened my stride, even heading up the hillside as I was, and she had to scurry to catch up. "Where are you even going?" she asked. "I thought last time you went downhill, to the north."

"Well, I didn't find them that way," I said. Now it was my turn to carefully edit the truth. "I'm thinking they must prefer higher ground."

"What did it look like?"

"Didn't you see the body?"

"No. Hawk said he put it in the cooler, but I didn't go and see."

I pictured one of them—not the one I had had such brief glimpses of, but the ones I remembered. "They have six legs," I said slowly. "But they can walk on two, four, or six, depending on how much of a hurry they're in. Their face is a lot like a cat's, with large eyes and pointed ears, but the mouth is different. They have fangs." I gestured to the corners of my mouth.

"What color?"

"Not really any color. The fur diffracts the light, so that they look like the color of whatever's around them. That's why they don't wear clothes when they're out in the woods."

"That's your theory?"

I froze for a second. "Of course." I continued walking. "That's what I told Hawk, when he asked why they didn't wear clothes if they were intelligent. They might very well wear them at home." In my head, Tsaft smiled and inclined her head. A silver chain hung from her ears and down around her neck in a sparkling waterfall. Her image didn't fade as before; now that my mind had a place to put her, it seemed it was capable of keeping hold of her.

Hopping over stones, we got across the stream without getting our feet wet and into the unburned forest. Sybil glanced at everything idly.

"I have to admit, I had no idea what you guys even meant by 'the wild' before," I said. "But here in the woods, it's just so different from what I had imagined. I can see why you'd like it."

"It's nothing like Earth."

"It's more like Earth than anything on Proxima. I mean, look at how the trees are spaced. There's a big white one…two small red ones…a big white one…no conscious pattern. And yet there are ways it can and can't go. Two of the big white ones won't go next to each other. It's…it's like a pattern that creates itself."

"Emergent design," she said. "Yes. But not the design that we co-evolved with. It doesn't suit us the way an Earth forest would. Terra doesn't like it much either."

I led the way through the trees. Doesn't suit us? It suited me perfectly. This forest felt as familiar as the tunnels where I'd grown up—where the numbers had all rubbed off the doors of the different apartments, but I knew my own by the stains and dents. I felt completely different from my last trek through the woods. This time it all felt hauntingly familiar. But only if I didn't think about it too hard.

"You never said," I commented, as I helped Sybil scramble over a rotting log, from which new saplings were growing among shelflike fungi. "What did the goddess say to you, when you were praying in the hydroponics lab?"

"She said it was time to return to my mission. She knows my soul has been struggling lately, but she says I'm ready to get back to work."

I paused. "I don't see how that connects to coming out here."

"Well, obviously if we're going to get rid of all the native life, we have to make sure we've dealt with the predators first."

"I thought you believed me, that they're intelligent!"

She quickened her steps, not looking at me. "All the more reason if they are. They're not going to sit back and let us terraform everything."

I stopped and stared at her in horror. "So you're just following me to find out where they are, so you can kill them?"

She frowned. "Figuring out how to deal with them is going to have to come later. First we have to get some sense of how many they are, and what sort of technology they have."

"No."

"What do you mean, no?"

"No, I'm not leading you to them. I didn't agree to this."

"I thought we were just going to explore and see what we found! Maybe we won't even see any on this trip."

I folded my arms. She had lured me in with her friendliness, her harmless eccentricity. But that was a mistake. She was smart and capable;

she'd founded an entire religion. She was good at playing people, and here I'd been assuming I was exempt from that just because I didn't buy her story. No more. I wasn't going to say a single word more to her than I could help. She'd only use it to manipulate me.

"Okay, fine." She hiked her bag up on her shoulders and turned around. "We'll just go back then."

"Not that either, ma'am."

Sybil turned, her dark eyebrows knitting together. "So what's your plan?"

"You go home. I go on."

"I'm not doing that!"

I pulled my stunner from my waistband and aimed it at her. "Start walking."

She gave an incredulous little laugh. "That's a stunner! Why should I be scared?"

"Because while you're knocked out, a predator will come and eat you." That was why I was threatening her, instead of just stunning her and having done with it. Angry as I was, I didn't actually want to hurt her.

"I don't understand why you care so much!"

For myself, I didn't. If I really believed that Sybil were capable of wiping out the predators without starting a war that blew back on the colony, I might be tempted to go along with it. It would be the wrong thing to do, of course. Genocide. But the colony was a single, fragile spot on a hostile world, and my kids were in it. I'm not a saint. I'd be tempted. I could let her do what she wanted and say it hadn't been my call and therefore wasn't my fault.

But I was more than myself, now. I had somehow gotten a piece of the predator trapped inside my head, and inside that piece was a memory of Tsaft. Someone had loved her. I remembered what that had felt like.

Of course there was no fucking way I was explaining that to Sybil. So I stood there and pointed the stunner until she turned and began to scramble back down the slope.

14

Robin

The predators didn't go in for cities, as it turned out. My home—the home I remembered—was beside a large clearing, but it would have been hard to prove for certain that anyone lived there. The trees had been fully uprooted and the ground smoothed, leaving a wide, perfect circle of pink ivy. In the center was a round platform of stone two feet high, blackened but swept clean.

No one was around, but I didn't feel surprised. Pausing for a moment, I tried to quiet my ego and figure out why I didn't expect anybody to be around. Nothing. Standing around in a mysterious clearing, wondering when a six-legged fanged creature might jump out at me was probably not conducive to a meditative state.

At the far end of the clearing was a vertical wall of stone, where the rock that made up the hillside protruded from the earth. But here, the rock face was intricately carved in swirling patterns. In the middle was a low double door, made of a dark, glossy metal.

I put my hand on the twisted handle, then half drew it back. What was I thinking? This wasn't actually my door. I couldn't just walk right in.

Then again, what *was* the etiquette for making first contact with an alien species? What was I there to say? I wanted to say we meant them no harm, but that would be a lie. The most important thing would be to tell them about the alien that had died. But it seemed the worst possible opener. What if they were angry? What if they killed me?

It had been stupid to walk here, with only a stunner, feeling safe simply because my brain was telling me I remembered this place. I should have waited till I remembered more. Of course, who knew if the opportunity would have come a second time. When an unpredictable prophet offers you what you want, you take it while it's hot.

I sat down with my back against the platform, smelling the faint whiff of ashes. It brought back a memory of a fire blazing, an animal turning on a spit, the clearing full of people singing and dancing. Closing my eyes, I tried to meditate. If I could just bring back something, anything useful …

Apparently hiking up the steep hill while pregnant had taken more out of me than I had realized, because the next thing I knew I was swimming slowly to consciousness. The first thing I was aware of were voices. Their language was hissing and husky, but I understood it easily.

"What is it?"

"One of the creatures Mrrka saw, obviously."

"Well, of course, but I meant what sort of thing is it? A bird?"

"Perhaps it lost its wings."

"It's so fat. What can be the point of bulging out in the middle like that?"

"It obviously has a pouchling in there."

"How would a pouchling breathe with its clothes over it?"

"It can't be here." The voice was flat, angry. "It shouldn't have been able to find us. Unless my mother brought it back."

A soft voice. "I haven't seen her since she left."

I meant to simply lie still, wait to hear more of their thoughts. Perhaps one of them would mention whether or not they meant to kill me. Though of course if they did, what good would it do? Any one of them could kill me with a swipe of its claws before I could get to my stunner.

But when I heard that the predator I had seen was someone's mother, I opened my eyes, still somehow surprised to have my impressions confirmed. I was surrounded by at least half a dozen of the creatures, some crouched on all six limbs so their heads were level with mine, others rising onto four or two limbs, so they towered over me. All of them wore jewelry, but most wore no clothes, only their thick, colorless fur.

They showed no sign of fear as I regarded them, but just kept discussing me. I wondered if they were any more aware of my intelligence than we had been of theirs.

If I could understand them, it ought to be possible for me to speak in their language. That knowledge was in my head, somewhere. The question was whether I could be both aware enough to decide what to say and passive enough to let the words come to me. I marshaled my thoughts, trying to think of some kind of polite greeting, for starters.

But as my eyes went around the circle, I spotted her. Tsaft. From my dream. She was wrapped in a sky-blue shawl, with a gold necklace around her neck. Words came into my mind and, rather than try to catch, assess, and translate them, I said them aloud. "Blue star," I thought was what it meant.

Tsaft's ears pricked forward and her eyes widened. She brought her hands to her mouth. "That was Mrrka's name for me! Tell me, creature, where is my wife?"

Shit.

A tall one in gold earrings cut in, "It probably can't say any more than what Mrrka taught it."

"Please," Tsaft begged me.

I shook my head slowly, feeling like the world's biggest asshole. Of all the things to lead with. "I'm sorry," I said, the words feeling odd and snarly as they came out of my mouth. "I came upon Mrrka when she was dying."

The angry one gripped my wrist. "How long ago? *How long?*"

I searched her face. I knew her. Kisht. My feelings around her were complicated: concern, guilt, care, frustration. I looked down. "Two days."

Tsaft collapsed in on herself, pressing her head to the ground. A low moan escaped her.

Kisht shook my arm in fury. "What did you do? What did you *do*? You *stole* my mother's memories! That's what you did! Or else how would you know all this?"

I looked from her to Tsaft and back again. My face was hot with shame. I hadn't done a thing to Mrrka, but my people had and I was all they knew of my people. And they didn't even know that yet. All they knew was that I had some of Mrrka's memories, however that had happened.

A stout alien interposed, removing Kisht's hand from my arm. "This is highly inappropriate," she chided. "Let your father mourn. Take her inside and mourn with her. I will deal with this creature."

She pulled me to my feet and led me away from the clearing. The others dispersed. I followed her in something of a daze. I knew I remembered her also, but my mind refused to give up a name. It annoyed me that this memory thing couldn't at least be consistent.

It was evening by now, and the trees gave a soft glimmer from their trunks. The glowing moss, or whatever it was, was artfully distributed so that it formed faint patterns. That didn't make enough light for me, though, especially following an almost invisible creature. More than once she had to turn around and wait for me, her large golden eyes gleaming faintly.

"You must forgive Kisht," she said quietly. "You see she was Mrrka's heir, and if she was not present at the death, she is disappointed in all her hopes."

"Hopes for what?"

"Her hope to be Eldest after her mother," the stout one said.

Eldest meant leader, I thought. Or at least first among equals. Fuck. We hadn't just killed a scout, we had killed the queen of the first intelligent species humanity had ever made contact with.

"I am the Second Eldest," she said. "Or I was. Mrrka and I have been

128

rivals, in many ways, for years. And her mother before her." The Second Eldest shook her head. "There has not been such a change in fifty generations. A line that old, completely died out. Memory lost."

"But I remember," I interrupted. "I do remember a lot of things."

Fesskh—there it was, after I'd given up on remembering it, her name was Fesskh—stopped and bent down to look me in the face. "You remember Mrrka's memories?"

I quailed, with those fangs so close to my face. She smelled like ginger, and a little bit like old people. "Some of them?"

"I see." Fesskh half-shut her eyes a moment, reflecting. "She couldn't get home, so she picked whoever was near to hold her memories for her. It makes sense. I'm only surprised that it worked." She continued walking.

"Maybe it didn't work as intended," I said. "I've been very confused. It's hard to say which memories are mine and which are hers."

"It doubtless didn't work properly," said Fesskh dismissively. "You aren't one of us. Your mind wasn't fit for it. You got scraps, no more. Kisht has no reason to resent you. It would have been no better for her if you hadn't been there."

It took the better part of an hour to get to Fesskh's house. These people did not like living close to each other, that much was apparent. She opened a metal door built into the hillside and preceded me inside. I balked, completely unable to see anything. It infuriated me because everything seemed familiar, I'd certainly been to this house before, but this time I was blind. Mrrka had been able to see in the dark.

"Ah," said Fesskh, "I'd thought you must be a daywalker. If you'll wait here, I'll get a brand from the fire."

"I have a light," I said. "If you don't mind my using it."

"You are my guest."

I pulled out my stunner, carefully checking the safety was on before switching on the attached flashlight. Within was a stone staircase, bringing me down to a large foyer. Fesskh led me through this and to a small room with a fireplace and a number of woven rugs. The rugs had a complex pattern of textures, but were all one color. I supposed that was unsurprising, given that they would often be seen in the dark.

Here, though, the fire lent some illumination, and I switched off my light. "Very comfortable place you have here."

Fesskh lowered her eyelids. "It has belonged to my family for ten generations." She settled herself on one of the rugs, four legs tucked in and the topmost pair spread out in front of her. She looked like the Great Sphinx.

I sat down on another, tailor-fashion, because it was the closest I could do. Scanning Fesskh up and down, I asked, "Why did you take me here?"

She tilted her head to the side. "You are the first of your kind to speak with us. I wanted to talk to you."

"Alone?"

"Later, we will gather all of the Elders for you to speak with them."

But Fesskh wanted first stab at me. It made sense. If Mrrka had been queen, what did that make her? An ambitious earl? "I will be happy to do that, but," I stifled a not-entirely-fake yawn, "I should tell you I am very tired. My people sleep at night."

I couldn't say why I mistrusted her. Perhaps only because Mrrka had. But the mere fact that Fesskh wanted an advance version of every-thing I knew seemed reason enough to deny her any such thing.

With a faint backward flick of her ears, she said, "Of course."

From off down the hall, I heard a voice crying, "Hai hai! Fesskh! Open up!"

Fesskh gazed at me a moment, in no apparent hurry to go upstairs and open the door. Contemplating a course of action, it seemed to me. But in the end she placidly rose to her feet and went out.

Kisht's voice loudly declared, "What do you think you're doing, Sec-ond Eldest? The second you hear the creature has my mother's memories, you swoop in to take it from me!"

"I merely wanted to give it a chance at a better impression of us than your emotional attack. And give you a chance to calm yourself."

"You've brought it here to kill it, I know you have."

I jumped to my feet when I heard that. Of course that would be a natural course of action, wouldn't it? She had said that, without her mother's memories, Kisht couldn't inherit the title of Eldest. Then who would? Fesskh, probably. I wanted to kick myself for being so stupid. I'd been so grateful for some friendly treatment from one of these people, I hadn't even considered what her ulterior motives might be.

"Me?" Fesskh was all innocence. "I could never do such a thing! Why, it's our only chance to learn anything about its people!"

"Let me see it then."

"What a high tone you take toward an Elder."

"I only speak what my mother would, if she were here."

By then they had reached the room, and I tried to look relaxed and not at all worried about being clawed to death. Kisht favored me with only a single glare. She didn't want Fesskh to kill me, but that didn't mean she had to like me.

"I am afraid I must ask you to stay awake longer, if you can," Fesskh apologized. "It seems the only course of action that will satisfy Kisht is to gather some of the Elders right away. I suppose here won't be acceptable?" She cast Kisht a questioning glance.

"It will have to be," the other grumbled. "I'm not troubling Tsaft's mourning for this."

"One wonders why you trouble your own mourning."

"I can't mourn properly until I have found out what happened and why and what can be done."

That last line gave me hope. "So you think you might be able to take the memories back?" Then again, that might be the worst possible thing. What if they accessed *my* memories? What if they learned what Sybil and Hawk wanted to do to their planet?

Kisht snatched my hands and inspected them, carefully running her fingers over every inch. "Look," she said to the Second Eldest, ignoring me. "No tendrils. So how could she?"

"She couldn't," said Fesskh decidedly. "Her people don't share memories."

Dropping my hands, Kisht turned away. "We'll ask the others. If any such thing can be done, one of them will know."

"By *we*, I assume you mean me," said Fesskh to Kisht. "*You* won't be there."

Freed of their attention, I turned to my pack and dug out a thermos. Had Sybil thought to pack . . . yes, bless her. There were several cafbev packets, and I dumped two into a thermos. That made it even nastier than normal strength, but I clearly was going to need it. If it took this much arguing to even decide what to do with me, I wasn't getting any sleep tonight. That nap against the fire circle was going to have to hold me till morning.

They organized the meeting with surprising efficiency. Fesskh summoned two servants by pulling at a long rope in the corner of the room, and they hurried off to collect the attendees. Now that I was free to question things without having to carefully not think while remembering them, I wondered what that meant about their society. It seemed very normal to me that there would be servants, but I couldn't call to mind how many one might have or how they lived.

Kisht crouched on the rug glaring at me, apparently only there to ensure Fesskh didn't either kill me or ask me any questions before the others got there. I stared back, refusing to let myself be intimidated by her. This would be my daughter—Mrrka's daughter, that is—and even if she was much bigger than me, with fangs and claws, a part of me still felt like she was a kid.

The meeting wound up being utter chaos. I got the impression that usually Mrrka would have handled it in a much more orderly fashion, but nobody was willing to listen to Fesskh or take turns to ask their questions.

"Where did you come from?" one demanded.

"Why did you set the forest on fire?" shouted another.

"What happened to Mrrka?"

Perhaps the chaos could be to my advantage. I answered the first two questions as best I could, and by the time I had gotten through that, there were more questions to distract from the one I didn't answer. What the ship was. Why we were planting green stuff. Was I a bird or what?

Fesskh managed to shut everyone up long enough to ask, "What is your rank? Are you an elder among your people?"

I blew out my breath. "I'm pretty important," I said. "I drove the ship that brought us here."

Everyone flicked their tails in annoyance. "So just the driver," grumbled one. The word brought up the mental image of someone hauling a two-wheeled cart piled with building materials through the woods. So not even the driver—the horse, kind of.

I wanted to argue that point—my title was *captain*, technically, or had been—but they had no word for it and no concept that an important person would do a hands-on task like that. So instead I said, "My spouse is of a high status. If I do not return, she will come to fetch me. With others."

"*Obviously* you will return whenever you wish," said one, earning a glare from some others. Not everyone seemed to find it so obvious.

An hour in, I was fighting sleep, my chin resting on my fists. An argument had broken out about inheritance issues which I definitely didn't need to be here for. Kisht, everyone agreed, couldn't be the Eldest without her mother's memories, but could she still inherit the estate? Piles of documents, etched on a fine white bark, were consulted and passed around. I yawned.

The door swung open, silencing everyone. Fesskh rose to two legs, ready to rebuke whoever had interrupted, but when she saw who it was, she settled back to her haunches. "Tsaft. You honor us."

"My apologies for interrupting the elders," she said quietly. She had donned a woven shawl of a deep red, which tinted the refractive fur around it the same color. Was she really more beautiful than any of the others, or was that Mrrka's memories talking? "Your servant claims the right of widow to speak to my wife's heir."

"The Elders need—" began someone officiously, but Fesskh smoothly interrupted, "Of course. We have much to discuss which is not for its ears anyway."

I scrambled to my feet and gathered my pack. It was certainly well after midnight now, and my eyes burned. But the caffeine shivered in my veins, making me wider awake than I had any business being.

Going with Tsaft ought to be safe, anyway. Not just because I instinctively trusted her, but because I was the last that remained of her wife. She would want to protect me for my own sake, which I couldn't say of either Fesskh or Kisht.

When she found out my people had killed her wife, I wondered if she'd change her attitude.

15

Robin

I sat on an ornate circular rug, sipping water from a delicate silver bowl. Tsaft had offered some other beverage, but I had declined, remembering Aspen's warning. For all I knew, it would kill me.

"I only remember bits and pieces," I was saying. "Fesskh said it was to be expected."

"What do you remember?"

"You, mostly." I cast my eyes downward bashfully. "I can tell that what you two had was something special."

"It was everything," she said. "To both of us. We were closer than is common. Mrrka and I slept in the same bed every day."

I remembered that. Remembered how the heat from her body looked in the darkness, to eyes that could see in infrared. How was Tsaft going to get to sleep in the morning? "You don't have to talk about it," I said lamely. To me she looked cool and collected, but I had a sense that it was probably a front.

"It helps me," she said. "I spent some time tonight keening for her, and some time in silence, and now what I want is to talk. I will keen for her again later."

Yes, that was like her. Like when her daughter had been mauled by that earthshaker, she had stayed perfectly calm until the healer had told us—told them she would pull through. It was only afterward that she had broken down.

"I don't remember Kisht very well," I said. Speaking of daughters. Though by their rules, each of their two daughters would be considered primarily the offspring of the parent that had carried her. Kisht would have been Mrrka's. "I have very conflicted feelings toward her, but I don't know why."

Tsaft blew across her drink and set it down. "Kisht...she's an odd one. Her mother and I, you understand, had an unconventional relationship. I'm a second child, I had no memories to inherit. My daughter will receive only mine. Whereas Mrrka was the heir to the Eldest, it was understood that she was born to greatness. She should have made a much better match."

"She never could have."

One ear pricked forward, a pleased expression. "You would think this would have made Kisht understand that not all social rules are carved in stone. That sometimes making a break with tradition is the right thing to do. Our rebellion brought her into the world, after all. But instead, I think Kisht has always been ashamed of me. She is proud of her lineage and I am contrary to what many of her ancestors would have wanted and expected. She fears change."

"And that was a cause for conflict?"

She inclined her head, making the firelight dance in the translucent tufts of fur on the tips of her ears. "Always. Mrrka feels—felt that class hierarchy stagnates us. All the advantages belong to elders, but the young people, with no memories, are the quickest to try new things. Science, for instance. Mrrka was fascinated by it but her mother always discouraged it. Said it was disrespectful to their ancestors to look for new answers to questions they had already solved. Whereas my family had no such concern, but we were too busy trying to get enough to eat, without land.

Who does that leave to try new things?"

"But Kisht disagreed."

"Kisht was only waiting for her mother to die," said Tsaft bitterly. "No. That is unfair. They loved each other in their own way. But Kisht did look forward to getting her own chance."

"I can see now why Mrrka felt so conflicted."

Reaching for a broad, squat pitcher, Tsaft refilled my bowl. "Do you have any daughters?"

"Yes." For a second that was all I could say. Lily would be sleeping now, I hoped. But I had worried about her since the moment I had gone. Thinking about dying and leaving her without me—I couldn't. I pushed the thought away. "I have two, actually. And will have a third soon."

"A pouchling!" Tsaft leaned forward, delighted. "Can I see?"

I laughed, rubbing my belly. "I'm afraid we're not made that way. It can't be looked at for some time yet."

"That must be difficult. How can it feel real, if you can't see it?"

I shrugged. "It doesn't, really. When it's born is soon enough." As if to contradict me, the baby did a slow roll, its head shoving hard against my belly.

For a moment I started to feel relaxed. Hanging out with a mom friend. We could be any two women, talking about our families.

But she was only disarming me. After a little more casual conversation, she met my eyes earnestly over her bowl. "Anything you can tell me about my wife's last moments would mean the world to me."

I dropped my eyes to the water swimming in my bowl. Shit. How could I? But how could I not? She had the right to know.

Tsaft set her bowl in front of her, seeming to sense my reluctance. "Mrrka is—was," she corrected, her voice catching only slightly, "so curious. So eager to know. She was the first to spot your vehicle falling out of the stars. Many others wanted to stay away, but she wanted to know everything she could about you."

"Was she the one destroying our plants?"

She sighed. "Yes. The council insisted. After the fire, their chief goal was to harass you and drive you off. Because you were taking up valuable hunting ground and making it unusable. Mrrka refused to allow anyone to attack you directly, but to get that, she had to agree to destroy your buildings and growings."

"That's our food, though," I said. "We eat the plants."

One ear went back, in surprise or maybe disgust. "Like animals do?"

"Yes. But unlike them, we cultivate our own. We needed those plants. Soon we'll be out of the food we brought with us, and by that time we need to be able to eat the plants we've grown."

"So you killed her." Tsaft's chin went up. "You killed her to spare your own lives."

I opened my mouth and shut it. Took a long drink. Hesitantly raised my eyes to her face. "They placed a trap," I said. "They didn't know you were any more than animals. They made a trap that would kill any animals that came too close. They didn't know!"

"They," she said. "*You* knew?"

"I thought maybe they were wrong. I went out looking for you, thinking if I had proof of what you were, we could try to speak with you instead. And that's how I came upon her ..." Tears sprang to my eyes. It had gone so wrong. If I could have found Mrrka first, none of this would have happened. Of any one of her people, she was the furthest from our enemy.

Tsaft watched me crying, head tilted to the side. I scrubbed at the tears furiously. How could she be in more control than I was, when she was the one who had lost her wife? "I'm sorry," I said. "I should have found a way to prevent this."

"You are not to blame," said Tsaft. "And if you were, I could do nothing. You are all that remains of my wife. She wanted peace with your people. For her sake, I must forgive all of you."

Reaching out, I put my hand over hers. Her ears flicked back for a moment, but she tolerated the touch. "We have no right to expect forgiveness."

"The only other option is war," said Tsaft. "Which I will do all I can to prevent. Fesskh wants to destroy your people. Without my wife holding her back, it will be hard to stop her. You threaten our order, our way of life."

She didn't know the half of it. Sybil, seeking to destroy them all. Our need to take more and more of their land and terraform it to feed ourselves. The goats in their incubators, ready to be born within weeks, and all the other embryos we'd brought. Enough to recreate Earth—or the closest thing to it, with the species that weren't extinct. And we couldn't just not do it…not if we wanted to feed the children.

"Thank you," I said quietly. "I cannot speak for all of my people either, but I will do what I can to ensure peace between us."

And God help me, I meant it.

16

Aspen

A frown creased my forehead. In the dish in front of me was one of the first samples of the new lichen. It *should* adapt to the conditions outside, but would it? If I were back on Proxima, I'd test it in sterile soil first before seeding a small test plot.

But these were hardly lab conditions. If this batch failed, I needed to know in time to make another before the lights went out. And they had to be productive before the colony ran out of food.

I selected six of the samples, leaving ten in reserve. Time for a field test.

It was damp outside, which was ideal. No dry heat and no torrential downpour either. Just a fine, soft mist, as good as a greenhouse. The plot I'd picked was too small to be any good for a field, between the stockade and where the new school building was going up. The freshly-cut wood was lavender in color and smelled more like hay than like pine, but it seemed to be enough like Earth wood to build the same. The school was fully framed now, and the workers were fastening on siding with the loud slams of air-driven nail guns.

I sifted the damp soil between my fingers. It would do. Carefully I transferred a tiny, gray-green lichen off the plate and snugged it into the soil. It had hardly any roots as yet. Hopefully those would extend out once it got comfortable.

I watered them in with a bottle of nutrient solution. The ammonia scent stung my nose. No natural plant would ever handle that much nitrogen, but this was engineered to always be starving. The more it ate, the more high-protein food it could grow for the children.

Sitting back on my heels, I surveyed my work. Six colonies the size of a thumbprint. It was ridiculous to think they could succeed out here. It had taken a large team of botanists years to develop the original bioscrubber. This lichen was a quick and dirty alteration: heat and cold tolerance added, some of the hungriest genes ripped out. I had added all the genes that had gone into the farm crops, what I called the "Eos tolerance package," but those genes had barely been tested.

But Terra, I reminded myself, was a goddess of long shots. Hadn't she guided the very first cells as they evolved in the hellish landscape of the Archaean Epoch? Hadn't she preserved the first few intelligent apes despite any number of threats?

Dear goddess, I prayed, closing my eyes. *I know these things aren't the kind of life you like, but this once can you help them to grow? We need them if we're going to survive on this planet.*

I opened my eyes and spotted Hawk approaching. I scrambled to my feet, ready to update him on the lichen's progress. But all Hawk asked was, "Heard anything from your wife?"

I shook my head. "I'm worried. But on the other hand, it's like her not to call. She gets caught up in what she's doing. I'm telling myself, if she got herself into any kind of trouble, she'd have called."

"Could be," said Hawk. "Sybil left a note saying she didn't know when she might be back."

"Robin said tomorrow. If she isn't home by then, I'll know there was trouble."

"You don't think Sybil might convince her to stay out longer?"

"No," I said firmly. "She promised."

Cloning seedlings was tedious work. It was after midnight when I finally staggered off to bed. My whole body sagged with exhaustion and my eyes burned.

But once I hit my bunk, I couldn't sleep. My worry about Robin, put on hold all day so I could focus on my work, flared to life. What had I been thinking, agreeing to this plan? Couldn't Sybil have taken somebody else? Somebody who wasn't pregnant and a mother and my wife?

Since we had landed, nothing had been right. I had made my peace, long ago, with her need to roam, to do dangerous things. You couldn't put a woman like that in a box. But if you were lucky enough to love one, she always came back to you, with the smell of space on her flight suit. Those trips made her come alive, made her passionate and happy and fulfilled. I had never wanted to clip her wings.

But she had *wanted* to come out here, I reminded myself. For the kids, mostly, but also so she could pilot the *Resurrection*. And it had been a relief to find she hadn't sunk into a depression when the job was done. She had simply found other things to do.

But did they have to be so dangerous?

Maybe that was the appeal. She had to believe something that made it necessary for her to go out in the wild, because otherwise there was nothing for her but boring, safe drudgery like taking care of plants.

Unless the appeal was getting away from *me*. Because that was a thing she'd also been doing since we landed. We hadn't had an evening to ourselves since we were in orbit. And sure, I'd been busy, I'd been working late, but somehow every time I thought that maybe we could spend together, she ended up being busy. Maybe she was angry at me. Maybe she blamed me for ending her career.

No. I turned over onto my side, pulling the blanket over my ear. I was overthinking. Robin would have teased me for it, if she'd been here. Smoothed a finger over my wrinkled forehead and told me I looked like an old man. I could never work out why she liked a boring guy like me, but she had picked me, hadn't she?

All I wanted was Robin home safe. Tomorrow, by noon. She had promised. And Sybil had said it was what the goddess wanted. What the goddess commands, She makes possible. That was a favorite line of Sybil's. Robin was in the hands of the goddess, carrying out Her wishes, even though she wasn't a disciple. Surely that meant She would look after her, just like She'd be looking after Sybil.

Rolling onto my back, I decided to meditate. A little prayer would be a comfort right now, and probably help me get to sleep.

The children, in their bunks an arms' length away, breathed in little sighs. I slowed my own breathing, feeling my chest rise and fall. I pictured a forest scene, maybe with a little creek flowing through. The calls of long-extinct birds through the trees. That was my interior temple to meet with the goddess. She was the force flowing from the soil to the trees, to the birds, and back to the soil, binding it all together, bringing a higher order out of chaos.

Usually that idea was enough for me. I wasn't one to anthropomorphize the deity, picture Her as a friendly mother-figure or a destroying angel. But for once, I wished I'd picked some other religion, one that actually promised miraculous intervention instead of the slow pushing-upwards of sprouts. I wanted a legion of angels looking out for Robin just now.

"I'm not a baby," she would have said. "I can handle myself."

Normally I believed that. I would back her against any number of asteroids. But I thought of the pictures I had seen of the giant herbivore torn up by predators, and I wasn't sure.

17

Robin

I slept in Tsaft's house for a few hours, while she went somewhere deeper inside the den. Keening for her wife, I assumed.

She shook me awake from a sound sleep. "You want to go back, yes?"

I rubbed my eyes. "I have to," I said. Oh god, what time was it? If it was afternoon, Lily would be beside herself.

"Fesskh is saying you must be kept here," said Tsaft. "But if we are to make peace, you will have to bring that message back."

I gathered my things, still groggy and confused. Why would Fesskh want to keep me here? Did she want me, or only want to keep me from tipping off the others about their location? "Can we slip away without her finding out about it?"

"If we stay on our—on Mrrka's lands the whole way," she said. "Only her servants and share-hunters will be here."

"And Kisht?"

Tsaft paused with her hand on the door. "We must hope not."

Outside, it was cold and damp, with gray light filtering through the trees. Just before dawn. At least this time I could see, rather than following an alien's tail whisking ahead of me in the dark.

Tsaft left me at the edge of the burned area. We had seen no sign of Kisht, nor anyone else. From there it was an easy walk down the hillside toward the colony. I felt strange, disconnected. Between the lack of sleep and the experiences of the past night, I didn't feel like myself. Somewhere inside me was Mrrka—her memories, at least. Maybe that was why I felt I both had and had not walked this way before.

I couldn't stop thinking about Tsaft's offer of forgiveness. Maybe, if she and I were the leaders of our respective peoples, we might be able to hash out some kind of compromise. But instead the decisions would be made by Sybil and Fesskh—two people with no interest in common ground. Of the two, Sybil was probably worse.

I had to get back as soon as I could and tell Sybil what I had found. I hoped at least she would believe me; that she might be swayed on her plan to wipe them out. That still wasn't much; Sybil would certainly expect to be able to dictate who had what land and where the Eosians would be allowed to live. And, dammit, there wasn't that much land. Not on a planet this cold, with only the middle habitable at all.

I didn't doubt that, if it came to a fight, our side would win. The Eosians were far from primitive, but they seemed about medieval in their technology. No sign of guns, electric lights, cars. We might be few, but we understood things they couldn't imagine. We could even engineer viruses to attack them or their ecosystems…

For a second I froze. We wouldn't, would we? Aspen wouldn't. He would never. Not even for Sybil, for his goddess. Would he?

No. No, of course he wouldn't.

Starting down the hill again, I tried to let the matter go. Hopefully it wouldn't come to that. Not if I could get Sybil to listen to me.

Lost in thought as I was, it was no wonder that I didn't hear her coming. The first I knew I was flat on the ground, a heavy weight on my shoulders, sharp claws just pricking my skin.

I struggled, instinctively rolling onto my side and wrapping my arms around my belly. I didn't cry for help. I wasn't raised in a place where crying for help was a useful thing to do. Any more than it was here.

She clambered off me and hunched nearby, one paw extended in case I tried escaping.

"Kisht," I said, sitting up and checking myself over. A muscle in my side hurt, but my belly seemed fine.

"My father let you go, didn't she."

"I don't belong to Tsaft," I said. "I go where I want."

Kisht narrowed her eyes. "That's for us to decide."

She hoisted me in her forelegs, like a fireman, and started off. Honestly a relief. My legs were tired. And her four-legged gait was impressively smooth. It ate the ground across the burned land, and flicked easily between trees once we reached the forest. But we were going further from the colony again.

The den she brought me to wasn't Mrrka and Tsaft's home. It was more of a—hunting lodge, I decided. A small place, with crossed spears over the fireplace.

Kisht crouched on the hearth and dug through my bag. "What's this?"

It was my stunner. "A flashlight. My eyes are no good in the dark."

"This?"

The radio. "Medical equipment. I need it in case I'm hurt."

She stared at the items, back at me. Finally she took one of the spears from over the fireplace, turned it butt-down, and smashed both devices. Then she stared at me again, as if daring me to say anything about it.

It was like her, Mrrka's memories reminded me. Contrary. Stubborn. Sassy. For a second I was almost overwhelmed with how much I loved her, how much I wished things had been different. Or how much Mrrka had.

What would she have done in this situation? Surely she knew how to handle her own daughter. But the only thing that occurred to me was to cuff her upside the head. I needed a discipline tactic that still worked when outweighed by a factor of two.

"I'm a mother," I ventured. "I need to get back to my daughters." I thought of Colt begging to come too, of Lily and her alarm clock. It would go off in a few hours. I needed to be back by then. We'd finally overcome her separation anxiety; if she couldn't trust the alarm clock, she'd fall to pieces.

She glared at me. "They're better off without you."

Yikes. Wrong subject.

"You'll leave when I say, if you leave at all," she continued. "I need those memories out of your head. You were wrong to steal them from me."

"I never asked for this," I said. "I don't want them."

"Good," she said. "Then you'll cooperate in everything."

18

Aspen

It was five minutes to noon, and I sat between Colt and Lily in the cafeteria. Normally I'd have eaten lunch in the lab so I didn't have to stop working, but without Robin here I felt I should eat with the kids. Lily wasn't showing any sign of anxiety so far, but she had her alarm clock on the table in front of her, counting down the last few minutes. If Robin didn't appear…

I spotted Flint, walking by with a tray, and jumped up to intercept him. "Who's guarding the gate right now?" I asked.

"Nobody," said Flint. "Hawk pulled me off. Said he didn't need anybody at the gate anymore."

"With Sybil and Robin out there? Who's going to let them in?"

He shrugged. "Hawk told me not to worry about it."

I pulled at a handful of my braids. Of all the things to worry about, I hadn't thought to spare a moment on whether the colony would be watching for Sybil to get back. Why wouldn't they?

"Sit down, Dad," said Colt, pulling at my sleeve. "Hawk is gonna say something."

The room quieted down as Hawk stood up. "Some of you may have noticed that Sybil left the colony yesterday. She is taking a retreat in the wilderness, the better to meditate and commune with the goddess. I'm not at all worried about her safety, since she took Robin with her. By now I think we could all agree, Robin's the leading expert on Eos's wildlife."

Just then Lily's alarm clock went off. She snatched it up and shoved it in my face. 0:00:00. With a sinking feeling in my stomach, I made a grab for it to turn it off, but she pulled it away from me and clutched it against her chest. "Mommy," she said sternly.

Nobody but Mommy could turn it off, that much was obvious. The shrill beeping rang out in the quiet room. Hawk gave an annoyed look, but kept talking. "The goddess spoke to me last night and revealed that Sybil is safe…"

That was garbage, I realized. Then a stab of guilt. That was a disrespectful thing to think about a person like Hawk. But it still seemed suspicious. I'd heard him say he never heard anything from Terra. She wasn't the kind of goddess who constantly revealed things to people. Only Sybil ever had messages from the goddess to report, and even then it was the kind of inspiration that bubbled up inside a person, not newsflashes on current events.

I didn't catch Hawk's next words over Lily rapidly muttering, "See, look those numbers countin down. When reaches all zeroes, whole way across, tha's when I'll be back."

"I know that's what she said, sweetheart," I whispered. "She must be just a little bit late. If you can just hang on a few minutes…"

"WHEN IT REACHES ALL ZEROES THAT'S WHEN I'LL BE BACK!" Lily roared.

Colt turned worried eyes to me. "She's *missing* again?"

Hawk stopped talking and glared at me. "I don't think it's fair for one young disciple to interfere with the edification of everyone."

That was as good as an order. Scooping up Lily and grabbing Colt's hand, I beat a hasty retreat.

I brought both the kids upstairs to my lab. By now Lily was crying in earnest and chewing on her sleeve. Where was her bunny? That might help. But if I left her to go find the bunny, that would probably be worse.

Setting her down on the counter, I said, "Mommy is late coming back, okay? I'm going to have to look for her."

Colt asked, "But how can you look for her? You couldn't last time!"

It was a good question. "Well, she might be back in the colony by now," I said. "Maybe we could look around?"

"We could ask people to help."

I sighed, staring at the ground. One thing was becoming clear, through all the distractions and the beeping timer and Lily's crying. Hawk had chosen not to wait for Sybil to return. If he'd cared at all, he'd have search parties out everywhere already. He had always seemed like Sybil's most devoted disciple, her right-hand man. He had handled everything.

Then again, I'd seen his frustration with her recent seclusion. He hated having to do everything himself, while all the while everyone just wanted to see Sybil. Could this be as simple as spite?

"I don't think we can ask people to help," I said at last. "Let's see what we can do ourselves. Can you run outside real quick, just check around everywhere and see if she's there? Don't ask anybody if they've seen her. Just say you're checking on the plants for me."

His brown eyes got big. "You want me to *lie*?"

I took a breath and let it out through my nose. "Of course not. You can check on the plants *too*, okay? Just don't tell them you're also looking for Mom."

Colt dashed off, and I was left with Lily. Big tears poured down her face and she had already worked a hole in her sleeve with her teeth. I wrapped my arms around her. "I know, baby," I said quietly. "I want Mommy too. We're gonna get her back, okay? We're gonna find her somehow. Maybe Colt is finding her right now."

I didn't really believe it. Hawk wouldn't have spoken with such confidence without checking around. But what could I say? Lily's sobs kept up steadily. Automatically I started reciting mantras. She often liked those. "Terra, mother of all, Terra, soul of Earth, Terra, refuge of all creatures…"

Lily's sobs quieted a little against my chest. I closed my eyes and tried to meditate. If I could get just a minute, just a little quiet, I'd know what to do.

I breathed in. I couldn't get to my mental forest. I could only imagine what Robin would do, if she were here. She'd be out after me in a heartbeat. Herself.

I breathed out. It was insanity to think I could find them out there. Even Robin didn't know what she was doing out there, and she at least had done it before. But damn it, there were no other options. Somebody had to do it, and Hawk wasn't going to.

I'll do it, I said at last, half to the goddess, half to myself. *I'll find her.*

I opened my eyes. What was I going to do? Leave the kids here, with their teachers? I couldn't. Not with Lily like this. What if the worst happened and neither of her parents came back? But taking them out into the wilderness was dangerous too. I had no idea where to go.

Letting go of Lily, I started puttering around the lab, getting things together. On my notepad, I left a long to-do list for my assistant. The work had to go on regardless. Only the cloning would be delayed, nobody else knew how to do it, but I had at least four hundred embryos done and that would have to do for now. Planting them was a job other people could do.

What else, what else? I harvested some scrubber lichen. It looked worse than ever, and wasn't regenerating anywhere near the usual rate. No time to work on that now. I bagged up the chunk I'd cut off. Dumping some tools out of a duffel, I put the bag of lichen in.

Lily was watching me. "I'm packing up to go find Mommy," I said. "What other food can we bring?"

Without taking her sleeve out of her mouth, she pointed to a shelf of cucumber plants. I picked a few and put them in. After a while she slid down and started to help, picking a few pea pods and a bell pepper. "Perfect," I said, holding open the bag for her. As long as she was working on this, she wasn't crying. Now the only noise was the steady beep-beep-beep of the alarm clock. I decided to let it be for now.

Colt came running back in. "She isn't anyplace," he said.

"We'll just have to go outside and find her."

"Outside the fence? I get to come? Really?" He jumped up and down with excitement.

"That's the plan. Don't tell anybody, 'kay? We'll have to sneak out … somehow." I shoved my blowtorch in the bag. It was for killing weeds, not shooting predators, but it would have to do. My radio was on my belt at all times anyway.

Just then there was the clank of boots on the ladder. I shoved the duffel under the counter and pretended to inspect my notepad. Didn't look very casual, but it was the best I could think of on short notice.

"Sorry about having to ask you to leave," said Hawk.

I looked up, as if surprised. Overplaying it, probably. "I understand."

Hawk nodded toward Lily. "I can see she's taking it hard that her mother's absence was longer than expected."

"Well, Robin promised. I felt sure she'd be here by now."

"Probably would have been smarter if she hadn't set an exact time. Sybil can't always foresee how long she's going to need to meditate."

"I'm sure they'll be back soon," I said. Got to sound like I wasn't too worried. Let Hawk think he had some time before he needed to think up a new excuse.

"I was just thinking," he said. "Since your work is so important and Robin isn't here, you could probably use some extra help. I could assign somebody to Lily full time. Just to help manage her."

My lips tightened involuntarily. "Manage" her? "Oh, maybe," I said. "But I'm gonna just keep her in the lab with me today. She likes watching me work."

"But Colt, at least, shouldn't be in your hair. Go on, son. Get to school."

Colt looked up at me for confirmation. His brown eyes held volumes of hope and fear. Would the promised treat of a trip outside be withdrawn? Should I say something? I gave him a tiny headshake. "Go along to school," I said. "We'll talk later."

Hawk stood with his hands in his pockets, watching Colt go. When he was fully out of earshot, Hawk said, "You're not thinking of going looking for her, are you?"

"Why should I? You've said the goddess told you they're safe."

"Of course." Hawk stood for a moment, frowning at the floor. Then he crossed over to me and pulled out the duffel. I tensed, watching him unzip it and dig through. "These aren't your usual tools. You're not being honest with me." From his crouch beside the bag, he stared up coldly.

The game was up. "If I were, if I asked permission to go, would you let me?"

"Of course not." Hawk straightened up. "I need you here in the lab. There is far too much to do to spare you."

"Then send someone else. Send a search party. Put Flint in charge of it, maybe. You could spare him to guard the door before."

"Things are getting too busy now. You know that. Replanting everything, and while the building is going on, too. We need houses. Keeping everyone in the ship is burning power that you need here in the lab. You've said that yourself."

"But Sybil and Robin—"

"Are safe. You have Terra's word on it."

I swallowed. "I don't, exactly. I have *your* word that She said so."

"What reason could you have to doubt me?" Hawk's eyes were wide. I was hardly less surprised. Me, questioning Hawk, whose voice had been almost equal to Sybil's all these years. Robin wouldn't have believed it.

I turned back to the counter, scooping up Lily and her softly beeping clock. Her chewed sleeve was damp on the back of my neck. "I think this is all a little too tidy," I said. "You don't want Sybil to be found. You want to handle everything without her."

"I want *someone* with sense in charge!" Hawk fired back. "What has she done for the colony since we landed? Nothing! She's hidden in her room and left all the work to me. But she still feels free to waltz out when she pleases, impress everyone with her spiritual act, and fly off into the sunset! What does that do to the people she's taught to rely on her? She doesn't even know, and I'm dealing with the fallout every time. People who only want her, even though she's done nothing for them like I have. It must be like you felt, when Robin was always off in space, but you'd better believe the second she walked through the door, the children went running to her."

For the first time since Hawk had come in, my temper flared. "You don't know anything," I said coldly. "*My* relationship isn't founded on envy. Which is why *I* want my wife back."

"Wife back," echoed Lily firmly. How much of this conversation was she understanding?

Hawk folded his arms. "Fine," he said. "I thought you were going to be reasonable. Let your wayward wife come home whenever she's a mind to, since that's what she'll do anyway. But if you're going to be so difficult, fine. I'll send Flint and Cliff. It's all I can spare. Will that make you happy?"

I eyed him suspiciously. It would be easy enough for him to ensure Sybil and Robin never came back. Cliff, though, was friends with Robin. He surely wouldn't agree to anything sketchy.

"All right," I said slowly. "I suppose I couldn't expect you to spare any more than that."

Hawk nodded and turned to go. Then he paused and looked over his shoulder. "Can't you silence that damn alarm?"

"Sure," I said. "When Robin comes home."

19

Robin

I sat in front of the fireplace, trying to stretch the aches out of my hips and shoulders from sleeping on the floor. Kisht had left me alone for some time, probably while she got her own sleep somewhere else.

I had no sense now of what time it was. I had inspected the room, tinkered with the lock, inspected the chimney (firmly grated; no good), and looked for tools. I thought maybe, if I could find anything to stand on, I could get the spears off the wall. They were seven feet long, with wicked, curved blades, but I could probably rest one end on the ground and menace an Eosian with the other.

If I could get them down from there, which I couldn't.

Then I had slept a few hours, because I was tired enough I could have slept through a brass band. I'd dreamed of horrible things happening to the children. Whenever I'm anxious about them, that's what I dream. They're lost, or they're on a cliff edge and being careless, or they fall in a well and drown. The only constant is that I'm frozen and unable to help.

So. I wasn't very rested. Whatever time it was, surely it was after noon by now. Lily would be crying. Aspen would probably be angry at me. He couldn't know I was being held here. He'd trained me very early in our relationship to always call when I was late. Every time I didn't, he would carefully explain all the terrible things that could have happened to me, and how did he know it wasn't one of those?

He didn't. He couldn't. But he also stood no chance of finding me, in an underground den somewhere in the woods. I hadn't even told him what direction I'd meant to go.

At last, I heard soft footsteps on the stairs. More than one Eosian, I thought. I stood up, bouncing on the balls of my feet. It was the closest I could get to an assertive, threatening pose before creatures who could rear up on their hind legs to the size of a grizzly.

"Here it is," Kisht was saying. "I don't care what happens to it, so you're welcome to try anything."

The other Eosian was older than her, I thought, with fur half-opaque with age and a gray shawl around her shoulders. "I'm not the kind of scholar that cuts animals to bits to see what's inside," she said, somewhat snippily. "If it can be done at all, which I doubt, it can be done without hurting it."

"You have to find a way," Kisht insisted. "The reward will be very great."

"It had better be," the scholar muttered. "If it doesn't work, and Fesskh is angry with me for trying—"

"Fesskh isn't going to know."

At last the scholar approached me, ducking her head politely. "Can you understand me?"

"Yes," I said. "You aren't going to hurt me?"

"No. Can I see your hands?"

I showed them to her, and she inspected them minutely. "You see, she doesn't have—"

"I know," interrupted Kisht roughly. "But what about the rest of her?"

The following inspection was unpleasant. The scholar had a whole theory about my pubic hair that I was forced to sharply debunk. "If it were possible for my people to pass memories to each other, don't you think I would know that?" I demanded as she moved on to the hair on my head.

"I wouldn't have thought you were capable of receiving memories either," the scholar said. "It's a stroke of luck for Mrrka they were compatible. If I were doing the experiment, I'd have wanted to do it in a more controlled way."

"It's not her fault she was *dying*," said Kisht acidly.

"Let me try something," said the scholar. She held her hands close to my face, where I could see the long, snakelike tendrils sprouting from between her toes. That was what allowed them to be so dextrous and run on the same foot—toes for grip, tendrils for detail work.

But watching them brought back another, closer memory. This was what Mrrka had done. She had shoved the tendrils into my face, into my eyes and ears and mouth, and—

"No," I said, backing away. "I don't want you to do that."

"I won't hurt you," she said. "I won't try to give you a memory. I want you to focus on one of Mrrka's memories, and try to pass it to me. Maybe it will work this way."

I looked at her, and then at Kisht, who was standing over me looking menacing. Clearly she wasn't going to take no for an answer. And in any event, I wanted to be rid of the whole mess. Having an alien's ghost in my head was complicating my life unduly. Perhaps if I gave them back, the Eosians would feel more friendly toward the colony.

"All right," I said, drawing a shaky breath.

The tendrils went all over my face, but this time there were no strange sounds, no flashing lights. I tried hard to think of one of Mrrka's memories. The only thing that came to me was Tsaft…Mrrka mating with her. Now that would be a nice thing to give Kisht. Just as a special little present just for her. *Hi Kisht, here's my memory of when I fucked your mom!* Well, dad. Well, not-really-gendered begetting parent.

But a moment later, the scholar withdrew the tendrils. "Nothing. I can't sense anything from her."

Kisht's tail lashed from side to side. Inches from a tantrum, or would have been when she was younger. "Maybe if we cut—"

Mercifully, I never heard what part of me she wanted to cut. Footsteps came down from above, and Fesskh's voice thundered, "Kisht! For shame!"

Kisht instinctively cowered, before drawing herself up and attempting a little sass. "I'm only trying to take back what's mine."

"If you were going to attempt such a thing, you should have asked me."

"As if you would ever have allowed it. Not when you stand to inherit if the experiment fails."

"I didn't kill it, did I?"

"I have an idea," I broke in. "Let me leave. That way Kisht won't have me, and Fesskh won't have me either. A compromise?"

Fesskh scowled at me. "There is no need for compromise when we both know who's the elder here. Come with me. You will stay with us until council has made a ruling."

I looked helplessly around the room. Kisht and the scholar were both slightly crouched, acknowledging Fesskh as their better. There would be no fight, during which I could sneak off somehow. I shouldered my pack—what was left in it—and followed Fesskh outside.

20

Aspen

I stowed my packed bag under my bunk and went on with my day. If I'd really believed Hawk's plan of sending Cliff and Flint would work, I probably would have unpacked it, but ... I couldn't shake the nagging feeling in my gut that he didn't really want Robin back. He'd resented her since she'd first starting talking about the aliens, and he'd as good as said he wanted to be rid of Sybil.

But if he'd been suspicious of me before, now he was watching me like a—well. Everywhere I went that day, there he was. Staring at me as I sowed alfalfa from the construction site across the way. Popping up in the barn to "check it would be ready in time for the goats." While I worked in the lab, interns kept casually sauntering in, looking around, and sauntering back out again.

He could surely have been more subtle if he'd wanted to. This was intended to intimidate, and I certainly felt it.

Lily stayed glued to me all day. Not a chance she'd ever consent to going to school. She was afraid another parent would vanish and not come back. She did let me wrap her alarm clock in a sweater and put it in her backpack, where its beeping was mostly muffled. At bedtime, she cuddled up to the entire backpack and fell asleep in five minutes. Those feelings must have been exhausting.

Once she was out, and Colt was reading with a tiny light, I tiptoed out. I needed to make some kind of backup plan. How long would I wait for Cliff and Flint to come back? How would I sneak past the watchers Hawk always kept by the gates? Should I bring the kids or not? It wasn't safe out there, but I didn't want to leave them with Hawk acting like this.

So I went upstairs to the bridge. That was Robin's special place. It would be a good place to think and make a plan. And Hawk wouldn't think to look for me there, so maybe I could get an hour without the man staring at me.

When I walked in the door, the person in the pilot's chair startled guiltily. "Cliff," I said. "I thought you were—"

"Shit," said Cliff. "I mean—I can explain—"

I folded my arms. "I'm not really sure you need to."

Cliff paused. "Maybe *you* should explain to *me* then. I was told to stay out of your way today. Nobody said why."

"I was told you were out looking for Robin and Sybil."

"But Hawk said they were safe?"

It was a tricky question. I didn't want to say Hawk had lied. Who knew how Cliff would take that. Robin was always getting on me about the "greenie groupthink," how nobody could criticize people seen as important within the church like Sybil or Hawk or Pine. I mostly shrugged it off. I mean, it's natural to respect people you see as authority figures. It doesn't make it a cult. But for once I could see it had become a problem.

"I feel like the goddess is calling me to go to Robin," I said at last. Which was the honest truth; whatever in me was closest to Her was certainly the part that knew I needed to go look for her. "I think Hawk was trying to reassure me by telling me you were out looking for her. But obviously finding you here doesn't make me feel any better."

"Sorry," said Cliff. "I screwed up. I thought you'd never find me here. Nobody comes here but Robin."

"It's okay," I said. "I won't tell Hawk. I know he meant well." That was my hook. I had dirt on him now. I was keeping secrets from Hawk for him. That meant he owed me.

I know, I sound like a manipulative bastard. I'm a person who thinks before I talk and have a good sense of the effects I have on people. Usually I use that power for good, like talking Lily through things she doesn't want to do or understanding why Robin's so mad when the only words coming out of her are turning the air blue rather than explaining anything.

Today, I was going to use it to find my wife. Which was also for good. So. "Are you guarding the gate at all today?"

"Night shift," he said unhappily. "Hawk isn't convinced the wire is enough to keep the predators out. But if one of those creatures gets over the fence, what am I supposed to do about it? Not sure a stunner is going to cut it. I saw the thing in the freezer. It's not small."

"Probably just a precaution," I said. "If you see one, run like hell and shout. It's what I would do." My fingers were twitching with nervousness. If I saw one, and it was threatening Robin, would I have the courage to fight it?

Time for the squeeze. "It's just for predators, then?" I pressed. "You're not trying to keep people from going in and out?"

He shook his head uncertainly. "Well, if I did see someone, I'd have to tell Hawk."

"Sure, sure," I agreed.

"But …" I had him now. "I guess I would have to stay by the gate and keep watching for predators. I'd have to tell him after the shift was over."

I nodded. "Yeah, good idea. After all, protecting the colony is much more important than … whatever the reason is Hawk doesn't want people going out where Sybil has gone."

"I mean," said Cliff. "I guess I know the reason. It's because it's dangerous out there. And not everyone's going to have divine protection the way Sybil does."

"Of course. Only someone who's really called to be out there should be going out."

He nodded. "And if they did, it's kind of on their own head, isn't it?"

I got the kids out of bed at three-thirty in the morning. Colt was too sleepy to even ask excited questions about where we were going. Lily didn't want to walk, so I let her ride on my back and bury her face in my neck. I'd wrapped her alarm clock in a second sweater before burying it deep in her backpack, so nothing could be heard from outside. It seemed a safer course than to turn it off and face a meltdown when she noticed.

It would make a lot more sense not to bring them. It wasn't safe out there. But I couldn't take away their other parent, when they were already missing one. And I didn't trust Hawk with them. He couldn't easily keep me from leaving, but it would be trivial to keep me from coming back.

The hallways were dark except for the blue lighting around the baseboards that signaled sufficient oxygen. No one was around. Outside, it was cold and a little damp, as the dew fell. The clouds had cleared away, and the stars shivered slightly in the interposing atmosphere.

Cliff paced along the wall, not looking my way. But he must have seen me, because he turned and sauntered away from the gate. I wondered what had tipped him over to my side. Knowing that Hawk had given a different story to him and to me? Or that Robin was his friend?

In any event, he had apparently decided to take no notice of me at all. Maybe he'd still tell Hawk after the fact, but it didn't matter. People would notice I was gone by morning anyway.

I opened the gate and slipped through, holding Colt's hand tightly. "Don't walk yet," I said, taking out my flashlight and watching for the wire. In this darkness, it was all but invisible. Lily got restless, letting go of my neck with one hand to rub her ear. She could probably hear it buzzing.

My heart pounded as I edged forward. My brain kept helpfully supplying ideas of what might happen if we didn't see the wire in time. At last, I saw it, glinting damply in the beam of my flashlight. "Time to crawl like a snake, Colt," I said. "Can you do that? Do you see the wire?"

His eyes widened. It wasn't often he took me this seriously, with no questions. Kids can sense sometimes when you mean business. If only I knew how to sound that way on cue, instead of only when our lives literally depended on it.

I moved Lily to my front before crawling under myself, so she hung under me like a baby sloth. I just couldn't be sure she wouldn't stick her head up right under the wire.

On the other side, I straightened up and stood for a moment, looking back at the colony. Who knew when I would be able to come back. If I found Sybil, it would be hard for Hawk to keep her out. But I didn't even know where to begin.

I aimed uphill, because I knew Robin had gone downhill the first time. She wouldn't have retreaded the same direction. Colt came more awake as we went along, bouncing and springing along burned tree trunks like an overexcited goat. Even Lily eventually decided she wanted down, though she clung tight to my hand.

The sky slowly grayed, and then all at once the sun sprang into the sky. Pink ivy was growing over the burned trunks already, and little purple bramble bushes, just like the ones that kept popping up all over the farm. The forest springing back, the way living ecosystems do. In ten years, you wouldn't know there had ever been a fire.

I stopped at a creek bordering the burn zone for a rest. The fire must not have been able to cross here.

"Why did we have to sneak out like that, Dad?" asked Colt, as he started in on the snack I'd brought. "Why didn't Hawk want us to go?"

"He thought it was too dangerous."

"Is it too dangerous? Are we going to see wild animals?"

"Maybe. I'll keep an eye out, and you stay close to me."

"Do you know where Mom is?"

"No."

He got bored of my short answers and started playing at the edge of the creek. First he dropped rocks in, one at a time. Then he tried to catch minnows. The next thing I knew, he'd taken off his shoes and waded in. Lily was pulling at hers to join him.

I sighed. This was hardly good exploration procedure. There were probably leeches or something else unwholesome in the water. But looking at the excitement on Lily's face, I couldn't make myself say anything. Instead I sat, for a good half hour, and watched them splash.

This is what I'd left Proxima for. Not to see new plants, and not just for the church. But because my children deserved wide open spaces and fun that wasn't rationed. Their idea of wading was a chlorinated splash pad with five hundred other children, which cost ten dollars to get in. But nobody had had to tell them what you do with a creek. They knew.

Eventually I made them get out and put their shoes on, with some regrets. I'd have preferred to stay here, listening to the different chirps and buzzes from the forest and cataloguing all the different trees I could see. But clearly this wasn't where Robin was.

I followed the creek uphill, on the burned side to avoid the dense underbrush on the other. The kids followed after, flagging a little. I couldn't expect their short little legs to make good time. But I was careful not to pull ahead, instead spending my energy searching the trees across the river and the scorched hillside for predators. My hand stayed in the pocket where my stunner was. If something came at the kids, I had to be ready.

The bluffs to our left drew closer and closer to the river, till eventually we were forced to cross over. I took off my boots along with the kids and splashed through the icy water, cold enough to make my whole body feel a chill, as if my bones had been turned to ice.

The other side was still lush with violet and magenta undergrowth and vast, feathery trees. I sat down to put on my boots, trying not to get too curious about the different kinds of trees. If I got too interested, I'd want samples and I didn't have that kind of time. Lily stared up at the canopy with her mouth open. "Plants?" she said quizzically.

I grinned. She had finally figured them out. "Plants," I agreed. I plucked a leaf I recognized—the pink star ivy that covered the ground everywhere—and handed it to her. She stood still, twirling it in her fingers. "Pink plant," she said softly.

"It's scary in here," said Colt with relish. "Are there going to be predators?"

"Let's hope not," I said, and we went back to walking along the edge of the creek. Colt ran ahead and then back to me, keeping up a running commentary about being an explorer in a strange new world. I guess even he couldn't think of anything more exciting to pretend than the reality. Lily sang quietly to herself, holding her leaf in one hand and my hand in the other.

I was tempted to ask them to be quiet, but then I wasn't sure whether noise would draw predators or scare them away. I'd always read you were supposed to make a lot of noise when traipsing through bear country, so they knew to avoid you.

Suddenly the forest canopy opened up into a clearing. Here, the creek formed a broad pool. At the far end, a little waterfall came splashing down, making a constant shushing sound.

And beside the waterfall, on the bank, was a person.

It was Sybil, and she was flopped unnervingly on the ground, her dark hair tumbling around her. I hurried over, hoping to get to her before the children did in case—well. It would be easier to explain a corpse if they weren't the ones who had to turn it over.

But she raised her head as we approached, blinking blearily. "Oh— are you messengers to guide my spirit? Or am I awake?"

"You're awake," I said, kneeling down beside her. "Are you all right?"

Her pupils were dilated, but she managed to focus them on me. "I think so," she said at last. "Though I don't have any food. I lost my pack."

I quickly dug in mine and gave her a cucumber and a chunk of scrubber lichen. "Did you touch any of the plants? You seem…" I didn't want to say drugged, but she seemed drugged.

"I ate one," she said, with a little cringe of embarrassment. "Those berries over there."

They were turquoise and didn't look delicious to me, but I guess she'd been pretty hungry. "How long ago?"

"Last night. I'm fine, all right? They weren't good for food, but they made me high and sometimes? Sometimes it's good to be high." She gave me a knowing smile.

I sighed. She could be worse than Robin, when it came to doing impulsive things. "Start from the beginning."

"I got separated from Robin," she said. "I wanted to see the aliens. I wanted to be rid of them, if that's what it was going to take. I wanted to make this planet a home for Terra."

"I know," I said. Robin had had moral qualms on that count, but I knew Sybil didn't.

"But look at this place," she said, earnest. "Really look!"

I sat back on my heels and looked. The sun was shining brightly through the drops of spray from the waterfall. Different birds, or bugs, or something, were making little chitters and cries. Violet leaves drifted down from overhead and touched down lightly on the surface of the water, slowly drifting across the pool.

The kids were already taking their shoes and socks off again, squishing in the mud at the edge of the water. "I'm looking," I said. I didn't feel very patient with this meditation. I wanted to bring her back to the colony, and hopefully Robin also. "What am I looking for?"

"What is Terra, anyway?" she asked. "The harmony of life. The balance between predator and prey, growth and death. The circle between the soil, the tree, the animals, the soil again. Water rising into the sky and falling down, and rushing to the sea. Carbon and nitrogen cycling through earth and air, through living flesh. All of this is Terra."

Nothing she said was new to me. "I understand all that."

"What if we didn't have to *build* a new home for Terra? What if we only had to *find* one? What if this is her, here, right now, in a place we never knew? What if she's much larger than a single planet, what if she's everywhere life has ever been?"

Gooseflesh rose on my arms and the back of my neck. I'd had a few great moments of enlightenment in my life, and this felt like one of them. But chief among my emotions was relief. I didn't have to build a wall between myself and all this beauty. I was allowed to love it. I was allowed to recognize it was the same, for all its foreignness, as all the natural things I'd loved all my life.

I looked over at her, eyes shining. "Do you really think so?"

She nodded. "I've been praying since I found this place. It feels like a temple of Terra, so much more than the old place we had back on Proxima. I've had visions…I need to get back to the colony. I need to tell everyone the plans have changed."

That brought me back to earth. So to speak. What would it even mean to preserve this place rather than terraforming it? We still had to eat. "First we need to find Robin," I said firmly. "Where is she?"

Sybil shook her head. "She left me back by the colony. I was trying to follow her, but…" She made a vague gesture to her surroundings.

I bit my lip. I didn't want to go back without Robin, but it also felt vital to deliver Sybil back to the colony. "Hawk has been…weird, lately. He didn't want me to come out looking for you. I had to sneak out. If we go back now, will you let me go out whenever I want? I need to keep looking for Robin."

She scrambled to her feet, brushing purple leaves off herself. "Of course. You have to find her."

"Even though you don't like her?"

"Of course I like her." Sybil looked puzzled. "I wish she liked me."

21

Robin

I sat on the floor of the room they put me in, wrapped in a large purple shawl and nothing else. Hashta, the servant of Fesskh's who had been tasked with guiding me, had taken me to a warm, bubbly bath underground. Somehow my clothes had gone missing while I was washing. When I asked for them, she had given me the shawl with a number of awkward apologies about it not being what I was used to. I finally worked out that she had sent my clothes away to be washed. Fair enough; I hadn't had a shower in two days and I didn't have a change of clothes. I must have been pretty ripe, and Hashta's manners hadn't permitted her to tell me so.

I dug through my pack anxiously. Sybil had packed enough food for maybe three days. Though, with the amount I was eating lately, maybe only two. What was I going to eat when that was gone? Would they let me go? Would I be able to make them understand?

They seemed to eat mostly animals. Which made sense, they certainly had the teeth of predators. Perhaps I could safely test some of their meat, if I had to. I knew the plants were full of indigestible sugars and starches, and some of them might have toxins, but meat was meat, right? I wished I'd listened to Aspen more.

Really, I wished I was anyone but myself. Every other person in the colony had spent the two-year voyage studying ecology and survival skills and anything else they might need. Most of them were already college-educated when we had left. Whereas I was only good at one thing, and it was the most useless skill on the planet.

I shook myself. Enough self-pity. I had goals to achieve while I was here, and I needed to be working on them. First, to figure out what Fesskh and her council had planned, and convince them not to attack the colony. Second, to work out what their technology level was and what weapons they might attack us with. At first they had seemed primitive, but after having had a warm bath indoors, I was beginning to wonder if I simply underestimated them because they didn't have cars or roads or big visible buildings. Why would they have cars if they could run, or aboveground buildings if they didn't like cutting down the forest? It didn't mean they didn't have guns. I had to find that out.

And most importantly, I should take any opportunity to escape. Sybil didn't care whether the Eosians were sentient, but the rest of the colony might. I needed to spread the word and get a real referendum on what we should do. I wasn't sure how the colony would be at opposing Sybil, but I had to try.

But the real reason I longed to get back was more simple. Lily needed me. I had promised. I was already late. I wondered if she had slept at all last night.

Wrapping the shawl under my armpits, I tucked it to make a simple dress. I looked like I was wearing a towel, but it didn't really matter. This was just so I didn't feel naked. The Eosians didn't care.

Hashta was waiting for me outside my room. She rose up onto her haunches as I came out, but didn't speak. I had figured out after some awkwardness that it was impolite for her to speak first since she was, in her estimation at least, the lower-ranking of the two of us. "Can we go out?" I asked. "I want to see everything."

172

She blinked. "Everything?"

I sighed. Even though I was able to speak their language, I kept inserting idioms she didn't understand. "I want to see…" My brain refused to spit out a word for town, city, village, anything like that. Maybe they had no such word. "I want to see where people live and work."

"Perhaps the honorable stranger would like to go to the edge of the common," she said. "Those with no patron live there."

We set off. With the sun still some hours from setting, I could tell our direction a little better than last night. But our way was anything but straight. Hashta kept turning abruptly to one side or another, even when a clear path was visible just ahead.

"Why is it taking so long?" I asked after a while. "We've hardly come any distance."

She regarded me blankly. "Because you walk so slowly."

I picked up the pace a little and she easily matched it. Of course her longer legs, four of which she was walking on at the moment, could easily outpace me. "I meant, why don't we go directly to where it is instead of making so many turns?"

"Your servant doesn't have permission to cross all these estates," she said, with a gesture to either side. "Certainly the honorable one wouldn't, being a stranger."

"What would happen if we did anyway?"

She recoiled with horror. "We just wouldn't!"

"Of course not," I reassured her. "I just wondered what happens if people do."

"Feud," she said. "Or war. A person's estate is—well, it's her *land*!"

A feeling so strong she had no metaphor for it. This didn't bode well for me, for the colony. If they went to war for land, would they go to war for the plateau we were on? Whose land was that?

"Do you have land of your own?" I asked. "Or does your family?"

She arched her neck. "The Second Eldest is our patron. We have rights to hunt on her land, to build our dens there."

So no. Haves and have-nots, even when the thing to be had was so valuable they'd kill to protect it. What happened if everyone decided you couldn't cross their property? Did you have to stand perfectly still lest you trespass on something?

My question was answered when we arrived at the common. All I could see was a stretch of field, sparsely planted with trees, and a few earthen structures. "This is where the landless and patronless live," said Hashta. "Everything in this direction is their hunting grounds, but they have to live here, so they don't frighten the game by their numbers."

Even when we got closer and I started to see the holes of their dens, burrowed into the sides of small mounds, I didn't think the numbers were that impressive. No two holes were closer than a stone's throw apart. It was like a suburb in a movie of old Earth. Nowhere on Proxima is that spaced out. If you get three feet and a soundproof wall between where you sleep and where your neighbor watches television all night, you're lucky.

The sun was getting low and a few of the Eosians were getting up and moving around. "Your servant's apologies for addressing the honorable stranger," said Hashta, "but your servant sees her friend Tisket over there. Do you care to be introduced?"

"Oh, certainly," I said, following her to a small building, where smoke was curling out of the chimney. A youngster about Hashta's age was starting a fire inside what appeared to be some kind of forge.

Tisket straightened and turned to face us, and I saw her startling blue eyes. "Ah," she said to Hashta, "the creature. My mother told me about her." To me she bowed silently, dropping to all six legs and lowering her head. "Forgive me, I don't know how to address ..." She trailed off. It took me a moment to piece together her problem from what I could remember. Her language had half a dozen words for "you," each with a fine gradation of superiority or inferiority attached. There was no word for equals that my mind could dredge up. I wasn't sure they had any such concept. Any two of them always seemed to know who was "elder."

"You can call me whatever you want," I said without stopping to think about the pronouns I was using.

That cleared up the difficulty. When I spoke without thinking, I always ended up using the forms Mrrka would have used. I was pretty sure I had used the most condescending one, a pronoun a far superior would use to a far inferior. "Thank you," she said, piling honorifics onto both words. I cringed.

Her face was familiar, and I ventured a guess. "Your mother is . . . Tsaft?"

"Yes, honored stranger," she said, straightening up.

"Why don't you live with her?"

"I do live with her," she answered, taking up an accordion-like gadget and giving the fire some air. "I work here. I'm apprenticed to Rashesk."

"How is your master?" asked Hashta. "I can bring her something from home, if she doesn't have enough."

"I brought her a brush-creeper," answered Tisket. "Once the fire is going, I'll roast it for her. You can join us."

"I couldn't," said Hashta. "I have food at home."

"It would make it easier," urged Tisket. "If it's a gathering, rather than something she thinks is only for her."

I was hit by a surreal sense of deja-vu. Here we were on a pink plain dotted with purple trees, watching six-legged translucent tigers converse in a language my mouth could barely pronounce. Yet it was the same conversation I'd heard a thousand times, in soft voices, down in the tunnels.

"The Nkumbes don't have enough to eat right now."

"We could bring them something."

"Nobody's supposed to know about it, they'd be humiliated if they knew we knew. Let's have a dinner and just happen to invite them."

Sometimes my family gave those little dinners . . . mycosteak, algae tots, lemonade made with a quarter scoop of mix. Stretch it to make it go around. And sometimes we were invited to them. My cheeks would burn with secret shame, knowing we were starving, knowing the neighbors knew we were starving, but as long as you didn't say it out loud, it wasn't really real.

My eyes prickled and I swallowed hard. Hashta was looking to me for confirmation that we would accept the invitation. "Of course," I said, clearing my throat. "That's very kind."

Tisket started dressing the animal, a nasty process I tried not to watch. Vat meat was one thing; real animal flesh was entirely different.

"Why do these people live on the common?" I asked Hashta.

"Because they have no land of their own," she said. "Second children, or one of their ancestors was a second child. The estates can't be divided too much."

I took a deep breath. "I meant, why are there estates at all? Why isn't it all common?" What I wanted to say was, What the hell, I didn't fly three lightyears from Proxima just to find more haves and more have-nots! I had thought the tunnels I grew up in were the result of bad choices, that things could be different. But if the same inequality diseased the Eosians, it made me wonder if there was something innate about it. Was any sentient species bound sooner or later to stratify? Generations down the line, would the colony sport a row of fine houses and streets of slums?

But my command of their language wasn't good enough, and I didn't want to start a fight.

Hashta settled onto her haunches. "If it all was common, the landless would overhunt the prey animals. It's what they always do. The estates serve as a breeding ground for them, because otherwise whenever the landless got hungry, they'd kill the young or the mothers, instead of the older beasts like they should."

"Don't be unfair," Tisket put in. "They can't help doing it, because they're pressed by hunger the way the Elders aren't."

I leaned on the wall. The conversation had gone well beyond me. I wondered if Mrrka had had a solution for any of this. It wasn't coming to mind.

"Anyway," said Tisket, looking back at me, "it isn't so bad as that, usually. Rashesk sells her work to the Elders. She doesn't live only off hunting. More and more people are turning to crafts these days, and I think that's wise."

"But she still doesn't have enough to eat?" I asked.

"Well…" Tisket hesitated, looking at Hashta. "You see, a great part of the common was burned. It's causing trouble here."

Like her mother, she was too polite to lay blame, but I felt it nonetheless. That was one thing I couldn't blame on Sybil. No one else had set the fire. If I had repaired the cooling array better…if I had predicted the atmosphere would put too much strain on it…

Though, fire or no fire, we were taking land out of their hunting grounds, weren't we? And our intention, from the moment we had landed, was to take more and more. My hand drifted to my belly. Eos was supposed to be the place we could have as many children as we wanted. A place of space, of abundance. But the only way to have abundance for ourselves was to take away their sufficiency.

Eventually Tisket's master showed up, a large old creature with muscles rippling in her arms. After a suspicious look at Tisket, she accepted the offer of a meal together with good grace. If she recognized the ruse, she was willing to let us believe she hadn't.

The two adolescents were silent at the meal, letting Rashesk talk. She wanted to know about metalworking among my people. She probably thought she was being polite, but I gnawed my lip and struggled to think what to say that wouldn't give away just how advanced we were. With some difficulty, I managed to turn her to talking about her own work, the innovations she had invented.

What I found out was horrifying. Rashesk didn't make plows, didn't make pruning shears, didn't make wagon axles. She made almost exclusively weapons: weapons of war and hunting weapons. Warming to her subject, she showed me barbed spearheads for taking down the big earthshakers; arrows with slender points for birds, fired at high speeds by a specialized shooting gadget; long, delicate knives for an Elder to make the ceremonial kill at the end of a root-digger hunt.

I admired them all, trying not to show my nervousness. We had far superior technology, certainly, but none of it was in this direction. The fabricator should be able to print weapons of various kinds, but it would take time to do, and we weren't prepared at all. I wondered if the battery power was even up to printing at this point.

Trying not to think too hard about the animal it had been, I tasted a single bite of the meat. My plan was to try a tiny bit now, more tomorrow if I had no ill effects. It was delicious, rich and smokey, even with no seasoning.

Too soon, Hashta stood up and announced she had to take me back. I followed her reluctantly. I wasn't eager to see Fesskh again. I doubted I could dodge her questions forever.

22

Aspen

As I expected, the gates were hardly thrown wide for our return. I had to jimmy the lock with a stick poked between the planks of the gate. But once we were inside, everyone came running to see Sybil. Even Hawk, with a vein jumping in his forehead. He hadn't wanted to see her again, but of course he couldn't show it.

Sybil wanted to gather everyone together right away, to tell them her new revelation. I urged her to wait a little bit, maybe recement her authority in the church. After her recent breakdown, and the time she'd spent away from everyone, I worried not everyone still felt as loyal to her as I did.

But she was insistent, so once the kids were settled in the schoolroom, I agreed to help gather everyone in the freshly-built chapel. Autumn and her husband caught a seat next to me, and I scooted down the pew to make room. "Do you know what all this is about?" Autumn whispered.

"She wants to tell us what she learned outside."

"I wouldn't expect the goddess to have spoken to her there, so far from Earth-origin life."

I shrugged. "The goddess can do what she wants."

Hawk came to the front and led everyone in a meditation, directed out of his book of scripture. Technically, Sybil's book—Sybil's words. But I thought of it as his. It certainly hadn't been her idea.

The door swung open, making a long beam of sunlight on the floor. Hawk's voice paused for a moment, but he finished out the prayer as Sybil came toward the front.

"Thank you," she said in her warm, alto voice, squeezing Hawk's arm. "You've done so much for the church, for all of us, by shepherding the community while I was praying in the wilderness. I know Terra will bless you for it."

Hawk blinked at her, frowning a little. But he cleared his throat and said, "Thank you."

Sybil began to speak, her voice rich and hypnotic as she talked about the beauty of the planet, about its natural ecosystem. My spirits lifted as she went on. It felt so right, thinking of the natural life as belonging to Terra too. Why else was it so fierce, so determined to survive? That's a Terra virtue.

We wanted a living planet in all its messiness, not just a bigger zoo. And wouldn't our attempt at terraforming have been the latter? We had carried with us everything we could get our hands on, but that was a tiny fraction of the genetic diversity Earth had had. Even if we'd had it all, it would still end up being a model, a copy, artificially created. Not real and wild, not naturally evolved.

We'd planned all along for a hard struggle maintaining the balance of our new world. Generations of our children would be tending it, saving creatures from extinction and culling plants that became unexpectedly invasive. But that wasn't nature. We had all accepted that, accepted it was the best we could get. But what if it wasn't?

Autumn's head bent near mine, and she hissed, "What the hell is all our work for if she's going to devalue it like this?"

I took a breath to whisper back, but I couldn't think of anything to say. I needed some time with these ideas; to turn them over in my head and pray about them. There always had to be a role for Autumn and me, even if we didn't try to wipe out the native ecosystem, because we had to eat. But I couldn't say that to her. Planning the fauna of this planet had been her life's work. She wasn't going to be content with a stockade of goats, or whatever we settled on.

"I want to talk about this with all of you, my dear friends," Sybil was saying. "I know this revelation is strange, and not where we thought the goddess was leading us. We need to take some time in prayer to ask her what she wants of us now, how we are to preserve our past without disrupting this living ecosystem."

There was a short bark of laughter. "What is it, Pine?" asked Sybil.

"Sorry, it seemed like you must be joking," Pine said, in a voice I recognized. Privately I called it the bless-your-heart voice, known to church ladies of every religion. "If we're keeping the purple trees we can't very well preserve our past, now can we? It's one or the other, and the goddess called us to bring Earth back to life, not adopt other ecosystems."

"I confess, I don't understand the theology behind this," Hawk put in, caressing the cloth cover of his scripture book. "We know that Terra is the spirit of Earth, that she grew weak when Earth's ecosystem began to die, that she came with us as a bodiless spirit to Proxima, and to Eos. We know that she needs a body, and that body is a living, Earth-origin biosphere. This one," his wave took in the lavender planks of the chapel, as well as the forest outside, "isn't going to work. She can't live here any more than she could in Aspen's gene-modded lichen."

Sybil's eyes widened below surprised eyebrows. She hadn't been prepared for this. And why should she? We had always listened to her revelations before, hung on her words. I felt ready to learn from her, but clearly not everyone was so open. "I understand not everyone feels ready for this," she said.

"It's not a matter of being ready," Pine said, the church-lady voice overtaken by an increasing coldness. "It's a matter of holding fast to what we were taught. We are keeping the faith of what you've taught us before. Being 'ready' for new ideas sounds like being ready to go astray from the

Revelation."

"Haven't I always told you speaking with the goddess is like a conversation?" Sybil insisted. "In every conversation, there are words we don't understand, moments when we have to backtrack and re-explain. The goddess is trying to enter into that conversation with us, and we can't learn if we're too focused on repeating what we already know."

"In every *conversation*, we talk with the same person the entire time." Hawk's voice had gotten fierce and snappy, losing all the softness it usually had when he talked in church. He tapped his scripture. "But the words in this book are the conversation up to this point, and they sound nothing like what you're saying now." He flipped it open, expertly bringing it to the passage he wanted. I doubted Sybil could have ever done that, even though the words were hers. "Sermon 129. 'No one is perfect, anyone might go astray. Even I might wake up and lose the way, stop listening to the goddess and start listening to the voices of doubt.' I think that moment is now."

For a moment the chapel was completely still, as if everyone at once had caught their breath at the blatant challenge. Then the babble broke out. "Can you *believe* this?" Autumn demanded, of the room in general.

"That he's claiming she isn't inspired?" I ventured.

"That she's abandoning the Revelation!"

My heart sank. I had come to Sybil's church, so long ago, because I had felt the ring of truth in her words. She seemed to understand the living macro-organism a biosphere was supposed to be, in a way I had thought only scientists like me ever could. And she breathed a kind of life into it, a spirituality that could inform daily living.

I still felt that truth, in her words today. But, judging by the hubbub going on around me, not everyone did.

Maybe not anyone.

23

Robin

At Fesskh's den, I was given back my clothes, now clean and dry. Hashta watched me dress without a hint of embarrassment. I turned my back on her to pull on my pants. "What comes now?"

"A full council," she answered, in awed tones. "Fesskh summoned them to rule on her new rank, and on the honored guest of course."

Once I was ready, I had to wait for over an hour. "They aren't ready for the honored guest," was all Hashta could tell me each time she returned from checking on them.

At last I was summoned to the council chamber. At least two dozen Eosians crouched around the enormous rectangular table, eyes glittering in the light of a small brazier, apparently brought in out of consideration of my infirmity. Thoughtful of them. Facing all of them at once was terrifying enough with the lights on.

Fesskh directed me to the empty foot of the table. There were no chairs and the table itself was at chest height. I leaned my elbows on it. It was going to have to do.

Fesskh herself sat at the head of the table. I wondered if that meant she was officially the Eldest now. Bad news for me if she was; at least if Tsaft was correct that she wanted to destroy us.

This time, I wasn't asked any questions. Instead Fesskh announced without prologue, "We have decided you are not guilty of trespass on Mrrka's land. Since you received her memories, you would have been drawn to the place. And in any event, her widow welcomed you after the fact; she doesn't wish a feud with you."

I blinked. It hadn't occurred to me I could be held responsible for blundering into Mrrka's territory. "Thank you," I said, because they seemed to expect some response.

"But we must charge you, on behalf of all your people, for burning public land and setting up your dens in the place you have been inhabiting."

Shit. "Whose land is that?" I asked. From what Hashta had said, and what I remembered, I thought it was only on the common.

"If you had trespassed on an estate, the matter would be between you and her only. But the place is on the common."

I breathed a sigh of relief. Anyone could go on the common, right? That was for everyone, even if you had no patron at all.

"As such," Fesskh continued, "we are all at feud with you."

"What?" I cried. "I thought anyone could go there."

"Anyone can hunt there," she said. "No one can build there. And all of us have sworn to defend the common. There has been hunger among the landless since you arrived. We must hold you accountable for that."

"But we didn't know it was the common!" I heard the pitch of my voice rise, desperate.

"What kind of person simply *assumes* land is there for the taking?" she countered. "Land is blood. Land gives life. Of course all of it belongs to someone."

All of it. Well, that wasn't promising. If all of it belonged to someone, where could we go? "I need to go home," I said plaintively. "I need to tell the others what you've said."

One of Fesskh's ears flicked backward. "Not as long as the feud lasts."

I closed my eyes. *Mrrka, got anything for me?* Images of feuds past bubbled to the surface: a longstanding quarrel with another family that had lasted several generations, a brief argument, a boundary dispute. Further back, I remembered a single combat. Teeth pressed lightly into my neck. Not to kill, to demonstrate she *could* kill. I remembered the words that had ended it all.

"I submit," I said suddenly. I bowed my head and raised my arms, my best imitation of the gesture I remembered. It galled, because everything Mrrka had remembered was telling me Fesskh was my inferior. But this was what I had to do to end the feud. I had to accept her dominance over me.

She blinked twice. I could see she hadn't expected such a quick victory. Would it make her suspicious? She couldn't conceive, I realized, that humans didn't care as much about rank or dominance as they did.

But the others were looking up at her, ears pricked. They expected her to accept my surrender. Eventually she shook herself slightly and said, "Very well. You may go, and tell your people they have submitted to us."

I cringed internally. What would Hawk say? Would he even understand what had happened? I wasn't even sure I did. One thing I did feel certain of: if Hawk showed aggression toward them, if he began any terraforming projects or harvested any more trees, it would almost certainly nullify our agreement.

Tsaft was waiting for us back at her den. "I hear you are to leave us."

"Yes. I'm sorry we didn't get to talk more. But I am eager to get back to my daughters. I have been very worried about them."

She put up a finger. "Please wait, I have something for them." She left the room for a moment and came back with a . . . stuffed animal? It was lumpy and shapeless, clearly much-loved. All I could tell about it, at this point, was that it had six stumpy legs. "This was Tisket's," she said, handing it to me.

"You don't want to keep it?"

She bowed her head; a regretful negative. "I need to get rid of as much as I can. The other decision of the council tonight was to give the estate to Kisht. She won't be Eldest, but she will have Mrrka's lands. And she doesn't want me to stay here. I will be moving to the common soon."

My jaw dropped. "How could she do that to you? She's your own daughter!"

"No," said Tsaft, "not my daughter. I only provided the seed. And she resents me for that. She didn't want me where she would have to see me every day, even as a bonded servant."

Her voice held sadness rather than anger, but I could barely contain my fury. "It isn't right," I said fiercely.

"I will be all right," she said calmly. "I will live with Tisket. I only feel sad. It is hard enough to be without Mrrka; to lose even the home we had together..." At last her composure failed; she lifted her face upward and let out a low wail.

"I'm so sorry," I said, wishing I could hug her. That, certainly, didn't feel like the sort of thing her people would do. But I nervously extended a hand and touched her elbow. "I will remember her always."

She lowered her head again to meet my eye. "It gives me great comfort to know her memories live on in you," she said huskily. Then she whisked around, tail flicking outward, and left the room.

Hashta led me as far as the creek that edged the burn zone. She offered to come further, but I thanked her and let her go. I knew the way from here, especially as the sky was beginning to lighten.

Just as I was scoping out a path to cross the creek, though, I spotted something odd in the gray half-light. Little brown objects were clinging to all the violet leaves in the undergrowth. In the predawn silence, I could hear a soft munching sound. I bent close and pulled one off a leaf. "Oh *fuck*," I said aloud. I knew these bugs. Locusts, for the terraforming effort. They weren't supposed to be released outside the colony yet. We were supposed to focus on the colony itself first, making it sustainable and growing food for ourselves.

Another thought occurred to me, more disturbing than the last. Had Aspen engineered them? Autumn had said she couldn't engineer the bacteria herself. Aspen had done a small batch to keep down the weeds.

This, though, wasn't a small batch. I looked up and down the creek. They were clinging to every leaf. Thousands of them. I wondered how fast they could defoliate a tree. And how soon the Eosians would notice.

I snatched a single locust and stuck it in my bag. I wanted to throw it in Aspen's face. I wanted him to know I knew he hadn't believed me, that he had chosen to follow Hawk when he should have trusted me.

Fuck him, and not in the good way.

24

Robin

The gate was locked when I reached it, but peering through the logs, I could see Cliff hanging around nearby. For a second I was afraid to call out. Would Sybil be angry at me for turning a stunner on her? Would she keep me out? After all, I did the colony no good now that we'd landed.

But that was paranoia, and this was Cliff. My friend and colleague for years. "Hey, Cliff!" I called, and he came over to let me in.

"Thank the goddess you're back," he said. "Aspen has been beside himself."

Once inside I went straight to the hydroponics deck. Aspen was sitting on a stool, bent over a microscope. And beside him, perched on the counter—Lily. One sleeve was in her mouth, getting gnawed to shreds. In the other hand she held her little clock, beeping steadily.

I rushed over, for a second able to see nothing but her. She leaped into my arms, making me stagger. "I'm sorry baby," I said, resting her butt back on the counter so I could keep holding her. "I'm sorry."

She let go of me with one hand, offering me her clock. I swallowed hard and silenced the alarm. "You won't need this for a while," I said, pocketing it. "I'll be right here, okay?"

Aspen had pushed back from the counter and was watching me. "She's been a mess," he said.

"You think I don't know that?" I snapped. "I suppose you think I just lost track of time!"

This wasn't the reunion I wanted to have with him. I'd been longing to see him again, to have someone on my side again. And now I didn't feel like he was.

"I told Hawk you hadn't," said Aspen. "I told him you would have come if it was humanly possible for you to." He looked up at me with a question in his eyes. So he wasn't actually sure. All our years together and he didn't know I'd be there for Lily when I said.

"I found them," I said. "I was right about everything. They're people. A whole civilization, and Hawk wanted to treat them like animals."

Aspen's eyes widened. "Did you make contact? Try to communicate?"

I gave a short, sharp huff. I'd almost forgotten how much he didn't know. "Yeah, I talked to them." I let go of Lily to put my pack on the counter. "They wouldn't let me go at first. I finally managed to convince them we weren't enemies, and they let me go. But all of that relied on us not antagonizing them. And then I find this." I dug out the locust and dropped it on the counter.

"That's a locust," he said, touching it with one finger. "One of Autumn's. Where was it?"

"Outside," I said. "I thought you were using them to eat the plants *inside*."

"Yeah," he said. "Autumn clipped their wings and everything. So they wouldn't get out before phase two."

We both looked at the locust, slightly mashed from my bag but alive. Its wings definitely weren't clipped.

"Are you telling me you didn't engineer the bacteria for this batch?" I demanded. "I know Autumn couldn't."

He stared at me. "You think I would do that? When you said there

190

were aliens out there?"

I met his eyes. "I don't know. I don't fucking know what you would do if it was a choice between me and your religion." I kept my voice level, not wanting to scare Lily, but I could feel her fidgeting and knew my anger was seeping through. She never missed that.

"Well, I didn't do it. I guess you don't *fucking know* whether or not to believe me, now." His tone was like ice. Aspen wasn't like me. When he swore, it meant trouble.

I sighed and stared at the ceiling. Shit. This wasn't how it was supposed to go.

"Did Sybil make it back?" I asked, in a quieter voice.

"Eventually," he said. "Things have been—complicated, lately. You should talk to her."

"Later," I said. "I'm going to bed. The aliens are nocturnal and kept me up the past two nights. See if you can stop anybody from doing anything else hostile."

"Take Lily with you and see if she'll nap," he said, turning back toward the counter. "She was up at three-thirty this morning."

I bit my lip. Of course. And there was no rest for Aspen, after all that. I hoisted her down from the counter and took her hand. "How about that nap, baby girl?" I said as we reached our room. "I'll read you the botany book." Yeah, my kid is seven and her favorite book is Principles of Botany, Fourth Edition. I got bragging material too, it's not all alarm clocks and not talking.

When we got to our room, I took out the lovey Tsaft had given me. Lily's poor bunny had completely lost both ears. "Look, I got you something."

She looked doubtful but grabbed it, tucking it under one arm. "I'm packin' up to g' find Mommy."

"Did Daddy say that?"

"I want m' wife back," she said.

"Why didn't he come then?"

She nabbed her battered bunny from her bed, got into mine, and cuddled up with one toy under each arm. "Principlesobotany fourthdis-hon," she said. That was all I was going to get.

I woke up a couple of hours later. I could have stood to get more sleep, but there was too much to do. I had to find Sybil and tell her what I'd found out. And if possible, find out how to do something about the locusts. When the sun went down, the Eosians would be waking up, and they might discover the damage to their trees. If not tonight, within a few nights. We didn't have much time.

Yawning, I slid open the door that led out to the playground. On the bench beside the door, Aspen was sitting, staring at his hands in his lap.

I sat down beside him. "You been waiting here this whole time?"

He shook his head. "Saw you on the baby monitor. Lily go down for you okay?"

"Took eight pages, but she did pass out eventually. She needed it."

There was a long silence. He hadn't come down here to talk shop. I opened my mouth, trying to frame some sort of apology.

He beat me to it. "I'm sorry," he said. "I shouldn't have snapped back at you like that. I was tired, and worried and—well, you know."

"You came down here to *apologize*?"

He ducked his head sideways, as if afraid of my reaction. "Yeah?"

"You don't need to apologize for not rolling over for me, okay? I came in and started yelling at you, and it turned out I was wrong. You don't have to sit and take it every time. It's okay for you to tell me off."

He shook his head. "I don't feel good about it. That's not who I am."

"But it is who I am?"

The question hung in the air. He didn't want to answer it. "You and I are really different," he ventured.

"That's not me being my special self. That's me being a dick. You shouldn't have to deal with it."

192

He shrugged. "I feel like I owe you everything, after all you've sacrificed to come out here."

"So you just have to enable me forever, so that I can play the martyr over having to quit my job? Fuck that noise. Tell me off when I screw up. I mean it."

"I'm not that guy," he said. "You can't put that on me. If you don't want to be like that, stop being like that."

I winced. He was right. He wasn't my dad. It wasn't his job to tell me when I was being an asshole. It was my job to do better.

"Okay," I said, putting my hand over his on his knee. "I hear you. And I'm sorry."

"It's okay," he said.

I waited, hoping he would say something else. Like "by the way, I would always listen to you over Sybil or Hawk." But I couldn't ask again. Not after the fight we'd had. Not when I still didn't know how to ask the question without getting angry. So instead I said, "Lily said you were going to look for me?"

"I did look for you," he said.

"You? Trekking through the bush?"

"Don't act so surprised. I'm not afraid of trees."

I shook my head ruefully. No, not scared of trees—but I hadn't predicted he would get up and take action. Particularly not if Hawk told him not to. "Did you see the aliens?"

He shook his head. "I found Sybil instead. I was going to go out again tomorrow and look for you, but I had to deal with a few things here first. It's…not easy, being torn between work and the kids and everything else."

"Tell me about it." Hadn't that been my life for years? I knew how he felt, but I hadn't been very considerate of it, despite that.

"I've been working on a solution for the locusts," he said. "I didn't want to ask Autumn, because I knew she'd just go straight to Hawk. If she wasn't firmly on his side, she wouldn't have hidden it from me when she thawed them all out. We have pheromone traps to collect them again, though I'll have to wait for daylight to put them out."

I took a deep breath and let it out. Could it really be that easy? "Okay. Okay. Maybe the Eosians will never notice."

"What are they like?" he asked, finally turning his hand over to weave his fingers through mine. "I want to know everything."

We sat there, hand in hand, and I told him all of it. The memories, the Eosian culture, everything I knew. It felt silly, now, that I hadn't told him earlier. I'd grouped him with Sybil, Hawk, everyone I didn't trust. But he was my *husband*. He'd been mine first.

25

Aspen

The next few days passed quietly. Whatever cease-fire Robin had managed to hash out, it seemed to be working. At least we saw no sign of the aliens, either inside the stockade or outside, when teams went to cut logs for our construction.

No one guarded the gate any longer, because no one seemed to know who was in charge anymore. In the cafeteria each day, the room was audibly quieter, as people scooted chairs close together and spoke in low voices. When I came into rooms, conversations stopped.

I wanted to talk it through with everyone. Share what I knew about the Eosians, what I'd experienced with Sybil out by the waterfall. Help them understand that this was where the goddess was leading us.

But I had a feeling most people weren't open to hearing something new. They seemed to regard me with suspicion, since it had become known how I'd snuck out against Hawk's orders. So I hung back and watched, as people sorted themselves into categories. Many, like Pine and Autumn, were staunch Hawk supporters. He'd been there for them while Sybil had hidden in her room. He stuck with the revelation they'd received before.

Others sought Sybil out. I saw her many times, walking along the edge of the stockade with a disciple, heads bent together in quiet conversation. Perhaps she was slowly winning them over, in her own way.

A few people, like Cliff, came and talked to me personally, hinting that they were on Sybil's side and checking to be sure I was too. I hated the feeling of being sorted onto one "team" or another. We were one colony, and could hardly avoid one another forever. And we were one faith, or ought to be. But I said I believed Sybil, that I thought the goddess had revealed something new to her. That satisfied her "side."

Plenty of others chose not to make a decision. They tried to muddle on without leadership, never outright disobeying either prophet, but lying low when they could. This group had most of my sympathy, even though I knew Sybil was right. What business of ours was colony policy anyhow? We were stranded on an alien world, a world that was more hostile than we had believed. Best to focus our efforts on survival. Fighting among ourselves would hurt our chances.

I went out each day to check and empty the pheromone traps, carefully recording how many locusts I got. Autumn appeared to have thawed out a couple thousand, which was less bad than it could have been. But I had to catch every single one. If even two escaped, they'd reproduce and wreak devastation on the forest.

Autumn came upon me one day on my rounds. "Undoing my hard work?" she said, in a tone I could tell she'd spent a lot of effort making light.

"Yep," I said in the same tone.

"Hawk told me to do it," she blurted out. "I took the gut bacteria culture you'd made. No hard feelings?"

"I figured," I said. "Why now? It wasn't time for phase two."

"He was worried there wasn't going to be a phase two. Not with Robin insisting there were aliens here, and then Sybil wandering out as well. I think he figured, if he got it kickstarted now, hopefully it would provide the momentum to keep going and nobody would be able to stop it later."

I frowned. "Prescient of him. But he's wrong. I can get this cleaned up." I finished counting the locusts in the pheromone trap and carefully shook them into the net cage I carried. Seventy-four in this one. We were getting there.

She was quiet for a second. "Are the predators really aliens?"

"Robin's met them. They sound … well, let's put it this way. We're a lot safer if we make nice."

"They can't be that advanced," she argued. "Not if there was no sign of them from orbit. No emissions, no roads, no cities."

"Funny thing," I said, putting down the trap and continuing toward the next one. "Species don't all advance in the same directions. While we were busy inventing cities and cars, they were perfecting their hunting ability. From what Robin says, they don't like living close together and they hate cluttering up the woods with buildings. But I wouldn't want to be up against those teeth and claws."

She frowned and came reluctantly after me. "But surely with guns and bioweapons and things—"

I stopped and turned around. "What are you trying to do here, Autumn? Do you just want to fight with me that much? I'm not going to help you destroy them or their forest. But I don't think I'm going to be able to convince you either."

She sighed. "I wanted somehow to make peace. I hate the way the colony is getting divided. I'm ready to take the goats out now, which will spare a lot of battery. But I had always meant to have you there."

I softened. We had been friends since we'd left Proxima. I didn't want to lose her over this, no matter how wrong I felt she was. "Just let me wrap up here, and I'll come. I wouldn't want to miss this."

There were tears in Autumn's eyes as we opened the long drawers that held the incubators. Against all odds, the kids had been brought to maturity. She set one hand, trembling a little, on the lid of the first. "Do you want to do the honors?"

"Me? These aren't my babies. Mine's still cooking."

She laughed and pressed the hatch. Under the lid, the goat fetus floated in its amniotic sac. One quick slash with a scalpel and the fluid gushed out. She reached in and took the goat, squirming and crying out. I passed her the clamps.

While she gave it a quick rubdown, the best substitute for a mother's care, I sat back on my heels. My eyes prickled. A week ago, I'd thought we'd have to flush the tanks and lose them all. Now here was this creature, warm and beautiful and alive. In a year or two, if the colony survived that long, my children would have milk. In ten years we could have a whole flourishing barnyard of animals.

Well. Of goats anyway. With the strain of the gestators off the battery, and energy usage cut down even more, we had a couple weeks of power left. That wasn't enough to try for cows or chickens or anything. But maybe by then we'd have worked out some other solution. I chose to hope.

"Got a name?" asked Autumn.

"Seriously? You didn't pick them when you started them going?"

"Sometimes the embryos don't take. You don't want to get attached too soon."

I looked at the baby goat, which had already stopped bleating and started sucking at the bottle Autumn offered it. It was white with black markings, some breed good for mothering. "Call it Lucky," I said. "Because it's taken so much going right to get her here at all."

We decanted the whole rack of incubators. Not a dud in the lot—and no wonder, Autumn had checked and re-checked each embryo. I went outside, reeking with amniotic fluid and vernix, carrying one in each arm. We had a barn for them already, a fresh-built, airy place smelling of wood shavings.

Robin was already at the barn, scattering sawdust. "I don't have any hay for the hayrack."

"That's fine," said Autumn. "They won't eat hay for a while yet. We have milk powder for them for now."

"There will be hay by the time they need it," I said cheerfully, carefully setting the kids down on their wobbly legs. It felt like madness to be happy at a moment like this. We had divisions within the colony and threatening aliens just outside. The scrubber lichen was a little smaller every day. Pink weeds were cropping up everywhere, and the seed-bugs were thicker than ever.

But the goats staggered around their paddock completely unafraid. Maybe they knew something the rest of us didn't. Maybe we'd be all right somehow.

"Have you seen one of these big bugs before?" Robin asked Autumn, pointing to a fat one as long as her finger that perched on the paddock fence.

Autumn squinted at it. "No. I should get a net and catch it. If I sequence it, I should be able to find out what kind of tree it comes from."

"There's a heck of a lot of them out today." Robin gestured, and I could see what she meant. Big, blundering things like cicadas, with a faint buzz.

"Why don't they just land?" I wondered. "That's what the tiny ones do."

"Some of them have to mate first," said Autumn.

One of the cicadas landed on a goat—the first kid, Lucky. Lucky twitched her ear and danced around, trying to figure out what was touching her back.

The bug raised its wings and gave a deafening drone. "Holy crap," said Robin. "How much noise can come out of a bug that small?"

"Earth cicadas sound a lot like that," said Autumn. "Kind of amazing how they do. I guess it's probably calling a mate. Look how some of the other bugs are coming over."

It was true. At first it was just a few neighboring ones buzzing over individually, but more started crowding in, looking like a murmuration of starlings the way they swarmed together in an undulating mass.

"I'm not comfortable with this," Autumn said nervously, trying to brush the buzzing cicada off the goat. But it clung fast with its feet, and Lucky skittered around the yard to stop Autumn from touching it.

A moment later cicadas were landing all over her. Robin grabbed the broom out of the barn and tried to sweep them off, but it was no good. They clung fast, more and more until Lucky was covered with the shiny brown creatures.

Lucky screamed, an odd, human-sounding cry. The heap of bugs on her moved and pulsated, making a clicking sound that supplanted the buzzing of the original one.

We all watched in horror as Lucky staggered about the pen before falling down still. Her body still seemed to move, but it was only the flow of brown carapaces stumbling over each other, their jaws clicking horribly.

It was only minutes later that the cloud of cicadas lifted. Lucky was gone. In her place was a pile of wet bones.

Robin screamed in horror and started running around the pen, grabbing the other goats and bringing them into the barn. Autumn stood paralyzed, weeping silently.

I scanned the sky for other large bugs, but for the moment they seemed to have dispersed. Then I went around the outside of the barn, slamming the shutters and pulling off my shirt to stuff in a gap left in one window frame. "Is that all of them?" I asked Robin as she came out.

She nodded grimly and pulled the door shut. "We need to warn everyone."

Most of the colonists doing outdoor work had crowded around to see the bugs, and those were running for the ship. But we ran everywhere, checking behind woodpiles and half-built houses. I barged into Sybil's house, which was finished except for the attic windows. "You have to come into the ship *now*," I said.

She had been sitting, having tea with Ivy, one of the teachers. Trying to win her over to her new revelation? "Why?"

"I'll explain on the way," I said. "It's an emergency."

That got her moving.

We huddled inside the ship, having sealed the doors and vents. Someone went around counting heads. The schoolchildren had been inside the whole time; that was a relief. A few people had been in the new church building, but Cliff radioed them and they reported they were all accounted for. He suggested they stay put for the time being.

"Can you explain what has happened?" Sybil asked, taking charge without hesitation.

"These bugs are actually the seeds of different native plants," Autumn explained. "It's their way of reproducing and spreading. We theorized that perhaps the plants could detect a bare patch in this area, and specifically increase seed production to try to deal with it."

"But these ones eat meat," Robin put in bluntly. "If they eat goat, I doubt they'd turn up their noses at human."

"Probably not," Autumn agreed. "They must feed before planting themselves to improve their energy stores before germination. I suspect they are the seeds of a very large tree."

"I thought our life and theirs were incompatible," said Sybil. "We can't eat the plants here."

"The starches are incompatible," I said. "They're the isomer of our starches—they're inedible to us. But the proteins are the same as ours, so technically they should be able to digest Earth animals just fine."

"So I could have had dinner with the Eosians the whole time?" Robin put in. "Damn, and I was really hungry too."

"We should be safe in here," said Autumn, "as long as all the doors are closed."

"Unfortunately, we need to breathe," said Robin. "The scrubber lichen was struggling to keep up even with the doors open. The emergency mechanical scrubber is an energy suck, and we have less than a week of battery life left. Keeping the doors closed isn't a solution."

"I'll make screens for them," Cliff suggested. "How big are the bugs?"

Autumn held up a sample bag, in which one bug scrabbled to escape. Robin gave a little yelp. "You brought one *in*?"

"I wish I'd gotten more than one. The more we have, the more we can learn about how to control them. Don't worry, I'll keep it secured."

Robin

As soon as Cliff had the screens printed, I grabbed a pile and went around, covering each airlock. Luckily I could fasten the screens on the inside, and open each door only after. I didn't see any large bugs through the windows, but I couldn't be rational where those creatures were concerned. Just thinking of them made my skin crawl.

I should be able to be more help than this. Surely these weren't new, right? The Eosians must know them as a regular hazard they had to combat. How often did the trees make these killer seeds? Annually, or only when there was a fire? No one I had spoken with had suggested the fire did anything more than just destroying hunting grounds.

They had to be a danger to the Eosians as well. They seemed to be attracted by movement, or perhaps body heat and odor. They'd attack the Eosians as well, and their prey animals. So there must be some solution they'd devised.

But if so, it was possible none of the younger Eosians knew. That was why they needed to be led by the oldest, the ones with the longest memories. If anyone knew how to handle this threat, it would have been Mrrka.

But Mrrka was dead. And no matter how much I racked my brain, I couldn't come up with anything. Maybe I was just too panicked, too caught up in my own much-closer memory of the bugs eating Lucky alive.

On the other hand, maybe Mrrka hadn't given me that memory. She hadn't had long to spend with me before she died. Maybe she hadn't gotten that far.

I finished installing the first screen and pulled the lever to roll back the airlock door. Fresh air streamed in, making me realize just how stuffy it had already gotten. I peered out through the screen anxiously. We'd have to give the goats their milk soon, and that meant crossing the compound to get to the barn. That had never seemed a long distance before. Today, it seemed like miles.

Interlude

The council chamber was in an uproar. Fesskh had agreed to the meeting, but as soon as it had begun, the others lobbed more questions at her than she had any hope of answering.

What it amounted to could be summed up in the words of the Third Eldest: "You promised us you had the invaders handled. They submitted to you. Then why are they still on the common? You should have ordered them to leave again, and forced them if they refused."

"It isn't that simple," Fesskh protested. It had been so much easier to be the opposition, to be the one slinging accusations and not the one responsible when things went badly. "I have to gather the warriors, put together an appropriate show of force."

"Why is force needed? Why accept her submission if you didn't trust her to honor it?"

Because all of you were staring at me expecting it, she thought. Aloud she said, "We don't truly know their strength. Some of the things their ambassador said gave me pause. We already know they killed Mrrka, apparently without even trying. We must test their defenses."

"It's just a thin little boundary," said one of the younger members. "If you come close, you can hear it buzzing. As long as you don't touch it, it can't hurt you. Mrrka came in and out many times without harm."

Fesskh sighed to herself. She didn't want to confess the investigations she'd made on her own, the seamless construction of their ship, or the tools they used to build houses in mere days. She'd bluffed the ambassador into submission, but it was clear to her that one was only an underling. Sooner or later she would have to confront their Eldest, and she wanted to be prepared.

Just then Tisket came running into the council chamber. "What are you doing in here, youngster?" Fesskh demanded. She was in no mood to deal with Mrrka's family any longer. As far as she was concerned, Tsaft, Tisket, and Kisht could all walk onto the ice and not return. They were nothing but trouble, even Kisht.

Tisket stood for a moment, gasping for breath. She must have run flat out. "It's Hashta," she panted out. "We were stalking a fowl together. With permission," she added hastily, glancing at Fesskh. "An insect landed on her and started to scream. Then more came...I've never seen anything like it. They—they *ate* her, Eldest. Down to the bones."

The room fell silent, and everyone looked at Fesskh. She was the Eldest now. She ought to remember something about this. But she did not.

"I—remember something," the Third Eldest said. "One of Mrrka's forebears told me about it once. It's called the Devourer. It comes when too many trees are cut or burned. She told me always to replant the white trees after a fire."

Fesskh glared at her. Who was Eldest here, herself, or anyone who happened to remember something Mrrka had said once? Even beyond the grave Mrrka had to test her. "And what did she say to do when the Devourer is awakened?"

The Third Eldest's eyes widened. "She never said."

26

Aspen

We survived for several days inside the ship. Someone sewed a few make-shift beekeeper's suits so we could go out to feed the goats and check on the plants. The group in the chapel made their way, a couple at a time, back to the ship in the suits.

The children hated being cooped up in the ship again, after having finally gotten to play outside for the first time in years. Doubly so, since we couldn't spare the battery power for them to watch a movie or play a computer game. Colt spent hours lying on the floor whining and kicking the wall, the first day.

Cliff rigged a makeshift generator up to an exercise bike and challenged the kids to see who could bike the longest to help charge the batteries. "The actual electricity it makes is peanuts compared to what we need," he whispered. "But at least the kids can feel like they're accomplishing something." And it did seem to interest the kids. Colt did four miles on the thing without stopping.

I wanted to say something about the wisdom of encouraging them to burn energy when our food levels were so low. I didn't want them to work up too much of an appetite. But I couldn't bear to break up the fun. Perhaps they'd manage to keep the bioscrubber's grow lights on another day, with how hard they pedaled.

Several white saplings had appeared around the colony, pushing their way up fast enough to see. That would be the seed-bugs that had fed on Lucky, doing their best to reestablish the forest.

I debated whether or not to destroy them. On the one hand, I didn't want something else that could make clouds of carnivorous bugs. But on the other, I suspected the seed-bug swarms wouldn't stop until they had established a healthy grove of trees. So, for the time being, I left them sprouting in the middle of my grass patch and my pumpkin patch and my kudzu.

The bioscrubber continued to struggle. Every day I harvested enough for the colony to eat. Every day it regenerated about half that much. It had been stressed too hard, and the grow lights couldn't draw enough power to shine at full capacity. I had tried to grow them outdoors, but every single sample had gone yellow and died. Without the nutrient pumps feeding them nitrogen 24/7, they couldn't get enough.

At the current rate of harvest, it would last six days. Could I put the whole colony on short rations on my own authority? The battery, at least, would last a bit longer now that the incubators weren't drawing power anymore.

I found myself staring at the pen of locusts I'd trapped. "I don't know if it's worth the energy to freeze these again," I said to Autumn. "I don't even want to open the freezer if we don't have to."

"We could let them go," she suggested, watching them crawl up the screened sides of the enclosure. "I know you wanted to preserve the forest, but it's clear now the native life is dangerous."

"No!" I snapped, more harshly than I meant to. "For all we know, releasing the locusts is what triggered the trees to release their seeds anyway. If we want this to stop, we first have to understand what's causing it. That means not disrupting the ecology any further till we know what we're up against."

She conceded with a tilt of her head. "Fair point. I'm still studying the bug I got. I guess in the meantime you could just feed the locusts whatever weeds you happen to pull? They're engineered to survive off native plants, thanks to your gut bacteria package."

I tapped on the screen, knocking one crawling green bug to the ground. "So what you're saying is, we have a tiny machine for converting native starches into Earth protein."

"What?"

"I mean we could eat them."

Her lip curled. "I suppose technically, but—"

"With how the bioscrubber is doing, I predict we'll soon be hungry enough to try them."

Robin

Autumn eventually had one piece of good news about the bugs: they couldn't fly in heavy rain. We didn't have enough water or power to simulate the effect with sprinklers, but we could at least wait for a rainy day and go outside.

The first good rainy day we got, Sybil insisted on a funeral for Mrr-ka. She asked my permission first.

"You're the one who knows most about the aliens," she said, eyes soft. "Do you think they would object?"

I shook my head. "They only care about their loved ones' memories. I don't think they'll care one way or the other what we do with the body."

Most of the colony—Hawk's people—didn't come. They said it was a farce, pretending a wild animal was a person just to support our anti-ter-raforming insanity. But a couple dozen Disciples showed up, and that was more than I had expected.

Sybil spoke awhile, her vocabulary larded with Greenie-isms, but for once I tried to listen. I wanted to know if she understood what we were up against, what the Eosians wanted.

The answer was, not much. She talked as if Mrrka were some kind of noble savage, living totally in harmony with nature. That the Eosians were a higher form of life than we were, because they didn't cut down trees and "bring the wrath of Terra down on us, in this plague of locusts."

The bugs weren't locusts, we literally had locusts in Aspen's lab. And I knew by now that the "wild forests" Sybil admired weren't wild at all. They were very carefully tended to make them good habitats for the kind of animals the Eosians liked to hunt.

"I believe we can coexist with her people," Sybil concluded. "I have to believe that, because both they and we are here to stay. Perhaps we can learn from them, ask for them to share what they have. In the end, I believe in the power of love to bind our two peoples together in friendship."

I audibly scoffed, and then quickly covered my nose to pretend I had sneezed. Fesskh share with us? It was all I could do to convince her not to kill us outright.

Sybil poured a damp shovelful of wet soil atop Mrrka's shimmering fur, which turned earth-brown as it refracted the color.

Tsaft should have been here, I thought. Not that she would have gotten much out of it. She'd been robbed of the kind of closure she should have had, a chance to say goodbye and her memories being passed down to Kisht, to stay in the community forever. Not that Kisht would have been remotely decent about it.

Once the last of the mud had been mounded over Mrrka's body, I wandered off to where Aspen knelt, hurriedly yanking radishes. "Can't stop," he said. "No telling how long this rain will last."

I knelt beside him. "That's why I came to help. Do they all come up?"

"These two rows."

I only broke off one radish top before I got the hang of it. "How are we doing, on food?"

He shook his head without answering. Little drops flicked off the ends of his braids.

"That bad?"

"We should be on short rations already," he said. "But Hawk won't agree, so his disciples won't abide by it, so the kitchen is serving the usual amount. Which means we run out after dinner tomorrow."

"And then it's eat bugs or starve?"

"Yeah. I hear the kitchen's experimenting with ways to make them edible. The kids can't know what they are, or they'll starve themselves rather than eat."

"I don't know about that," I said thoughtfully. "I think Colt—"

"*Don't* tell them."

I sighed. "I won't."

"Autumn would know better than me how long the locusts will last. They reproduce only once a year, so they're not an infinite resource. After they're gone—"

"The goats."

He nodded, yanking out radishes like the heads of his enemies. We'd only had them a few days, but by now we were all attached. I wasn't sure I could stomach goat.

But already I was eating far more than my share. I couldn't be picky. Baby had to eat, whether I liked it or not.

I spared a wistful thought for that roast animal at Tisket's. It had been edible the whole time, but I'd missed my chance.

Or had I…?

27

Robin

That idea was how I found myself, after the rain had stopped, leaving the colony in a beekeeper suit. In one hand I had a spear Cliff had managed to jury-rig for me out of scrap metal.

My memories of hunting were some of the sharpest. My mother had given me—Mrrka's mother had given her memories of hunting early on. It was how they learned, or part of it. A record of hunts gone past spanning generations. I remembered Mrrka's mother leading her out hunting brush-creeper the first time, and a time she'd led the whole village after an earthshaker on a festival day.

Neither of those would do this time. A brushcreeper was no bigger than a turkey. I'd need to bag dozens to make a single dinner for the colony. And an earthshaker was dangerous even for a half dozen Eosians. Its whiplike tail had killed more than one who had been careless, and I was nowhere near as light on my feet as they were.

My plan was the creature I had called the hexadeer, which they called light-leaper. Six-legged, like most of the life here, and smaller than a cow. You could hunt whole herds of them with friends, but in a pinch one of the Eosians could take one down alone. We'd have to find out if I could too.

Aspen had given no objections when I offered to go. That told me, more than anything else, just how drastic the food situation was. This time, I wasn't being rash or foolish. Terrifying as it was, going out against wild animals and risking bug attacks was safer than the alternative.

I would confine my hunting to the common, in the hopes of keeping my promise with Fesskh. I had no idea how she saw our relationship now, what she expected or how long it would be before she appeared to make demands. Perhaps the murder bugs were hampering her efforts to deal with me at the moment. But I didn't feel like taking chances.

The hexadeer browsed along the hillside where I'd gotten lost in the rain, that one day. I made my way there, watching for their tracks and droppings.

It was cool and cloudy, which made the beekeeping outfit slightly more tolerable. Of the several upcycled versions the colony had managed to produce, I had picked one in vibrant fuschia, with a purple veil. Garish at home, camouflage here.

My hips ached, every step feeling like a waddle. Hazel said the baby had "dropped," which apparently meant shoved its head directly into my bladder.

I spotted some tracks—a small herd, six or seven animals, with their young along. I didn't want the young, but I knew a herd with young moved more slowly, keeping the young in the middle. Which increased my odds of taking down an adult, hopefully.

I followed them for a good hour, thirsty yet afraid to unfasten my bee veil to get a drink. I could see a bumbling cicada blunder through the air every few minutes, which meant they could come upon me at any time. But dehydration was giving me cramps in my belly. Hazel had always told me to drink plenty of water to keep those at bay. Then again, even if I snuck a drink, then I'd need to pee five minutes later. I didn't care to show the murder bugs my bare ass.

I had seen a movie once where they had hunted deer from a tree stand set above a salt lick, with guns. All you really had to do was wait quietly and shoot. But I'd never shot a gun, I didn't have a tree stand, and I didn't even know if hexadeer liked salt. I knew how to track them like an Eosian, so that was what I did: stalking quietly among the trees, following the tracks, keeping my spear ready.

The longer I hunted them, the more like Mrrka I felt. The thoughts that flitted through my mind were all memories of hers—other hunts, other feasts. I remembered when she was young and trekked far from home, alone, to prove she could. She had killed a river reptile with her bare claws.

I remembered taking Kisht out after hexadeer, just the two of us. She had still looked up to me then. She had still believed I knew everything.

At last I spotted them, browsing just below me on the hillside. There were seven of them, four adults and three young. I marked out the one I wanted, the one without a youngling tagging behind. Mrrka would have chosen that one, because the mothers would help their younglings survive to be old enough to hunt in their turn. Managing the hunting stock was vital to her. It meant food for everyone and no lean times.

I crouched down and waited for my moment. Light-leapers browsed in little back-and-forth patterns, so they would come closer in a few minutes. I squeezed my spear and tried to quiet my breathing. If they startled, I couldn't chase them down like Mrrka would have.

A murder bug blundered through, knocking itself against trees and bouncing off. They weren't very smart, Autumn had said. They knew how to tell something they could eat, how to scream when they found it, and how to flock to that sound when they heard it. That was about all.

I stayed very still. Autumn hadn't yet learned how it could tell food from nonfood, whether by motion or smell or something else. But perhaps being still would keep it from seeing me.

It did not. The bug blundered closer and closer to me, knocking on trees and struggling through brambles, before landing on my arm.

I stared at it, holding my breath, willing it to go away. It stood there, dancing slightly with its feet. Tasting me, probably. Verifying I was edible.

I swallowed and waited for it to scream. If all the bugs swarmed me at once, I wasn't sure the bee veil would hold. Surely they could bite a hole in it as surely as they could bite one in goat hide.

But, after a long moment, the bug flicked its wings back out and continued its blundering path. My sleeve must not have tasted good to it. I let out a shaky breath, trembling all over. That had nearly been it for me. That wasn't the way I wanted to go. Give me hard vacuum, at least.

The bug's screaming rattle drew my attention back. For a second I gasped, certain it was on me. But no, it was on a hexadeer, the same one I'd selected as my target. The other deer pranced slightly, flicking their ears in confusion. They hadn't learned yet what the sound meant.

There was a sound like hail, as the other bugs came blundering through the trees. At first I only stared dumbly, watching the bugs cover the animal like they had done to our little goat. But then I remembered why I was there, why I'd braved the horrible insects in the first place. We needed to eat, and those bugs were stealing my meat.

I picked a new target and hefted my spear. At the same moment, the swarmed light-leaper began to scream, startling the others. They dashed past me, and I had no time to stop and line up my shot. I threw the spear as hard as I could, hoping Mrrka's bequest had reached into my muscle memory.

There was a panicked scrabble, and the nearest hexadeer staggered and fell, its front legs crumpling beneath it. It wasn't a clean hit; I could see the spear hanging out of its side while it struggled, eyes rolling and white.

The other hexadeer were long gone, and I had to make the kill. Steeling myself against my strong desire to do literally anything else, I yanked out the spear and used the edge to slash its throat.

For a moment I only stood there, gloved hands red with its blood, unsure what I felt. Mrrka would be triumphing, which meant the tears were mine. I hadn't wanted to end the life of this beautiful creature. It was only that I had to.

28

Aspen

Sybil sought me out while Robin was out hunting. I wasn't busy. There's only so much work you can do to make plants grow faster. At some point you just have to wait for them to do it. And with the lights so low indoors, I couldn't grow much of anything in the lab.

But I was pretending to work, because I was anxious. Trying more things with the bioscrubber to see if I could help it recover. It was just too delicate, always had been. When I had been in grad school, developing the stuff, we hadn't spent enough energy making it hardy. It was supposed to be in a controlled environment! We hadn't thought that mattered. But things happen all the time on spaceships and stations. We needed something tougher.

"I hope I'm not interrupting," she said softly.

I startled, bashing my face on the eyepiece of my microscope. "Oh! No, I'm not really doing anything."

"You look like you are."

"Just … trying to figure out how to fix the bioscrubber. It's a whole ecosystem of its own, you know. A perfect balance. But too many fungi died, and then the algae bloomed too much, and now the algae is dying off because it isn't getting the nutrients it needs from the fungi…"

"Like Earth," she said quietly. "Or like Eos."

"Eos is stronger than us," I said. "We aren't throwing it out of balance. It's trying to scrape us off, and doing a pretty good job of it."

She took a seat on the next stool. "We came close to doing a lot worse than that. When I think of how ready I was to hurt the aliens—even Robin knew better! Why didn't I?"

"Robin had seen one," I pointed out.

"But why didn't the goddess . . . " She trailed off. "I guess what I want to know is, how did I get to such a point of spiritual blindness that I convinced myself it was what she wanted. If I can't tell the difference between what I want and what she wants—well, what good am I to any of you? You count on me to know!"

Her words were vehement, but her face remained calm. I could see it was something she'd been thinking about for a while. "It's a struggle for anybody," I said. Certainly I couldn't generally tell. I always assumed, if I had a thought, it was my own thought. If the goddess ever wanted to inspire me, she was going to have to work with that.

"All of this is my fault," she said softly. "I brought everyone here. I told everyone this was the plan. And now it's gotten too big for me to fix."

I waited, but it seemed that was all she wanted to say. "There was something else I wanted to ask you about." I took the slide off the microscope and put it aside. "Did you look at the alien, when we buried it?"

She nodded. "Not the same, I'm sure, as seeing a live one. But it still made me feel…"

"Did you see its ear?"

"What?" She blinked, taken aback.

"There was a little snip off its right ear, when we buried it. It wasn't there when we found the body. Someone took a sample of it."

"It wasn't you or Autumn?"

"It wasn't me," I said, with emphasis. "There's no possible reason we would need to study them like that. Not when we have Robin to give us firsthand information about how they actually live."

"But you're concerned."

"We brought the makings of some deadly viruses," I explained. "As part of the terraforming plans. During stage two, when we were going to start clearing the existing biosphere, we meant to get samples of the local animal life and engineer viruses that would target them. We have everything we need to do that, except the samples themselves. And if someone's taken them—"

"You're afraid someone's still working on the terraforming project," she finished. "Against my instructions."

"A lot of people are getting their orders from Hawk now."

Her mouth was in a firm line. "You think it's Autumn?"

"She's probably the only one with the ability to do it," I said. "The lab assistants don't have the training to engineer anything."

"Have you talked to her about it?"

"No. I didn't want to accuse her of anything without proof."

She considered a moment. "Don't talk to her. I will. Autumn's a good person, I'm sure I can get through to her somehow. I don't want to put her back up with accusations, I just want to explain to her why this isn't what the goddess wants."

Privately, I was skeptical. If even Sybil could manage to convince herself the goddess wanted us to purge the planet, Autumn could certainly do the same. Especially with Hawk in her ear, reminding her that this had been the plan all along. "Have you had any luck with anyone else?"

She shook her head. "A few. Mostly I'm just trying to keep the colony together. Hawk won't talk to me to work out any kind of compromise, just so we can keep the colony running. Did you know, we've been draining power with that electric fence this whole time? Cliff finally disconnected it for me this morning. A huge power suck that doesn't even keep the aliens from getting in if they want to. We need that energy for food."

"And the freezer," I said. Without really discussing it, Autumn and I had both prioritized the freezer above everything else. It took energy first, even if it meant the grow lights went dim. It symbolized all our hopes. Even if we weren't going to terraform, we needed the seeds and eggs just to support ourselves. Our goats were all female. To get more goats for the next generation, we would need the semen in the freezer. And we wanted cows and chickens too.

"Aspen ..." she said, a note of reproach in her voice. "Think about that a minute. We've got days of battery left. Even if Robin manages to catch something, it's not going to replace the bioscrubber. If we don't survive until harvest, it won't matter that the freezer lasted a few more days."

I stared at her, stricken. Of course she was right. A flourishing colony needed the things in that freezer. But we could probably survive on just plants. The goats would grow old and die and not be replaced, but we wouldn't die. Probably. "Do you want me to unplug it?"

"I'm not going to tell you what to do," she said. "I've done too much of that in the past. I thought, by believing in my dream—in what I thought was Terra's dream—and plowing ahead as hard as I could, I could do anything. For now I just want to make as much right as I can. I'm going to go find Autumn and talk to her. You decide what we do about the freezer."

She left me, and I was alone, heart aching, unsure what to do. I didn't want to give up hope for the future, but how long do you wait before you do? When the kids are already hungry and it's too late?

29

Robin

I had to radio back to the ship to get a few strong volunteers to help me carry the creature back. I hadn't thought of that when I'd left.

We brought the animal through the airlock and deposited it in the corridor. Sybil and several others gathered to see, looking a little green.

"The Disciples don't usually eat meat," Sybil said skeptically.

"Only because it's artificial," put in Cliff. "This isn't vat meat."

"True, it's just ..." She trailed off, staring at the hairy beast, blood drying along its side.

"It's this or bugs, ma'am," I said. "Once it's cut up and cooked, it won't look bad."

"Does anyone even know *how*?"

Someone went to ask Autumn, and she sent back two of her assistants. Too busy, I wondered, or too squeamish? Hopefully busy figuring out a poison or something for those horrible bugs.

The butchering job was sloppily done, and the cooks didn't handle the steaks right, so they were burned on the outside and a little raw in the middle. I ate two big ones and enjoyed every bite. Even Lily tried a little.

As I stacked up our plates, Aspen asked me, "Is this the plan then? You go out and hunt what we need every few days?"

My hands stilled, and I pushed the plates away. "I don't know. I don't know how long any of this will last." The game. The bugs. The cease-fire with the Eosians. Hell, in three weeks or so, if Hazel's math was right, I'd be laid up with a new baby and not able to do all this hunting. So what then? I tried to train Cliff to do it?

Aspen frowned. "With the bugs eating all the game, I don't know if you'll be able to find anything next time."

"The Eosians are going to have the same problem." I wondered if they yet had come up with beekeeping clothes, or whether they were still hiding in their dens, afraid to come out and hunt. They didn't have any more food stores than we did. Living in a temperate zone with no real winter, why should they? There was always some animal or other roaming the area for them to hunt.

He looked at me expectantly. As if, having saved the colony once, it was now my job to produce infinite miracles on cue. "If you could remember enough to hunt…I mean, maybe…"

"Maybe the answer to the bug problem is in my head somewhere?" I demanded. "It should be. This has had to have happened before, and Mrrka would be the most likely one to have seen it."

"Maybe you need to meditate more."

"I meditate every day. It isn't giving me anything new anymore. I just remember things related to the things I've already seen. Sybil says my ego is blocking me from remembering more. Because I know I'm not her. It's hard to feel like her when I'm here, surrounded by . . . this." I gestured to the cafeteria, the Disciples eagerly eating the first steak of their lives, the flat walls and sharp corners. We might be on a planet, but we were also on a ship. A place that was as *me* as anything could be. Just being here reinforced my identity, day after day. This is me, this is my job, this is my place among other people.

"But out there, you felt different," he said. "When you were hunting."

"You think I should go out again?"

"Not to the wilderness," he said. "To *them*. See if you can remember, if you're where she lived, talking to her friends and family."

My face fell. Not that I didn't want to go. I missed Tsaft, even if it was just Mrrka's memories making me feel that way. And I wouldn't mind getting away from all the Sybil and Hawk drama, the quiet grouping-off from which I was forever excluded, but expected to somehow navigate.

"They're very dangerous," I said, dropping my voice even lower. I didn't want the children to hear this. "I don't know how to predict what they'll do next. At least two of them want to kill me."

"I understand," he said, but something changed in his eyes. Like hope going out. He'd really thought I was somehow going to save the day again.

Damn it, if he had begged, if he'd tried to make me, I'd have said no. What kind of husband sends his pregnant wife into danger? But instead he had *believed* in me. I would have piloted into the middle of a meteor shower for him, with nothing else but the power of his trust.

Ever since we'd landed—no. Ever since he'd gotten involved in the church, I'd felt like I was always competing. That I would always come second to his goddess, and by extension to Sybil. I'd felt threatened by someone else taking up that much of him, even a goddess.

But he wasn't asking Sybil for help right now. He was asking me. There was nothing else he could have said or done to convince me I really came first for him.

Under the table, I squeezed his thigh. I didn't know how to tell him everything was better now, that the unspoken conflict rippling under the surface of our relationship had finally quieted. But I looked hard into his eyes and hoped he felt it.

"Okay," I found myself saying, as I got up from the table. "It's worth a shot."

30

Aspen

I saw Robin off and went to the chapel to pray. We hadn't bothered setting the alarm clock for Lily; its utility had been ruined once it was proved unreliable. But she seemed to understand when I said Mama would come back. Perhaps she had learned a more important lesson than trusting a clock, trusting Robin to come back no matter how long it had been.

Perhaps I had learned that lesson too.

The chapel was empty, which said something about what the schism had done to our faith. When you're fighting over your religion, you're not practicing it.

The potted trees that usually decorated the chapel were gone, put outside to get sun and spare the grow lights. The lights were turned back to barely bright enough to see by. The only decorations left were the painted walls. Disciple temples are made in arboretums, or made to look like them. So the walls mimicked a forest, painted maples and oaks and pines stretching up toward the ceiling. The ceiling was crisscrossed with branches, with snatches of blue for the sky, so we could feel we were in a forest understory rather than a cramped ship.

It didn't entirely work. I sat on the floor in the back, behind the seats, so I could look at the trees. No breezes stirred them, no creatures sang. Lifeless. The Eos life was real, so much better.

And yet I found myself here, because I was homesick for *these* trees. I wanted to lie under an elm tree and watch the seeds shake out like little golden coins. I wanted the smell of a pine forest. I had never been in a real one, but the arboretums of Proxima had been a decent imitation, as far as they went. They were real trees, making real oxygen. It had been a remnant of Earth, not a whole new thing like this was.

I knew Sybil was right, that we couldn't justify razing this planet to make an imitation Earth. But that didn't mean I wasn't still sad about it. I thought at first that I wasn't, in the early thrill of realizing I could enjoy the forest we had here. But homesickness had set in.

Robin had few good memories of Proxima. Growing up in poverty like she had, she'd been eager to get away, if only into space. But I imagined she was homesick too, for the deep stars and a cockpit where she could be in total control.

For a moment I let myself imagine we were free to make a decision. Pack up and go home. Would she agree? I thought she would. Back to that little apartment, to jobs, to worrying about bills, but never actually going hungry.

The door opened, and someone came in. I didn't look up. The chapel was open to everyone; if someone else was coming in to pray, that could only be a good thing.

But the steps approached me, and then Autumn dropped down to sit on the floor next to me. I looked up. "Sorry, did you need me?"

She shook her head. "Just thought I'd join you." I looked back at the murals, and she followed my gaze. "Do you miss the trees?"

"There are trees on Eos," I said.

"But you're not looking out the window," she pointed out. "You're in here."

I sighed. "Okay," I said. "You got me. I miss these trees. There was this grove, in the arboretum we used to go to, that was all elms. When the fans were blowing, the leaves turned all silver."

"We have elm seeds," she said. "Lots of them, in the dry storage. And maple, and pine, and sycamore. We could plant the sycamores by that creek that goes past here."

My heart hurt for a moment, imagining their white trunks marking out the curve of the river, their big green leaves drifting down to float down the creek like little boats. "We couldn't," I said. "Not without cutting down what's already here."

"It's natural for one kind of life to succeed another," she said. "Think of the end of the Cretaceous. The dinosaurs couldn't hack it, but we could."

"For a while," I said. "Then we destroyed the whole ecosystem, and almost ourselves too."

"Not quite," she said, with a smile. "That makes us survivors."

"We're destroyers," I said. "We all know that. Coming here and re-building was supposed to be some kind of penance, for what our ancestors did to Earth. But it's no kind of penance if we repeat the same mistakes."

She'd come to talk me around, but now that I was arguing with her, my regret was dissipating. Of course I was sad about losing our chance at an Earth forest. We should have picked a different planet, one of the boring rocky ones that had nothing to supplant. We could have planted acres and acres of forest and done no growing thing any harm.

But that wasn't the reality. We were here now, and we had to make the best of it. "I want to try living in harmony with the planet we're on," I said. "I think it's Terra's way."

"This planet won't live in harmony with *us*," she said.

She wasn't wrong. Our bodies couldn't break through the indigest-ible cell walls of a single plant out here. The aliens, of course, weren't too friendly. And there were the bugs to think of.

The damage had been done when our ancestors had let Earth die, given her up for dead and moved on. Nothing we could do now could heal it. Not staying on Proxima, not trying to recreate Earth here. We were cut off from our roots, and no matter what we tried to graft ourselves onto, that wound would remain.

"We have to try," I said. "Are you even trying? I haven't seen you in the lab."

"I have my own work space," she said stiffly.

"And your own side project, that Hawk is having you do instead of trying to solve the problem with the bugs?" I know. Sybil had told me not to say anything. But I wanted to poke just the slightest bit, to see what she would say.

She scrambled to her feet. "I'm *working* on the bugs," she hissed, so as not to shout in the chapel. "Maybe you should focus on trying to grow us something to eat." She stalked out.

Well. It was a reaction.

Turning back to the wall, I closed my eyes. Things had never been worse. At this point, what *was* there to do but pray? Terra was the goddess of coexistence, of symbiosis, of interdependence. She had to see us through.

I went to the lab after I had finished praying. It was time to do what Sybil had suggested and start defrosting things.

If I were a more practical person, I'd thaw everything: goat semen and songbird eggs and frogspawn. But I was still bargaining. I still wanted a tiny bit of hope. That maybe someday we'd understand this ecosystem well enough to know whether a few spring peepers would throw it out of balance.

Instead I resolved to do just the terraforming tools. Since there were people on this planet, there was no bargaining with that one. We needed to destroy them, and the sooner the better. I didn't trust Autumn not to try something if Hawk asked her to.

The lab freezer itself was a row of drawers in a cubby in the lab, so that we could access just one group of samples without defrosting the whole thing, "refrigerating the whole dome" as my mother used to say. At

228

least I could empty a few drawers, I figured, and shut those off.

The first drawer I opened was the phase-two drawer. An innocuous term for some really horrific things, if you didn't want to cleanse an entire planet of its native life. Plant viruses. Animal viruses, both broad-spectrum and customizable. The rest of the locusts. Defoliating agents, antimicrobials, insecticides. Even if we had kept with the original plan, we likely wouldn't have needed all of this. Though, given Eos's vibrance and adaptability, maybe we would.

I put on coldproof mitts and started removing items. The remaining locusts, I couldn't defrost properly without spending more battery power, but I set them aside. We could eat them at least. The antimicrobials I tucked into a different drawer; we couldn't yet be sure we wouldn't be infected by something here. I put the plant viruses in the autoclave.

I opened the next drawer and stopped dead. The animal viruses were gone. I checked for every ingredient Autumn would need to customize them—gone too. That answered that question. I wondered where she had set up her lab to work on them. I hadn't seen her in ours lately, even though she was supposedly working on the bug problem.

I kept working, my bottom lip between my teeth. So that was it, then. Hawk would go full-speed ahead toward genocide, and Autumn had chosen her side. I wondered how much time I would have to find and stop her before her weapons were ready to go.

31

Robin

By now, the way between the colony and the Eosian village was familiar. I tried to avoid estate boundaries, the way Mrrka would have, though I couldn't be sure I was doing it right. The razor-briar hedges were easy enough to spot, but I knew some of the trees were marked with fungi that wouldn't glow till the sun went down. And some of the boundaries would only be marked with smells, too faint for a human nose to detect.

My belly objected to all this hiking, cramping more than ever. It had been a mistake to do this the evening after the hunt; I should have left the next morning. Especially as the Eosians surely wouldn't let me sleep.

I meant to go to the common, to seek out the house where Tsaft would have settled in with Tisket, if she'd moved yet. But my feet seemed to know my way better than I did, and I landed once again at the door to Mrrka's house. Now Kisht's.

If treading across an estate boundary could start feuds, walking into Kisht's house without permission would be much worse. But if I called out, Kisht would come and answer, and I didn't want to deal with her. I slipped inside and down the stairs.

It was black as ink inside, but Mrrka's memories must be working for me because I knew, somehow, when I'd reached the last step. I knew which way to turn to reach the living room. But Mrrka's memories drew me past that. There was a room I wanted, one that felt safe, at the end of the hall.

It was like returning to my old ship's cockpit, with how familiar it all felt. Phosphorescent fungi in patterns on the walls lit it just enough to see. There was my bed—a hollow in the ground, lined with cushions and blankets, big enough for two. Chests against the wall held shawls and jewelry. But, for the moment, I passed those by and crawled into the bed.

This had been our bed, Tsaft's and mine—and Mrrka's. I could smell my wife still on the blankets, and a cozy, familiar scent I knew must be Mrrka's.

I had my own room closer toward the living room, and Tsaft had hers. This one had been *ours*. It wasn't usual for a married couple to sleep together, but that had been how much they'd loved each other, that they didn't want to be apart even for a day.

There was a sound at the door, and I sat bolt upright. Stupid, stupid, stupid! Kisht would never forgive me when she found me here, in her mother's bed.

But the door opened instead to Tsaft. She blinked. "How did you get here?"

I scrambled to my feet, picking up my bee veil from where I'd carelessly dropped it on the floor. "I'm sorry—I didn't want to bother Kisht—but I wanted—"

"I mean *how*," she repeated. "Does the Devourer not affect you?"

Three guesses what that was, and the first two don't count. I showed her my veil, and she inspected it carefully. "Your people are clever. I wonder if I have enough shawls to do the same."

I hadn't thought of that; the clothing-to-body ratio was much lower for them. With their fur, clothing was a decoration, not intended to cover.

"I came because I want to help," I said. "The bugs—the Devourer, you called it. Wouldn't Mrrka have known what to do?"

"Yes," said Tsaft, "she told me she was worried about it happening after the fire. She hoped we'd gotten it contained in time."

"But she didn't tell you what to do if it broke out?"

Tsaft ducked her head in a *no*. "She wasn't terribly worried about it. I assumed she had a solution. But she didn't say." She gave me an inquisitive look. Shouldn't I know?

"I don't remember," I said quietly. "It's so hard for me to remember, back with my people. I thought I would come here, see if I remembered better."

"Is it working?"

"I thought it was. I remember so much here. But not about that. About you, and Tisket, and Kisht. Family things." I remembered Tisket's birth. She'd been an embryo no bigger than a human's thumb, shiny and hairless like a jelly bean. I'd licked a trail up Tsaft's belly to her pouch, smoothing the way for the tiny embryo to climb inside. What a journey for a creature so small to make. Yet it was strictly forbidden to take the embryo and place it inside. That risked helping an infant to survive that was too weak to make it to adulthood. So parents did what they could to smooth the way, and they hoped. When Tisket had slipped inside, Tsaft and I had joined hands and called aloud, so joyful to have a daughter that would live.

"If you need to remember ancestral things, you need to look at Mrrka's heirlooms." Tsaft opened one of the chests. "Ah, these are just my old shawls. That's what I came looking for, you know. When Tisket brought word of the Devourer, she and I just stayed here. Half the Council is here too, because they had gathered here. You're lucky you didn't run into them instead of me."

The next chest held much richer garments, soft as silk. The colors were hard to make out in this light, but the patterns of the weaving were delicate and impressive. "These belonged to your foremothers," said Tsaft. "This one here, your fourth foremother made by hand. This one I think was a wedding present to your ninth." *My* ninth. I appreciated that she included me in Mrrka's family tree. Fesskh never had.

She left me looking over the shawls while she went through her own. I fingered the fine fabrics and tried to empty my mind. A part of my brain was wondering what they made them out of, what their looms looked like. Another part worried if Lily would go to bed all right for Aspen, how long the hexadeer leftovers would last. I steadied my breathing and just looked at the shawls, one by one. Did Mrrka do this when she wanted to remember? It felt like she did.

The memories came tickling back, one at a time. Weaving on a great floor loom, my back aching as I stood for hours, passing the shuttle from one hand to the other, while my middle legs worked the beater. There was a baby in my pouch, peeking out from time to time, but too clumsy to grab at the delicate threads. I meant to wrap her in the shawl at her naming, when she was old enough to venture all the way out. I had time.

I remembered the wedding gift. It was Fesskh's foremother who gave it to me. Both our families were pleased. A union between the Eldest's and Second Eldest's lines was a positive thing, hopefully to reduce strife between the families. But there was so much bad blood between the families that even giving the wedding present had put my intended's family in a huff.

The relationship had begun to sour as we'd each received our ancestral memories. Grudge upon grudge was handed down. We tried to see the other's point of view, but it was hard with the memories of the original quarrels vivid in our minds. In the end, she had returned to her own den and we had ceased speaking. But I felt sad, fingering the shawl. I had really loved her, and I thought, somewhere deep down, she had loved me.

The door slammed open, and a voice interrupted my reverie. Fesskh's. "Tsaft. I knew I smelled something amiss in here. How long have you been sheltering that creature in your wife's daughter's house?"

Tsaft drew herself up, laying down the shawls she was holding. "This is no courtesy to a widow. This room was mine."

"It isn't now."

"Neither is it yours, Second Eldest."

Fesskh winced. She didn't like being called Second Eldest, but for whatever reason she chose not to argue that case. "How did it get here?"

"She protected herself with shawls. Look!"

Fesskh inspected my cast-off bee veil before finally addressing me, in the tone of a superior to an inferior. "So what did you find, when you returned? Do the others of your house agree to submit and end the feud?"

"I think so…honored one," I managed. Shit, Mrrka was not up on her respectful honorifics. Been a long time since she'd needed them. "What exactly are you—is the Eldest expecting us to do?"

She tilted her head. "Leave, of course. Isn't that the cause of the feud? Your trespass? To end it, you will have to return where you came from. Back into the celestial sphere."

Shit. "We can't do that, Eldest," I said. "Our vehicle is broken."

"Fix it then."

"We can't, Eldest. It's—it's far beyond our ability." I thought of the reactor, melted to slag. No, not a chance of patching that up. The efforts of thousands, over many years, with access to all the resources of this planet, might serve to build some kind of shuttle, but an interstellar ship with an ion drive? Impossible. Not without experts we hadn't brought along. "I thought submitting to you—to the Eldest meant that we would be your servants. Like Hashta."

Fesskh snorted. "You? Being my servant is an honor, which Hashta's family earned through her foremothers' loyalty. I don't give it to people just for showing up. If I did, there are many I'd choose before you."

"So what are we to do?" I pleaded. "We'll go anywhere you want. But we have to go somewhere."

"Onto the ice, I suppose," she said. "Nobody wants the ice."

"We can't live there, Eldest." I thought back to Aspen's requirements for a landing site. "We need sunlight to grow our crops. And warmth."

She was quiet. "I am very sorry we couldn't come to an agreement," she said at last. She didn't sound sorry. "Being unable to resolve our differences with a feud, I must declare war."

War. It finally came to me, the difference between a feud and war. A feud was never deadly, or never on purpose. Originally you would fight without claws or teeth, trying to subdue your opponent without bloodshed. Later it had evolved into a kind of ritual harassment, destroying your enemy's property or humiliating them in public.

War was different. Fesskh's nation never warred among themselves, only with outsiders. And it was to the death.

I abandoned the deference. "That's a really bad idea on your part, Fesskh. You don't know how powerful we are."

"If you were so powerful, you wouldn't have submitted so readily. Look at you." She waved a scornful hand. "You're soft, toothless, clawless. Plant-eaters, beasts of prey. You knew you were no match for us."

Eyeing her claws, I resisted the impulse to take a step back. "Our weapons are much more powerful than yours," I said. "I submitted quickly because I didn't want anyone to get hurt. On either side. Don't you think Mrrka was enough?"

"Unlike you, we do not fear war," said Fesskh. "You should return to your people to tell them. The next time we meet, there will be blood."

Fesskh turned, dropped back to all six, and left the room. Apparently etiquette forbade her from killing me on the spot, but I couldn't for the life of me remember how long the truce was supposed to last after the war declaration.

"Will you leave?" asked Tsaft quietly, when Fesskh had gone.

"I can't," I said. "War will harm us both, but not as much as the Devourer will. And I am responsible for that. I have to be the one who solves it."

She put her soft, pawlike hand on mine. "And what if it can't be solved?"

"It has to be. If it isn't, we'll never survive. Not my people, and I fear not yours either."

I shut the large chest. Nothing in here was as old as the memories I needed. Cloth only lasts so long. I adjusted my position. How long had I been sitting like this? My back was killing me.

The small chest beside it looked more promising. I opened it and started looking through the jewelry. Big hoops for ears, golden necklaces, bangles in sets of six to go on each limb.

If the answer wasn't in here, I didn't know what I'd do.

32

Aspen

Ivy offered to spend the night with the kids, so that I could work late, and take them to school in the morning. I agreed because I wanted to try starting more sprouts. And besides, I'd seen Autumn go into the lab and wanted to check up on her. Surely by now she'd made some progress on the bugs. I believed in Robin—if she told me she thought those memories were there, I was sure she'd find a way to access them somehow. But we had to work on it on our end too.

When I found Autumn, she was emptying ashes out of the autoclave. "What's that?"

"Last batch of bugs I tested. I didn't want them alive and on the ship if I didn't need them anymore."

I wondered if she was lying. I had no way to guess. "So you've cracked it?"

She gave an uncertain little shrug. "I know a few things. For one, they're blind. They're not tracking our motion. But I don't think it's anything scent-related, because we shouldn't smell like any of their usual prey. And sure enough they didn't seem to follow scents."

Well, that was unfortunate. Most of the bug repellents I knew worked on scents, either masking ours or just smelling bad. "So how do they know where we are?"

"Carbon dioxide," she said. "That's why they keep tapping on the airlock screens. There's more CO_2 in here than outside. They fly toward carbon dioxide, and then they taste with their feet to see if we're something they can eat."

"We can hardly stop breathing!" I protested. "What else do you have?"

"That's it," she said simply. "That's what I know. I'll tell Hawk, and maybe he can put someone on some kind of solution."

"Me, I'm the one to put on a solution," I protested. "You should have saved some for me. I assume our insecticides won't work, but surely one of the herbicides will."

"Probably. But the ones I tested were only a day old. My guess is, the trees keep making them constantly until they sense the forest is sufficiently repopulated. And goddess knows when that will be."

She left the lab, and I stood there fuming. She should have left some of the specimens for me. I'd have to go harvest my own, which wasn't a task I especially wanted. It wasn't like her to fail to collaborate with me. But apparently I'd lost all her good will with my question in the chapel. Or else she'd guessed I knew what she was doing, and was done trying to pretend we were a team.

With a sigh, I checked the locusts' food and water. They had eaten all the leaves off a whole purple branch I'd given them, and seemed none the worse for the wear. That was something, at least my gut bacteria package was working.

Once I'd finished checking on everything—a much shorter list, now that so much was outside—I went to the closet where we stored the beekeeper suits. Time to go hunt down some specimens of my own.

Only one suit was hanging there. There should have been three, with Robin out with one. Who else was outside at this hour of the evening?

I put on the suit, grabbed a net cage, and went outside, knocking bugs off the screen before I opened it. Now that I knew what attracted them, it should be easy to catch them. Just go around to another airlock and scoop them off the screen.

Instead, I found myself pausing in the pathway. I'd heard voices. A moment later I spotted them, heading toward the gate.

I hesitated only a second. If it was Sybil or someone, I'd just say good night and go to bed. But if it was Autumn, if she was finished with her weapon and ready to deliver it—I needed to know. And with Ivy staying with the kids, I had the evening to myself.

They went out through the gate, and I waited a full minute before following. I ducked under the dead wire before looking around. There they were, making their way uphill through the burn zone. One of them carried a light that bobbed as they walked. That was good—made them easy to spot, whereas if I stayed in the shadows they'd never see me.

At the edge of the forest, they paused and consulted a map. I hung in the shadows of the tree and listened.

"There are X's here, here, and here," came Autumn's voice. "You're sure that's where Robin thinks the predators are?"

"I took the map from her room, so I don't know who else's it would be." Hawk's voice.

"She might just be crazy."

"She's certainly been out and seen something. Goddess knows what. But if it's any kind of large animal, we need to be rid of it anyway."

They walked on under the trees. Both of them carried large bags under their shoulders that clanked.

Autumn's biological agent? Could it really be ready so soon?

33

Robin

I sifted through old jewelry for hours, back aching from sitting on the floor and belly cramping because of…biological stupidity, I guessed. Hazel had told me little practice contractions were normal in the third trimester, but she hadn't told me they were this uncomfortable. Of course she also told me to handle them by not overexerting myself, which I'd definitely ignored. I wasn't used to pregnancy. Tanks were far more civilized than this mess.

Memories came thick and fast. Mrrka's family wasn't always the Eldest line; as other elders died by accident, without handing down their memories, Mrrka's line had advanced. I remembered coming to this mountainside, poor and with only a few generations of memories, and having to hunt scanty game on the common. I remembered being the one to take down an earthshaker that had killed an elder with a blow from its massive tail, and earning the right to hunt on a noble's land. She was the one who had given me the little gold shawl pin in my hand.

"It's getting cold," said Tsaft. "I'm sorry I can't light the fire for you."

I looked at her, mind slowly surfacing from centuries of memory.

Light the fire? Why would she not?

"We have been keeping the flues closed, for fear the Devourer will come down the chimney. It isn't screened."

That's when it came to me. I remembered lying on a bed—sunken, like this one, but not this one—and watching the fire. Bugs came bumbling and droning down the chimney. I was frightened, but my mother had said, "Look. They think the fire is something for them to eat."

The bugs had dived into the fire's heart, making bright yellow flares of light as they burned up.

I remembered bonfires everywhere. The bugs would swarm toward them hungrily and dive into the flames. Something about fire drew them. Fire had caused the problem, and fire destroyed them.

"Light the fire," I said to Tsaft. "We need to light every fire we can."

She got herself covered—so that was what she'd been doing all this time, stitching her shawls into a kind of robe. It didn't seem adequate, but it covered her face at least.

We went outside and started dragging branches to the fire pit out front. Around us, the bugs blundered and buzzed. Night or day, they didn't sleep. More appeared as we worked. Sure enough, they were drawn by our breath. We couldn't help that. But that would be why they came to fire. Fire, like animal life, produced carbon dioxide.

A bug landed on Tsaft, and I quickly tore it off her shawl and stomped on it. Its feet tried to cling to the fabric, but it hadn't yet gotten a good grip. "We need to hurry," I said. "I don't know if these clothes will keep them off us forever."

She went to light the fire, baring her hands for a moment to strike sparks against a stone that was part of the fire ring. I held my breath, afraid the bugs would catch her in that time. But her hands disappeared back beneath the robe unhurt.

The flames caught, slowly biting into the wood and rising toward the sky. Firelight bathed the front of Mrrka's house and the trees circling the clearing. I craned my neck till I saw them: bugs blundering toward the flames, zigzagging or swerving, but eventually plunging in and rising

244

upward like burning leaves as they flamed out.

This wouldn't be enough—I remembered fires on every estate and dotting the common. The bugs only had a short range. But as long as the fire burned, we'd be safe around it. The fire would be a bigger draw than either of us.

I sat down to watch it burn, and Tsaft sat beside me, throwing her shawls back away from her face. "It was a mistake for Mrrka not to tell anyone about this," I said after a while. "Memories are all well and good, but this was too important. It should have been a story. Or a song."

She looked at me, puzzled. "A song to teach a lesson?"

"Our people have so many songs for that. Old ones, where the purpose was lost a long time ago. There's one about why it isn't safe to hang your baby's cradle on a tree branch."

"Much safer in the pouch," Tsaft agreed.

"It seems like, instead of leaving all the wisdom with Mrrka, you could have had something easy to remember that you just told everyone. If everyone knew, every generation, it wouldn't be so easily forgotten."

"A story couldn't hope to compete with a memory," Tsaft said.

"No," I said. "I used to be a little jealous of you people. I have these memories, but I can't give them to my children. I wish I could be sure they would know how much I love them. That someday, they could understand how I feel about them now."

I swallowed hard. I'd told Lily I loved her a thousand times. I'd tried to show it. But it was so hard to know if she felt it. I wished I could touch my hands to her face and send a memory of how it felt to love her this much. I wondered what Kisht would feel toward her mother now if she could know just how much love her mother had felt for her. How hard she'd tried to listen.

"I never had any memories," she said. "But I know my mother loved me."

I found myself smiling. Thinking of my dad.

"My father was in love with the stars," I said. "Always running off into them any chance he could. But I knew he loved me too."

"Do not worry about your daughters." She freed one hand from her robe and laid it on top of mine. "They know. They can always tell."

I clasped her hand for a moment. I wanted to stay here, snuggle into her fur, maybe nap. But, now that my main mission had been completed, I needed to get back. "Can you spread the word to everyone else here? I need to tell my people to start fires of their own. We need one on every estate, some on the common, anywhere people or animals might be."

She rose to her feet and moved toward the house. "It is odd that no one has challenged us," she commented. "Since I got here, I haven't been able to move around the house without Fesskh or Kisht bothering me."

I didn't answer. Standing up had given me a cramp so bad I could barely move. My breath tightened in my chest. Here I'd been traipsing all over creation, assuming my body would keep being the functional instrument it had always been. What if it wasn't?

Dampness trickled down my leg, and that's when the panic really hit. "Tsaft ...?" I called, my voice quavering.

She came back over to me in an instant. "Yes, Hrobin. What is it? Does the Devourer have you?"

"I think my pouchling is ready to come out!"

34

Aspen

Autumn and Hawk hiked some distance further, periodically consulting their map. I tried to keep some sense of direction, but tailing people in the dark like this didn't make it easy.

There was no sign of any habitation. Robin had told me the Eosians lived underground, but that made it impossible to say how close we might be. We could be walking right over one of their dens for all I knew.

We seemed to have reached one of the spots marked, because Autumn knelt down and opened her bag. She took out a metal cylinder and propped it upright. Just a gas canister; that could be anything. Poison, a viral agent…had she managed to customize one so fast?

"I got this carbon dioxide from the emergency scrubber," said Autumn. "I guess it just stores it, in case we need it for the hydroponics later. But we never did, so it's perfect for this."

"And the bugs will be drawn to it?" asked Hawk.

"That's the idea. The more CO_2 they have in their area, hopefully, the more bugs will go over here instead of toward us. And that means any animals in the area will be their preferred meal."

They moved on, opening canisters here and there. It didn't seem the most efficient route. Carbon dioxide was easy to make, and the canisters didn't hold all that much. Would it really do much more than just breathing?

But it seemed to. Bugs kept landing on me, and I knocked them off with my glove. Then they'd blunder over by the canisters, landing on them and then taking off again, disappointed, only to try to land on them again a minute later. They weren't very bright, just little carbon-dioxide-seeking, eating machines.

If Robin was right, this wouldn't do the Eosians much harm. They lived underground, and they surely had discovered the bugs on their own. They'd be sitting tight indoors, like we were.

Their prey, however, had no such protection. They didn't shut their animals up in barns like our goats. This would be a major depopulation event for all prey animals, which would result in starvation for creatures higher up the food chain. Like the Eosians.

I had to put a stop to this somehow, but there were two of them and one of me. My best chance, I decided, was to keep careful track of where they left each cylinder and then go back after to collect them all. That was easier said than done in the darkness like this.

As they walked on, my feet landed on something I hadn't seen before on this planet. Paving stones. Autumn noticed also. "Hawk? This doesn't look like anything an animal could have done." Her voice held a note of alarm.

"I suppose you think it's equivalent to finding a whole city here."

"No," she protested, "but it's a sign of intelligent life. There's a whole circle of paving stones here. Here in the middle, this circle could be a fire pit."

"Who knows how long ago that was made."

"There are ashes in it. This thing has been used this season, at least."

Hawk was silent for a moment. Then he spoke, harsh and forceful. "You've just got to ask yourself, Autumn. Are we obeying the goddess, or not? Are we going to build a home for her here, or should we just lie down and die? Because our lives are worth nothing if she's not with us, if we're not carrying out her will."

"Of course I'm not saying that!" she protested. "It's just very different what you're asking of me, if the creatures have some kind of rudimentary intelligence. The laws back on Proxima—"

"We're not on Proxima. They'll know whatever we tell them. But our faith leads us, not their laws."

"Does our faith really demand this?" Her voice was small, worried.

"Sermon 43. 'We will bring Earth life to the farthest reaches of the galaxy, if Terra wills it. Those plants and animals that were the most fit on Earth will be the most fit everywhere. They will outcompete any other life we discover. We shouldn't mourn the dinosaurs, they died because they had less of the spirit of Terra in them. The spirit of Terra is survival.'"

I didn't remember Sybil ever saying anything of the sort. But that hardly mattered. Nobody remembered every detail of what she'd said, even herself. So Hawk could pretty easily include anything he wanted in his printed scriptures, and nobody was likely to call him on it. Especially Sybil, who had never taken any interest in the book.

"I suppose," said Autumn at last.

"I understand that it's hard," Hawk said, in a gentler voice. "Nothing of this mission has been easy. But we do it for Her. I know we'll be rewarded."

She bowed her head and moved away from him, her steps heavy. She took out another canister, set it on the fire circle, and opened the valve.

"It isn't enough, doing it this way," said Hawk. He stepped forward, shining his light on a door that stood behind the fire circle. Autumn gasped—she hadn't seen it till now, any more than I had.

This, I had to stop now. It would do no good to come back an hour later. I wanted to believe there was no one down there. But in my mind I could only imagine the Eosians being like us, huddled inside their homes for fear of the bugs.

Hawk opened the door before turning around to get another canister. Autumn stood there, wringing her hands and stammering. I didn't think she'd get involved.

I exploded toward Hawk out of the darkness. I wasn't much of a fighter, but surely with the element of surprise I could bowl him over before he got to the canister. My fists came up, ready to punch.

He went for his stunner before I was halfway across the pavement. The bolt of light hit me square in the chest.

The bee suit must have provided some protection, because it didn't knock me out. But my muscles locked up, twitching, and I fell hard to the ground.

"What are you doing?" hissed Autumn. "That was Aspen!"

"Trying to stop us. You know Robin's gotten to him. He can't really be counted on anymore."

He pocketed the stunner again and picked up a canister. Opening the valve, he pitched it into the dark doorway. There was a loud clatter, as the metal cylinder bounced down stairs within.

Some of the bugs around the clearing, disappointed time and again with the cylinder on the fire circle, headed toward the open doorway.

I held my breath.

From inside came a strange cry, then a bug's deafening rattle. Calling all its brethren to come and eat. After that, screaming.

Hawk pulled at Autumn's arm. "We have to go."

She yanked her arm away from his. "No! You didn't tell me you were going to do that. It's inhumane."

"We can discuss it later, if you're having scruples about it. I can pray with you. But we need to get out of here, before—"

A dark shape loomed in the doorway. Hawk pulled out his stunner, aiming straight for the middle of the shadow. But the bolt of light only scattered and sparkled in the creature's translucent fur—making the shape of it visible for the first time. A majestic, but terrifying being. Even more so now that it was glittering with light, the light of the only kind of weapon we had.

Hawk darted away, leaving Autumn on her own facing the creature.

Reared up on its hind legs, it was at least eight feet tall. The sparkles in its fur fizzled out, and still it did not falter or fall. It spoke incomprehensibly for a moment.

Autumn, rooted to the spot, started to cry. "I'm sorry! I'm sorry! We didn't know—we didn't mean—"

The Eosian struck out with one paw. A careless, quick gesture, like a punch thrown across a bar. But its claws were deadly. Autumn dropped to the ground.

Behind the Eosian, the bugs came buzzing out in a cloud, fat and ready to plant themselves. The Eosian stood still for a moment. Robin might have been able to guess what it felt. Grief? Anger? Who had the bugs fed on? But at last it turned, went back inside its den, and shut the door.

I lay paralyzed for some minutes longer, struggling to regain control over my arms and legs. As soon as I could move, I crawled to Autumn's side. The Eosian's claws had gone deep; blood pulsed out of her with her heartbeat. I pressed my hand to her side, but I knew it was hopeless. Not without an actual doctor here, and a blood transfusion.

Autumn grasped my arm. "I hope the goddess…understands…I was only trying…to do her will," she rasped out.

"I know she does," I whispered. "I know she does."

But Autumn was gone.

35

Robin

Tsaft whisked me into her arms and down the stairs inside, closing the door carefully behind. The house was abandoned; no sign of Fesskh or the others. I wondered where they had gone.

Tsaft set me in her bed and stood anxiously nearby. "I don't know how this works for your people. For us, it's—"

"A hell of a lot easier, I know," I said acidly. Then translated, because I'd accidentally spoken in English. Mrrka wasn't a big cusser, and I was. Some things didn't translate.

"How can I help you?"

I shook my head slowly. My plan had been to have Hazel dope me to the gills and just—handle all that biological nonsense. Aspen would be there to make soothing noises, and I wasn't going to have to do anything but show up.

It was bad enough to have to have a body birth at all. I understood that the goats needed the incubators, and I'd been game to try the natural way since it seemed to be the in thing with the Greenies. They talked about it like it was some profound, spiritual experience of oneness with the universe. But I'd seen at least one video. It looked a lot more like some kind of torture session, with body horror thrown in for dessert.

Tsaft clearly couldn't do much for me, and the best I could think of was simply hope my instincts would guide me right. I had some experience by now in sitting back and letting my hindbrain come up with the ideas. Maybe that would work this time.

"I can't go and spread the news about the fires," I said, after another cramp—I mean, a contraction—had let up. "This could take all night. You need to go and tell everyone."

"Will you be safe here alone?"

"Unless Fesskh comes and murders me." Tsaft stared at me, and I grinned. My sense of humor just didn't translate. "I will be safe. Please go."

It was the last thing I actually wanted. I was terrified, and Tsaft was familiar and warm and soft. If I had to have a birth coach who'd never seen a human give birth before, she'd be the one I'd pick. But getting rid of the bugs was more vital. Even without telling the colony about the need for fires, just spreading the word among the Eosians would help reduce the population.

Tsaft gave me a last, skeptical look and went out. I twisted my hands in the bedding and cried. Cried because I didn't want her to go. Cried because I wanted Aspen. Cried because the pain was building again and I didn't know how many times I was going to have to endure it.

Please, baby, be easy on your mama.

Aspen

I stumbled back toward the colony with tears streaming down my cheeks. Autumn had been my friend for years, my closest colleague. The only one who really understood how I felt about my work, because she was exactly the same.

I didn't blame her in the slightest. I knew Hawk's game, I was wise to it now. Faith lives so deeply in a heart, if you can grasp at it and use it as a lever, you can make a person do almost anything.

In another universe, I might have been exactly as vulnerable. If I wasn't, it wasn't because I had a deeper or better faith. It was only because—well, probably because I had Robin to steady me, to ask the questions I might not have otherwise wanted to ask. I still believed, but my faith was in the goddess, not Hawk or even Sybil. Only my heart could tell me what the goddess did or didn't want. If I'd been better at listening, I wouldn't have needed Sybil to tell me the goddess didn't want us to terraform the planet. I had felt it in my heart long before.

When I reached the edge of the forest, I stopped, doing my best to blink the tears from my eyes without taking off the bee veil. The darkness of night was already fading to gray, and I could see the shapes of the burned, tumbled trees in the burn scar.

It was a wound, a wound in a complex organism we'd never taken the time to understand. My focus in botany was always on larger systems: forests, mycelial networks, symbiotic organisms. Like the scrubber lichen, half algae, half fungi. Under a microscope, the lichen was an entire city, different organisms supplying different needs.

Eos was the same in larger scale. The trees feeding the herbivores and the herbivores feeding the Eosians, and, according to Robin, the Eosians planting the trees. All reliant on one another.

The forest would devour the animals to feed itself. It had to, in the long term; the animals couldn't survive without it, so a short-term sacrifice was necessary. As long as a few animals survived, the forest would be fine. But since some of the animals were intelligent beings, it wasn't a wonder of nature. It was a horrific disaster, a loss of unrepeatable souls.

Hawk couldn't grasp any of this, if he was willing to turn nature against people in this way. He had never understood the heart of our faith, which was interdependency, the respect for all life.

But, if he had been able to confuse Autumn, he'd likely be able to do the same to anyone. He'd keep escalating his "terraforming effort" into full-scale war.

I had to stop him.

36

Robin

The birthing videos Hazel had made me watch were of calm, serene women in bathtubs or gardens, breathing their way through contractions as their bodies opened like flowers or unfurling leaves or some hippie shit like that.

This … was not like that.

I couldn't lie down. I paced, I leaned on things, I crawled around on all fours like a cat. I found a pitcher in the next room and drank the whole thing down. Then a while later I puked it all back up. Kisht was gonna kill me for trashing her new place.

The house was, as far as I could tell, empty now, so after a while I gave up trying to be quiet. There was a lot of screaming. Between contractions I cried. The word "fuck" was the closest I had to a mantra, but I swear it helped.

At some point, about seven thousand eternities in, I heard a change in the noises I was making. Mid scream, the pitch dropped an entire octave, from "shrieking harpy" to "whale noise."

That, I remembered from the video. "Shit," I said. "Shit fuck fucking balls. *No.*"

The noise meant I was starting to push. I knew I wasn't supposed to do that now. I was alone. I didn't want to give birth alone. Plus, how was I supposed to know it was time to push without Hazel there to tell me so? In the videos the doctors always told them when to push. I shut the noises off and focused on panting.

I knelt there for god knew how long, elbows resting on Mrrka's scarf chest, damp forehead pillowed on my arms. I wanted to push more than I had ever wanted anything in my life. But I dreaded it enough to keep holding back.

I drifted, time counted only by waves of pain, each one a small infinity while it lasted. I wasn't me anymore, nor Mrrka. I was no one. I was everyone. I was a long line of mothers, marching back into the past, each one of them here, giving birth, hoping the little pouchling would make it this time.

There was a sound at the door, and I looked up hopefully. Somehow a part of me believed Aspen might stride into the room, take my hand in his, and make this whole nightmare not be happening. Or Hazel, somehow transported from the colony with my epidural in her hand.

But it was Tsaft, and that was enough. I burst into tears of relief, just to have someone else there.

"Are you all right?" she asked, bustling into the room. Don't ask me how a hexapod bustles; they manage.

I shook my head, but she didn't know human gestures and I didn't have the energy to explain, so after a second I croaked, "Yes."

"Where is the pouchling? Did it ...?" She fell silent. A lot of theirs don't make it into the pouch. I remembered that now. Remembered that three of Tsaft's had failed before Tisket. They're just so tiny when they're born, like little gummy bears. It's an iffy business, climbing those few inches, when you're a gummy bear.

"It's still in there," I said. "It takes a while—mmmm." Another contraction was building. "Come here, Tsaft. Just be here."

She came close, supporting me with one arm while I got a death

258

grip on the other. I hummed out whale noises, my self-control completely gone. That baby was coming, whether I pushed or not.

There was a terrible stretching pain, a brief pause, and then I was reaching down to catch a slithery little thing. I sat back, holding it in my hands. A baby. My god. I had somehow produced a baby.

I blinked at it for a moment, completely befuddled. Somehow in all the screaming and cussing, I had put the end goal out of my mind. But here it was. Squirming and fussing and screwing up its face like it didn't much like being here.

I looked it over. Two arms. Two legs. Swollen little testicles. "It's a boy," I said wonderingly, in English.

Tsaft tilted her head curiously. That was one announcement that wouldn't translate. That didn't really matter. "She's healthy," I said instead. "She's supposed to look like that."

"She looks better than one of ours," she said, with a note of humor in her voice. "May I give her a memory?"

I furrowed my brow a minute, trying to remember. Normally, mothers gave their daughters memories later in life, when they were growing old. But there was another time a memory might be given by anyone—early in life, when a child was peeking out of the pouch, or venturing out on its own. The mother, or father, or any caregiver really, might give a little pleasant memory to the baby, whenever it was fussy. A memory of peace, or a good meal, or just waking up from a cozy nap.

"Sure," I said, holding out the baby to her. She didn't take him, but put her hands on his face. The tendrils brushed over him for only a moment before she took her hands away.

He wasn't fussing anymore. His face screwed up in a different shape, almost a smile. Of course a reasonable adult would call that gas. But he sure looked happy to me.

I tucked him back against my body. "I guess that makes you his godmother." I said the word in English; it didn't really matter if she understood it. Now we needed a nature name, all the Greenies had nature names. It was lucky our family had already had them—nature names were popular on Proxima anyway. But I didn't want to name him after an Earth plant or animal. No, his home was here. The first human baby ever born on Eos. "I'll name him Lightleaper."

A little later, when Tsaft had rustled up a pair of ornate silver scissors for the cord (a baffling request from her perspective; she was afraid to cut it and made me do it myself) and tucked me into bed, I finally asked her what was going on outside.

"There is a fire now before every dwelling," she said. "It has done enough that people are going out with heads uncovered, and coming to no harm. But I told them to still be careful."

"They should be," I said. "The trees will keep making more until there are enough saplings filling in the burn scar." I told her about climbing the trees, harvesting unripe seedpods, carefully feeding them on captured brushcreepers, and loosing the fattened bugs in places that needed to be filled in. It was tedious work, but it would put the Devourer to bed till the next time.

"And…" she said slowly. "Fesskh's daughter has been killed. Tessth. That Kisht had wanted to marry."

"By the Devourer?"

"Kisht was there, she says your people were responsible. That they opened the door and drove the Devourer inside. I don't know whether to credit it—"

"I believe it," I said heavily. "My people are desperate. And I wasn't there to stop them." I felt a crushing weight in my chest. More guilt. How I could have prevented being stuck out here, how I could even have helped if I'd been there, I didn't know. But that didn't make me not, somehow, responsible.

"I did not see Fesskh at all," she said. "I went to every dwelling in the area, and all over the common. If Kisht knew where she is, she did not say."

I grimaced. I wanted to get right out of this bed right this minute and go find out. But I was also absolutely exhausted. The adrenaline from the birth had left me, Lightleaper had fallen asleep, and now I just wanted to lie here and sleep too.

"I will go and find out," she said. "Stay here and rest."

37

Aspen

When I finally stumbled back to the ship on tingling feet, everything was quiet. For a moment I thought it might be too early for anyone to be up, but our family's room was empty too. I went to the school to check on the kids, and to thank Ivy for taking care of the kids overnight. I owed her the mother of all favors for that.

In the school entryway, though, I saw only Pine. "Hey, I just wanted to check on my kids," I said, as I passed by her to get to the classrooms beyond.

"You can't do that," she said quietly.

I turned, puzzled, with my hand on the knob. "Why not?"

"Hawk doesn't think you're a very good influence," she said. "He feels Colt and Lily would be better under the care of a more devoted disciple for a little while."

It took a second for her words to sink in. I felt cold and then hot. So that was what we did now? Split up families? I turned my back on her to open the door, but it was locked. "Devoted disciple?" I demanded, my voice rising. "You know I'm as faithful as anyone."

"You've disobeyed Hawk's direct orders more than once," she pointed out. "Obedience is one of the most important virtues."

Now that I knew didn't come from Sybil. I didn't have the complete list of Terrestrial Virtues memorized, but they were things like interdependence, creativity, and the will to survive. You don't see obedience in nature, not the way humans do it.

"My children belong to *me*," I said, hating the way it sounded. They weren't a package. But they sure as heck didn't belong to Pine either. "I'm not letting you do this."

Flint's massive frame filled the outer doorway. The man would have been an excellent henchman in a 20th-century mob movie; he was all corded muscles. "Everything okay in here?" he asked.

"Aspen here was having a little trouble keeping his cool," said Pine. "Can you go with him and help him walk it off?"

I went with Flint unwillingly. Pine would have had him waiting nearby, knowing as soon as I arrived I'd blow a gasket. But there was no point in fighting him, even if I could have won. That wouldn't unlock the door.

With a little deep breathing, I managed to convince Flint I was calm by the time I got to the lab. "I just need to get back to work," I said. "We're going to need more seedlings to plant as soon as it rains again."

He went out, and I was left to ponder my options. Hawk was calling the shots at school, which might mean nothing. Pine was one of his most loyal followers. But he was also getting Flint to carry water for him. I had thought Flint was staying out of the conflict. Ivy, too—was she in on it? Had she been the one to let Hawk into our room to search Robin's papers? Had she handed over the kids knowing they were going to be kept from me?

I needed to find out where Sybil was. And, for that matter, where everyone was. What was Hawk planning next. He already knew where the Eosians were and was willing to kill. What he had done tonight wasn't much, compared to what I knew he could. I wondered if Autumn had finished customizing that virus before she died. I hoped not. The only other person here who could do it was me, and I knew I wouldn't.

Once Flint was out of sight, I went back down the ladder to the main level and started wandering around. The halls were empty. The cafeteria too, but there were leftovers in a covered dish as always. I served myself a plate. It was a featureless scrambled mass, heavily spiked with various seasonings we weren't yet out of. Locusts, I was pretty sure. I tried not to think about it as I choked it down.

I checked the different reading rooms and work rooms. Nothing there, but I heard voices from the chapel. I came near the door and listened.

"They killed Autumn," Hawk was saying. "The question of intelligence is irrelevant now that they've chosen to attack us. If you're right, Cliff, and Robin told us the truth…"

(*Good on you, Cliff,* I thought.)

"…then we're up against a species that's intelligent, but not civilized and highly malevolent. I wish we could coexist with them, as Sybil wanted."

(*No you don't,* I thought.)

"But they've clearly refused that option. We don't have the luxury of waiting longer while they come for us. If they destroy anything else of ours, we'll starve."

I moved away from the door. On that last point, he wasn't wrong. I fully expected an attack from them by tonight, if not sooner. I wondered where Robin was, what she was doing. Was she working to hold them back from attacking us? If I tried to do the same here, would I help make peace, or just make us vulnerable when they did attack?

How did I know she was even still alive?

My head was spinning. My eyes burned with exhaustion, but I doubted I could sleep if I tried. I decided to look for Sybil. She would know what to do. Or, if she didn't, she'd at least be an ally.

Her room door was shut, and I knocked. "I'm here," came her familiar voice, and my heartrate slowed a fraction. She was alive. I hadn't put into words my fear she might not be. "But the door is locked," she added.

I tried it from the outside. No good. We didn't even have proper locks on the bedroom doors, which meant Hawk had jury-rigged something, or found someone else who knew how to.

Robin could have fixed it in five minutes. I wasn't so skilled, but I knew where the nearest toolkit was. It took me a while to get the door panel apart, and then pick at things until something gave way and let me shove the door open.

Sybil stood in the doorway, her long hair loose, in her green dress. "It was locked when I tried to come out this morning," she said. "Did something happen?"

I told her what I'd seen out in the forest, and what Hawk was telling the people now. "You need to get out here," I said. "You need to get your people back from him."

"I don't know if I can," she said. "I've been trying since I got back. They like me better than Hawk, but they like his message better than mine. They feel I've betrayed them, first by being sick after the landing, and second by changing the message. They were comfortable in what they already knew about the goddess. They didn't want to learn a new thing. And then you get them scared like this, locked inside the ship, eating bugs for breakfast—they will always listen to the person who's giving them a way out."

"But he doesn't *have* a way out," I said. "He's going to get us all killed at this rate. Autumn figured out how the bugs are finding us, and instead of using that to save us all, he used it to target the aliens. Our best chance of survival is still with you."

She nodded slowly. "I'll do what I can."

"We need to think of who we have the best chances with," I said. "Gather the people who have been more on your side, like Cliff and Hazel."

Whatever had been going on in the chapel had long ended. We found Cliff on the engine level, in the workshop he liked to potter around in.

Sybil had apparently had something to say prepared, but when she spotted the large object on the workbench, she shut her mouth and paused. "What is *that*?"

It looked like a giant firework, or maybe a very small orbital rocket. Cliff sighed. "I'm sorry, Sybil. I know it's not your way. But Hawk has a point. The aliens already killed Autumn. The ship has sailed on making peace, I think."

She blinked. "It's a weapon, then."

"It's a delivery vehicle for one," he said. "Hawk says Autumn only prepared a tiny bit of whatever it was she made. The only way to disperse it far enough to do any good is from the air. So." He gestured to the rocket, which was about as long as his arm. "This should go up, explode, and shower down whatever biological nastiness she came up with. I'm sorry," he repeated, "it's not like I want to."

Sybil's eyes snapped. "Feeling bad about it doesn't actually change anything."

I broke in, "Hawk lied. The creature killed Autumn because he attacked it first." That did give Cliff pause, and I filled him in with everything I knew.

When I had finished, Cliff gave a heavy sigh, leaning forward so he could rest his elbows on the workbench. "Does that really make a difference, though? So we struck the first blow. Arguably I did that myself, with that damn wire trap. We're in too far to back out now. We don't even know how to say sorry to these creatures."

"Robin can—"

His dark eyes fixed mine. "Do you really believe she's still coming back?"

My heart raced. I didn't want to think about it. Didn't want to imagine what it might have done to her little outing to have Hawk starting a war while she was with the aliens. Didn't want to imagine it had maybe been her down there, in the dark, when the CO_2 canister had gone bouncing down the stairs.

"Yes," I said evenly, because it was the only option other than collapsing on the floor crying. If I believed it hard enough, I didn't have to think about any of those possibilities. And I trusted her—God, how I trusted her. She'd come back to me a thousand times. She could do it again. "We just have to hold Hawk back from doing anything stupid. Buy her a little time."

❦

Cliff didn't know for sure where Autumn's secret lab was, but he thought it was near the kitchen, in one of the bunkrooms across the hall. That narrowed it down a lot; I knew most of the families that lived there.

Sybil and Cliff had gone to find others they could convince, anybody who might take a stand against Hawk. Which left me to go find Autumn's work and destroy it.

If I was honest with myself, I knew Autumn had been a little bit right. We did need weapons. If the Eosians chose to attack us, we would need to defend ourselves. And the options were slim on the ground.

But biological horrors like this one were a bridge too far. I didn't know what, exactly, she'd chosen, but the different things we had available were all the same. Quick-acting, contagious, and universally fatal. It would be tagged to Eosian genetic markers, which would leave us safe, but every single Eosian exposed to it would die horribly. Whether they'd attacked us or not.

It was overkill. We needed some kind of defensive weapon that wasn't, if we wanted to live. But first I had to take this option off the table, permanently. If I didn't, I knew Hawk would find a way to release it. He was a man with a mission, and that mission was destroying every speck of life on this planet that wasn't us.

I had promised Robin I wouldn't let that happen, and I meant it. Even Autumn, I thought, would understand me destroying her work. She'd been shattered enough when she had learned the Eosians were intelligent. Had she been thinking about what she'd created, back in her lab? Well. I would take care of all that for her.

I tried the first possible door. Empty, except for bunks and some scattered clothes. The next one, someone was napping within—I quickly shut the door. The third one was locked. Luckily, I'd just learned how to take those apart. I had the door panel off and the catch disengaged in under a minute.

Inside, Autumn's assistant, Willow, was pipetting something into a number of dishes. She looked up at me with wild, guilty eyes. "You shouldn't be in here!" she blurted. "Does Hawk know—"

I stepped inside and shut the door behind me. "Willow, I know what this is," I said, as gently as I could. "Hawk wanted you to finish Autumn's project. The bioweapon."

"It practically is finished," she said, a note of pride in her voice. "All I have to do is scale it up. The bigger the batch we have, the quicker we can finish them off."

For a moment I paused, debating with myself whether to try to talk her out of what she was doing. But she'd been clearly in Hawk's camp for some time now. I couldn't take the risk. "I can finish this up," I offered instead. "I've done more with this microbiology stuff than you have."

"It's really okay," she said. "This part isn't hard. I'm just inoculating the cultured tissue to increase the batch."

I shoved in next to her at the counter. "Really," I said, pulling some of the petri dishes toward me. "I want to help."

Funny how your conscience can feel conflicted over the idea of releasing a genocidal bioweapon, but what really makes you feel guilty is ignoring someone's polite no and shoving your big burly shoulders into their space. Willow was a slight woman, with arms like twigs. I could just overpower her, grab the stuff, and throw it in the autoclave. Yet even crowding her like this made me feel like the world's biggest heel.

"No," she said firmly, reaching for the dishes I'd taken. "Flint!"

I hadn't noticed before, but this room was one of a suite. The door to the connecting room was against the opposite wall, and it opened almost immediately. "You!" he cried. The man was everywhere today. Or, I corrected myself, everywhere Hawk thought I might turn up. "I should have locked you in your room too."

I moved fast, grabbing every dish I could reach and throwing them in the autoclave. I twisted the dial, which automatically locked the machine. It couldn't open till the cycle had finished, for safety reasons.

But, as Flint's huge hand closed around my upper arm, I saw I hadn't gotten them all. The main beaker, from which Willow had been inoculating the rest, was still on the far side of her left elbow.

I'd failed.

There was a small crowd by the airlock when Flint dragged me there. As we got close, I could see why. Sybil was there already, her arm firmly gripped by Hazel. I stared. I too would have thought Hazel would have been a safe choice. She had stayed on the sidelines of the schism, more worried about providing medical care for everyone than being loyal to anyone in particular. But apparently she'd finally made up her mind, and the wrong way.

Hawk stood beside the airlock, mid-speech. "You've chosen the aliens instead of us," he was pronouncing. "There is a demon of this planet that you've chosen over Terra. She's bewitched you and turned you against the true faith."

In the crowd, I saw faces I knew, cold and hard. I wanted to believe this was only Hawk's doing, but I saw the heads nodding. Did no one understand anything about Terra, about any of it? This wasn't a medieval play of gods and devils, good-guy/bad-guy team sports! Terra was life, was biodiversity, was the pushing of leaves through soil and the fixing of nitrogen into the earth.

Hawk had twisted the faith into an unrecognizable shape in order to get his way, and what was worse, everyone was falling for it. Maybe Sybil had been right. Everyone was far too afraid to be reasonable. In their state of mind, the puppet show of gods and devils made more sense than my theology, or Sybil's.

But I couldn't get absorbed in the theological side of it. This was deadly practical. They could only have brought us to the airlock for one reason. They meant to put us out. I wasn't sure how many minutes we could survive out there, with the bugs flying.

"Does anyone," Hawk asked, "think we should forgive them? Give them another chance?"

Cliff, who had just attached himself to the outskirts of the crowd, opened his mouth as if to speak. But Sybil pinned him with a look and shook her head slightly. Speaking up wouldn't help us at this point, only hurt them.

I hoped that was why nobody else spoke out, either.

Hawk was still speaking, all vague sentiments and religious platitudes without meaning. I stared out the airlock, trying to make a plan. It was CO_2 that brought the bugs. How long could we hold our breath? How far could we run in that time?

At last Hawk decided he'd said enough, and we were shoved into the airlock. The inner door rolled shut, leaving us in the narrow gap before the plastic screen. Along the screen, bugs buzzed and bumbled. We could stay here, I supposed, at least until we got thirsty or Hawk came up with a way to drive us out. But I had my eye on the barn. It would be a better refuge, if we could get there.

I rapped on the screen with my hand, making the blundering insects fall to the ground. "Get ready to run," I said. "When I knock the screen out, hold your breath and run for the barn."

She didn't argue, instead sucking deep breaths in and out to prepare. I wasn't sure if she agreed with my assessment or simply was happy to leave the practical things to me.

After one last deep breath, I kicked the screen out and started to run. Sybil followed hot on my heels. Around us, the bugs wheeled and swirled, searching for something but not finding it. Some whizzed past us, smelling something promising in the airlock we'd just left.

We were halfway there. My lungs burned, but it was all right. We would make it.

Suddenly there was a thump behind me, and I turned halfway

around. Sybil had tripped, landing headlong and knocking her breath out. She panted hard, redfaced and completely out of breath.

I turned and came back, holding out my hand. "Go on," she wheezed. "They're coming."

The bugs were certainly coming. They circled closer and closer, tasting us in the air, homing in on our direction.

My breath exploded out of my mouth. Reaching down, I grabbed her arm and yanked her to her feet. We ran together, breathing hard, beating bugs away from us till we reached the barn. The second we got inside, I slammed the door behind us, searching for any stray bugs that might have gotten in.

For a second we both stood there, gasping. My heart was going a million miles an hour. We could have both died.

"Thank the goddess," Sybil gasped after a moment. "I thought it was my time to go."

"Not for a long time yet, I hope." It was a stupid, thoughtless thing to say. Here we were in a barn, with murderous bugs outside, no food to eat in the colony, and hostile aliens close at hand. If either of us lived a long time, it would be a miracle.

"I failed," she said after a moment. "I thought I could get people to listen to me. People like Hazel—I thought I stood a chance at getting through."

"You were right. They're too afraid to think clearly."

She looked at me appraisingly for a moment. "But you aren't. How do you keep the faith?"

I pondered that for a moment. I didn't think I had more faith than anyone else. Surely not more than Autumn or Cliff or Flint. "I have Robin," I said at last. "I trust everything she's told us. And she's not a peaceful person. If she says peace is possible with the aliens, I know it is."

There was nothing to do inside the barn but pet the goats and maybe try to nap. Bugs tapped periodically against the shutters, as if to remind us how stuck we were. We took turns peering out through the cracks in the shutters at the ship, to see if anyone was looking out the windows at us.

They weren't.

The sun went down, and it started to get dark. A light rain started, and my spirits lifted a little. Once it picked up a bit, the bugs wouldn't be able to fly and we could make a try for the ship. Or maybe somewhere else. I could even go looking for Robin again. Probably a stupid thought. If all was going well, she would be able to come back here whenever she wanted. She must not be finished. And if all was going badly—I cut that thought off. I refused to believe she wasn't all right. My mind couldn't handle it.

Suddenly Sybil gasped, abandoning the crack she was looking through for a different one on the far side. "It's them!" Her voice hit halfway between excitement and fear.

I joined her, peering through. At first I wasn't sure what I was seeing. It was like mercury, pouring over the stockade, a vague blur spreading over the dark wood.

Then it resolved into separate shapes, dozens of them. They slipped over the fence like lizards scuttling down a wall, utterly unfazed by the barrier. I felt suddenly very foolish. Here we'd spent all that effort building the fence, and it meant nothing to them. I had imagined them carefully struggling over the fence to come vandalize our things. Nope. It had been a walk in the park for them the whole time.

I moved back to look at the ship again. Did they see this? If they had any sense, they'd close and lock the doors. They couldn't in a million years outfight the Eosians, but they could wait them out. Then again, with neither the bioscrubber nor the backup scrubber functional, they couldn't do that for more than a day or so.

But they weren't taking that approach anyway. They came pouring out of the ship, colonists holding kitchen knives and brooms and anything else they could find. I scanned the faces for Pine or Ivy or any of the other teachers, but didn't see them. Good. Someone was still inside with the children. Hopefully a lot of people.

My stomach clenched, thinking about the kids, huddled inside the ship. I had no sympathy for Hawk. If the Eosians killed him, he'd deserve it. But it wasn't like the Eosians knew which of us had set the cicadas on them. I wasn't even sure they cared.

Was it too late for peace? If so, I should probably get out there with the others. I had the pitchfork at least. I eyed the closest Eosian. It was half again as tall as I was, but if it kept its heart in the expected place, I might be able to take it down.

If it weren't holding a spear with a curved, scythelike blade. But for the kids, I'd have to try.

The lead Eosian stepped forward and began to speak. Its words were just a snarl to me, consonants clashing. Hawk shook his head and spread his hands. I chewed on the inside of my cheek. For all I knew they were proposing a deal for peace. Or telling us what had happened to Robin. Or declaring us vanquished. If we had only known they were here, we could have brought some kind of translator, or an anthropologist.

Stupid thought. If we had known they were here, we'd never have come.

The lead Eosian switched to gestures. A broad sweep of a paw to the people, the colony, the ship. And then a stabbing gesture upwards. Impossible to misinterpret: *all of you, go back where you came from.*

Hawk stood firm, shaking his head. He gestured at the colonists beside him and then pointed straight down at the ground. *We're staying right here.*

The Eosian shook its—*her* spear, stepping forward. The two ragged lines of combatants were only yards apart.

Hawk turned half around, gestured to someone behind him. Flint came running forward with Cliff's rocket. A clear cylinder graced the top. So they had been able to finish it all off after all, without Cliff's help. There wouldn't be much in the cylinder, after all I'd destroyed, but the stuff was contagious. As long as they exposed some of the Eosians, it would get them all in the end. Whether or not any humans lived that long.

"That's Autumn's bioweapon," I said, pointing. "Like I told you."

Sybil didn't answer. For one second, she stared in front of her, her mouth a hard line of resolve. Then she threw open the door and charged out of the barn.

Outside, the fuse of the rocket was sizzling in the rain, sparking but not going out. The Eosians only stared, uncertain of what it was supposed to be. As a weapon, it probably didn't impress them. It wasn't even aimed at them, just into the sky at an angle.

When it went off, it would scatter viral particles over the whole area, infecting all the Eosians present, the water, the soil. An ugly disease, engineered to be both highly contagious and highly deadly, a combination that's rare in nature. But we'd left nature behind a long time ago.

Sybil's shoes squelched in the muddy ground as she ran. I ran out after her, screaming her name. It was like her, it was so like her to do a thing like this.

The fire made its way to the end of the fuse and reached the rocket a second before Sybil did. *She's too late*, I thought, but she made a flying leap and landed on top of the thing as it exploded.

I came panting up, too late to do any good. Carefully I rolled her off the smoking rocket.

"Did I get it?" she whispered huskily. Her chest and abdomen were a bloody mess. Her dark hair pooled around her head.

I tore my eyes off her and checked the rocket. The bottom half, where the explosives were, was blasted apart, but the viral canister at the top was intact. I snatched it out of the wreckage and gripped it tightly in my fist. "You got it," I said.

"I couldn't let him do it," she said. A little blood showed on her teeth.

"But what is there left to do?" I asked hopelessly. "They don't want peace."

"I couldn't take their home from them. Not even to save our lives. That's what people did back on Earth. The goddess was trying to show us a better way."

Tears fell down my cheeks, unchecked. Robin had never understood the thing that existed between Sybil and me. She thought Sybil was her competition. But no. Sybil was the mother I'd always wished I had.

Nobody else would have been able to see the truth so clearly. Back on Proxima, her critics had called her crazy. Like we didn't know she danced just on the outside edge of sanity from time to time. But there was wisdom in that outside place. There were things she saw so much more clearly than the rest of us, and she knew the dark shadows of the mind so intimately as never to believe them.

The goddess was real to me, as a force that bound us all together. But only Sybil could see past that to a person, hear the words that person was trying to say. Maybe the words had only ever been Sybil's—the person only a secret part of her own mind. Hawk hadn't understood how little that had mattered. I had heard truth in her words and that was the only thing, in the end, that really counted.

Sybil's green eyes stared up at me, as her chest stopped laboring to breathe. She was gone.

I laid her down carefully and turned to the Eosian leader. "I hope you appreciate this," I said, my voice half-strangled. "She did that for *you*. Don't you think you owe us something?"

Behind me, Hawk said coldly, "You can't earn the respect of these creatures. Force is what it takes. I had that. You just ruined our chances at survival. Your *children's* chances."

I ignored him and kept staring the Eosian in the eye. Her eyes were large and golden, reflecting the light from the ship behind me, like a cat's. "Please," I begged, though I knew she wouldn't understand. I spread my hands wide. "Look, I have no weapon. We've chosen peace."

She looked down at me for a long moment. Then she waved one paw toward all of us. Jabbed it at the sky. *Just go.*

38

Robin

I woke up to Tsaft bringing me a roasted brushcreeper. I sat up carefully in bed and started right in. I was starving—how long had I slept? It was crispy brown on the outside, slightly greasy on the inside, and tasted smokey.

Beside me on the bed, Lightleaper was asleep with his arms thrown over his head. At some point during the day/night/whenever it was, I'd managed to nurse him a little bit. I badly wished for Hazel to tell me if I was doing it right or enough, but the baby had gone to sleep and hopefully that meant his belly was full.

"It's started to rain," said Tsaft after watching me for a moment.

I blinked at her for a second. "Did it put the fires out?"

"Not mine, at least. It's big enough a little rain like this doesn't bother it. But the Devourer isn't flying." She was quiet another moment, seeming like she would speak and then thinking better for it. "Fesskh is gone," she said at last. "And Kisht, and many others. They went over the common, through the burn scar. Tisket said they had weapons."

I froze with a piece of meat halfway to my mouth. Now, they had to choose now. When I wasn't there to help. I'd spent a day focusing on just the baby, because I'd had to. But now all I could think of was Lily and Colt, hiding in the ship. Would Sybil and Hawk get along enough to organize a response?

The smart thing would be to lock themselves inside the ship, but they wouldn't have oxygen to do that forever. At some point, they'd have to fight back. And I didn't know what I wanted Aspen to do about that. Roll over and let Fesskh anywhere near the kids? Fuck no. But if they fought back, they'd only increase the Eosians' resolve. It sounded like this time Fesskh had only brought a few. Had she not been able to convince the council? If the humans killed everyone she'd brought, I couldn't imagine the council holding back after that.

All of this flashed through my mind in a second, while I sat in bed with a sore undercarriage and greasy fingers. Then I dropped the meat back onto the plate and wiped my hands on my shirt. "You have to take me there."

"Are you well enough?"

I took stock. I had managed to hobble to the indoor bathroom down the hall—proof they were a hell of a lot more civilized than we had been, a few short centuries ago. But my whole midsection was wobbly and sore. My hips felt dislocated. I saw stars every time I got out of bed. And I was currently wearing a diaper fashioned out of some of Tsaft's old shawls, half soaked in blood.

"No," I said. "But I have to. Do you have …I don't know, a wagon or something?"

Instead of answering, she picked up Lightleaper and put him in my arms. He twisted and rooted in his sleep but didn't wake. Then Tsaft scooped us both up in her top pair of arms, cradling me like a baby. "I will take you there," she said. "It may be dangerous. But I cannot keep you from protecting your wife and daughters."

She went upstairs and out into the rain. I adjusted the blanket I was wrapped in to keep the baby dry.

My mind felt perfectly clear as Tsaft's gentle, four-legged gait carried us across the estate. Maybe it was the sleep I'd gotten, or the way I'd forgotten myself entirely during labor, but I didn't feel like two people anymore. I didn't feel out of place in the dark. I simply felt like a person with a long, long history in these woods. I sensed when we crossed estate boundaries, and I understood why Tsaft had rights to cross these and not those. I remembered why this boundary was here, and when it had been set, and which of Mrrka's ancestors had been at the council where it had been decided.

I was one of them now. Without losing myself. I knew now that this was what Mrrka had wanted. Firstly, because she had known the Devourer was coming, and she hadn't yet prepared her people to face it. She had wanted to leave the knowledge with someone. And secondly, because she knew their only hope of coexisting with us was for one of us to know everything they knew. The only flaw in her plan had been how long it had taken me to absorb all that information. Either because of my incompatible human brain or my extra-defensive ego, I had only gained access to it in fits and starts.

We came out from under the trees and into the drizzle. It wasn't yet fully dark, but the clouds were blocking all of the sunset but a murky, orange glow in the west. Tsaft ducked under the wire, unnecessarily, since it was shut off now. Then she scrambled awkwardly over the fence, arms tightening around me to keep me secure.

The Eosians were drawn up in a rough line, facing inwards, and Tsaft pushed her way through to the front. No one bothered to oppose her; she was one of them and a respected one, despite her widowhood.

On the other side of the line was a few yards of empty space, and then a corresponding array of humans. Hawk, of course. Cliff. Flint. Hazel.

And between the rows was Aspen, rain dripping off the ends of his braids and sheening his bare chest. His face held a weight of naked sorrow I'd never seen in him before, not even when his mother had died.

As Tsaft set me down on my feet, I saw what he was crying about. Sybil. She lay, her body bloody and her hair a starburst around her head. *Fuck, no.* After all she and I had been through, I had come to respect her. And here something terrible had happened. And I hadn't been here. Again, I hadn't been here. Another thing I couldn't prevent.

I wanted to go to Aspen, to hold him, to say I understood. But that had to wait.

On trembling legs, I walked up to Fesskh. "What is happening here?" I demanded. No respectful terminology now. I understood why it wasn't needed.

"I told you, we are at war," she said.

"You thought I was too ignorant to notice," I said. "You thought I wouldn't realize who I am."

"Who are you?" she asked. Warily, now.

"I am the Eldest," I said. "And *you* are out of order."

Absolute madness, that I could be the Eldest. But that was how their inheritance laws went. I'd cut Kisht out of her birthright, and that sucked for both of us, but I'd be damned if that meant I let Fesskh have it.

She stammered for a moment. "You're not one of us."

"I know." It was delicate here. I didn't want to actually be the boss. Only for so long as it took to make everyone settle down. "I'm not one of you, but your law gives me the right to decide this."

"They killed my daughter!" she protested. But she'd started using honorifics again, the tone of a protesting inferior, and I knew I had won.

"I know," I said. "It will be dealt with. But not like this."

I turned to Aspen. "Do you know who killed her daughter?"

He was looking at me like I'd dropped in from another planet. Which I guess I had. "Hawk," he said. "One of them killed Autumn over it, but it wasn't really Autumn's fault."

Autumn too. Fuck.

Hawk burst out, "Well, what else were we supposed to do? Wait for them to come and kill us?"

"They wouldn't have been so eager to kill us if you hadn't started it!"

"They were always going to do this," he said bitterly. "From the moment we came, it was determined. This planet is only so big. Sooner or later, we would have needed to fight over it. Better sooner than later.

280

Study history. All the wars, in the end, are about land."

"Or we could have respected their rights to begin with."

"Why?" His voice cracked harshly. "Because they were lucky enough to be born into plenty, while we were born in an anthill under glass? I knew the planetary survey board would take that exact same view. They would have cordoned off this planet forever!"

Cliff and Aspen both turned to him suddenly when he said that. "What was that?" I asked.

"The Hermes data," he said urgently. "I was the first to see it. All my life I've wanted to get off that grubby rock. I processed so much data, looking for a place. Eos was perfect except for one thing. Except for five minutes of footage."

Then I remembered. "The probe saw an Eosian." I remembered being her, remembered one brief glimpse of the probe before it had passed out of our territory. If I had remembered that sooner, I could have shown up Hawk for what he was, at a time when it mattered. Now he was spilling his guts because it didn't really matter now what he said. He was out of tricks, and ready for the Eosians to kill us all.

"I snipped the footage out, and got the whole planet rated 4-B, low quality, even though it's a paradise. I rushed the approval through for Sybil's colony. I knew if we were down here, it wouldn't matter that there were primitives here. With luck, we'd have the terraforming done before we even found them. But Sybil wouldn't pick the colony site I wanted."

Everyone was staring at him in horror. Not just Aspen or Cliff, but even his most solid disciples. They were beginning to grasp the kind of person he was, and the mistake they'd made trusting him. Hazel backed away a step, the crowbar in her hands sinking toward the ground. Flint was staring at the ground, ears red with shame.

"Believe me," I said, with a heavy sigh. "That wasn't where you fucked up." I turned to Fesskh. "By law, you have a right to his blood, since he's taken your daughter from you. He's probably not worth it, but I leave it to you. The rest of us, though? You have no right to us."

"You are on the common," she said. "No one may build on the common. That's ancestral law. None of us can change it. Not the Eldest, not the council."

That stumped me for a second. But then I pointed out, "But I own an estate of my own, don't I? Not Kisht. It would go to her if Mrrka died unmemoried. A thing you kept insisting had happened, but it didn't. I'm her heir."

Beside Fesskh, Kisht bristled. "Council will have to decide."

"Council won't even hear your objection, when I prove I have your mother's memories. Mrrka chose me." I wanted to add something else. *I'm sorry*, at least. Sorry for the loss of her mother, sorry she had lost her fiancée. Sorry I had taken everything she had wanted in life. I still felt a certain tenderness toward her, which I knew must be Mrrka's. But I couldn't say any of this to her. I knew it would only anger her, coming from me.

"You will destroy all your buildings and growings and put them on Mrrka's estate?" Fesskh's voice was horrified. That was prime hunting land, the best in the region. Wild beasts couldn't be penned; if we built there it would disrupt hunting everywhere.

"I will petition council for an exchange," I proposed. I felt an odd thrill: Mrrka had so loved playing politics with Fesskh. I couldn't be sure whether this idea was mine or hers, at this point. "Mrrka's estate joins the common, and this land becomes my estate. It never was good land, was it? You shoved the have-nots here once the best had all been chosen by you and your friends."

"It's bad because the commoners don't care for it."

"But I will," I said. "My people will make it grow again. We can grow animals here that we can share with you, as needed. But Mrrka's estate can be good hunting for the common people. She was always generous with share-hunting in life. Let Tsaft keep the den. She can be common-warden." That was an old, old term. I didn't know if even Fesskh remembered it. Somehow the position had fallen out of use. In the old days, it was someone whose job was protecting the hunting grounds of the common, setting limits and determining seasons. It seemed to be needed, and it gave Tsaft a reason to have her old home.

Behind me, the humans were unsettled. All they could hear was me snarling back and forth with the Eosians, with no way to tell if we were making peace or war. I turned around. "Go back inside, everyone. We won't be fighting with the Eosians today. Hopefully not ever."

The crowd started breaking up, people clumping in twos and threes to whisper. Not quite going inside, but they weren't brandishing their ridiculous weapons anymore either. Even Flint, hesitating at first, was gently pulled away by Hazel.

Hawk, however, wasn't going to go. I saw it before he moved, saw the tension in his legs and shoulders, how he was about to bolt forward with his makeshift spear of sharpened metal pipe. I don't know if I knew it because of Mrrka's memories or because of my own past, when I'd sometimes had to dodge men like him in dark alleys.

But Fesskh saw it too. Faster than my eye could follow, she was upon him, claws opening him up like an envelope.

I looked away. I hadn't, strictly speaking, wanted her to kill him. But it did make things a lot less complicated for the rest of us.

Someone screamed. Hazel cried, "They're attacking us after all!" But a second later, Fesskh had turned and was heading back toward the wall, followed by the others. They glided over the fence like shadows in the darkness.

Tsaft lingered a moment. "Thank you for what you have done. I wish none of you had come here. My wife would still be with me. But if it had to happen, I am glad the falling star brought you."

"Thank you," I said, "Blue Star."

Her eyes widened. That had been Mrrka's nickname for her. Because her eyes were blue, like Rigel, which was visible from here like on Proxima. I hoped it wasn't rude to remind her I remembered everything they'd had. But I thought not, because she lightly touched her nose to my forehead before following the others.

I turned at last to Aspen. "I'm sorry about Sybil." There was so much to say about that later; the colony would have to grieve her and I didn't even know where they would start.

He nodded. "I was worried you were dead."

For a second I froze. He knew nothing about what had happened. I was here with a blanket wrapped around me and the baby in my arms, and he had no clue at all.

Lightleaper wiggled, farted, and made a little cry. Aspen's eyes widened. "Robin—what—"

I unwrapped the blanket, carefully, keeping a little tented over him so the rain wouldn't hit his face. "Sorry I couldn't come back sooner. I was a little busy."

Aspen's tears started up again, mixing with the rain on his face. God, how I had missed that face. He wrapped me in his arms, so the baby was snuggled tightly between us. "I knew you could do it. I knew it."

"Do what? Save the colony? Or go through unmedicated labor? Because given the option I would still like to go back in time and get that epidural."

Aspen only gripped me tighter. "You can do anything."

Epilogue

A few months later, the colony was booming. Everything within the stockade was thick with green: sweet potatoes, peanuts, beans, wheat, clover. Here and there, white trees with waxy dark purple leaves interrupted the greenery. I'd been afraid they'd shade out the crops, but their shadow was small for their size, and they had some kind of symbiotic relationship with the mycelia that made the soil much richer.

The goats roamed at will, noshing on grass and kudzu and the occasional pink star ivy. I'd given each of them a dose of the locust's gut bacteria mix, so they could digest the local plant life. If they did well on it, I'd start offering it to the humans. Some of the Disciples didn't like the idea of polluting their all-Earth-natural bodies with it, but most of us preferred to know we wouldn't starve even if our crops failed.

Behind our chapel was a little churchyard, where Autumn, Sybil, and Hawk lay buried. There had been some debate over it. Robin didn't think Hawk deserved to be there, and Pine wanted Sybil thrown outside for the scavengers. But most of us wanted them both with us. It felt like healing, after the scars of our schism. Many people were ashamed of what they'd done to Sybil, after all she'd done for us.

The Disciples weren't what we had been. After the death of both our leaders, we'd flailed for a while. Some people, desperate for another leader, followed Pine. But most took their religion a little deeper into their hearts, and talked about it less. We prayed, alone or together, in silence. I think we were afraid of getting it wrong if we said something out loud. Or afraid someone would find something to argue with.

I held Lightleaper on my chest, patting his back so he wouldn't fuss. He wanted Mama—our first child to like her better than me. But she was out on the river. Tsaft had given her a boat, and she and Colt went out on it when they could, braving rapids and dodging rocks. She said it was the thing most like space that existed in a gravity well, where the current was the thrust that took you out of your comfort zone, made your heart race. Colt, being a thrill junkie like his mother, always came along.

Lily stayed with me and helped with the planting. I'd never seen her so calm and happy. All her life, plants had been a precious thing we'd given her as much of as we could, rationed out like candy. Now she was out among them all day, every day.

We didn't see much of the Eosians. "Grudging tolerance" described most of their attitude to us. They had let us put a small hydroelectric turbine in the river, so we had power again. But they wanted none of our technology. The elders were convinced our corrupt ways would destroy their hunting grounds if allowed to spread off our own estate, and I couldn't say they were wrong.

Robin had been able to work it so that Kisht voted for her in the Council as her proxy. She'd felt terrible about taking the Eosian's inheritance, and she'd done what she could to make up for it. Once she'd gotten the land trade through the Council, she'd dropped the whole "Eldest" thing as much as they would let her. From time to time she visited Tsaft and told her stories. Memories that the Eosians could keep, the way humans passed them down.

It had been a mistake to come here. Without Hawk's lie, we never would have. Our little green patch in a purple forest looked, from high up the hillside, like a disease or a mistake. And it was.

But Sybil would have said mistakes are part of what we are. That so much of evolution, of life itself, is scarring over the broken places and moving on. That as long as we live, we create beauty and joy.

And we had. I had. I was deeply happy with our little snatch of Earth here inside the stockade, even if it was only a farm. The freezer full of deer and bear and songbird ova stayed frozen. If I wanted a wild forest, I went and walked in the common, listening to the trill of the batlike twigperchers and the drone of leaf beetles. It was enough.

The End

About the Author

Sheila Jenné grew up in Seattle on a steady diet of Star Trek and religion. Throughout her career, she's been a Latin teacher, content writer, editor, and a parent to four neurodiverse children.

When she's not writing, she enjoys crafting, conlangs, and wandering around in the woods.

You can stay up-to-date on her releases and science thoughts at sheilajenne.com.